Starting Over at the Crafty Bee Barn

Margaret Amatt

LEANNAN
PRESS
INDEPENDENT PUBLISHER

LEANNAN PRESS

First Published by Leannan Press 2024

Book Cover designed by Margaret Amatt

eBook ISBN: 978-1-914575-57-0

Paperback ISBN: 978-1-914575-55-6

PROLOGUE

Aidan

Long grass rustled at the side of the uneven path and Maya the husky shot through the overgrown garden towards the cottage door.

'What the hell happened here?' Aidan McBride muttered, slinging off his hiker's backpack and dropping it by the door. A knot formed in his stomach. Thirteen months away, and the place was unrecognisable. Lit by the sliver of moonlight, it appeared derelict. Abandoned.

He tried the handle. It squeaked in protest but with a forceful twist and shove, the door sprang open. *Not even locked?* Was this what his mum called 'looking after' the place? He fumbled around for the light switch. His fingertips landed on something dusty and sticky. He pressed it.

'Jesus Christ!' His hand leapt to his face. He'd never owned much furniture but the little that was left was covered in cobwebs. Damp patches bloomed over the walls and pooled in black masses around the filthy skirting boards.

Aidan almost retched. Thirteen months on an endurance walk in Canada and Alaska had meant sleeping in some dodgy places, but this took the cake. No way could he sleep here, which left only one option: he'd have to go to his mother's house.

He balled his fists. How could he face her after this?

'Come on, Maya. Let's get out of this hellhole. I can't bear it.' He closed the door behind him, squinting into the darkness. Was there even a tiny chance his bees were still there? He groaned. What did he expect? Maybe this was his own making, but it stung.

Time was a forgotten thing and didn't seem to mean much anymore. He'd hiked at all hours in all weathers. The sound of his thick boots on the pavement cut through the still evening as he strode down the hill from the cottage, along the narrow pavement at the side of a country road towards Glenbriar, passing houses so familiar yet strange. It had been so long since he'd walked these streets. Had he known his cottage would be in such a state, he'd have had the taxi drop him off at his mum's straight away. But not far now. Walking half a mile in a Scottish small town was nothing compared to what he'd just come from.

Before he'd gathered himself or considered what he was doing, he rapped hard on the door. Then again and again, until he heard squeals and voices from inside.

The door opened and a face peered through the gap above the chain.

'Oh my god, Aidan. It's you. What the hell are you doing here at this time of night? What the hell are you doing here at all? I thought you were still in Canada.'

'Hi, Mum. Are you going to open the door?'

She pulled back the chain and Aidan stepped inside, followed by Maya.

'Aidan!' another voice screamed, and arms wrapped around his neck.

'Hi, Scarlett.' He extricated himself from the grip of his half-sister and gave Maya a reassuring stroke.

'I can't believe you're back. Why didn't you give us some warning?' his mum asked.

'Would it have made any difference?'

'To what?'

'My cottage. What's happened to it? Have you been there at all in the last thirteen months? Did you look after the bees?'

His mother's expression sank. 'Oh, Aidan, I'm sorry. Bees aren't really my thing. I tried, but I couldn't.'

'You couldn't?'

'They scared me and it was so hard to find the time for the house. Not now I've started my own business.'

He frowned. 'Business?'

'I'm selling some of my crafts.'

'Don't get pissy with Mum,' Scarlett said. 'It's not like you've done much communicating in the last year, is it?'

'I've been in some rough places. I lost my first phone with all my contacts, the next one broke and most of the time I've been in places with no reception or I've had no way to charge anything. So communicating wasn't exactly easy or a priority.'

'And we get that, but it was your choice. You can't expect the world to stand still and wait for you.'

'That's not what I expected.'

'Just as well.'

'Why?'

His mother cast Scarlett a warning look and she gave a little shrug.

'What?' He glanced from one to the other.

'He's going to find out sooner or later,' Scarlett said.

'Find out what? Will one of you tell me what's going on?'

'Elise got engaged.'

Aidan froze, his heart slipping to the soles of his hiking boots. Not Elise. They'd been together before he left. She couldn't come with him, but she supported him. They'd not made any promises, but he knew she'd wait. Just one year. She must have waited. He hadn't heard from her for a while, but that meant nothing. They both knew that communicating would be hard.

'What?' he choked out. Scarlett must be making up stories. She'd always been into books and dramatics, and she sure knew how to spin a tall tale if she thought she'd get a reaction. She'd been doing that ever since she started talking.

'It's true,' his mum said. 'She's engaged to Finlay.'

Aidan staggered back until he collided with the door. 'Finlay? As in my cousin, Finlay?'

Both his mother and Scarlett nodded.

How was that possible? It made no sense. But the expression on their faces told him it was true.

Aidan closed his eyes and, for the second time in his life, the world collapsed around him.

Chapter One

Lilah

Lilah Clarke twisted her long hair into a tight roll, wound it up the back of her head, and pulled her baseball cap over it to hold it in place. She dodged a child with ice-cream all over his face and paused behind a row of food trailers and carts. The smell of fried onions, burgers, and something warm and sweet, possibly doughnuts, made her stomach rumble. The loose change in her pocket wouldn't buy anything that good. Make that anything at all.

Where is Jaxon?

She edged into a crowd of people jostling around the stalls. Her focus roamed over them, part taking in what they were selling or advertising, but mostly seeking the face of her brother. She averted her eyes from a cake stall with beautiful displays of tray bakes and cupcake towers and moved closer to a gazebo with a table covered in photographs of local woodlands. Bunting fluttered in the gentle breeze above a sign reading Forestry Land Trust Scotland. A woman with blue hair was talking to some passersby. Lilah moved on, passing a book stall where a signing was taking place. She vaguely registered a pile of children's books with a bright pink building on the front. As a lover of stories, she'd like to investigate further, but she couldn't afford anything here... And she needed to find Jaxon.

Finally, she spotted him, lurking close to a bright yellow stall. On the tables were display trees laden with handmade jewellery, trays of stitched goods made from 'bee' fabric and a large log decorated with little golden badges in the shape of bees. Jaxon's eyes darted about as he slouched around with his hands in his pockets.

Lilah ground her teeth. It wouldn't surprise her if he'd helped himself to some of the goods around here for free. How easy would it be to swipe something off the table while the stallholder was looking the other way? She made her way towards him. He lingered by the yellow stall, his gaze travelling over the table. Lilah couldn't imagine him bothering with a stall like that. He'd want something more valuable or that he could eat straight away.

Like he'd stumbled on something, he stared down and cursed. Beside him was a sandwich board sign reading The Crafty Bee.

Lilah put on some speed, darting past more people and moving in beside him. She placed her hand on his shoulder. He spun around, his fist balled and raised.

'Nice to see you too,' she said, pulling back out of his reach. Some people behind her muttered as she accidentally brushed against them. 'Sorry.' She didn't look around as she spoke, but kept her gaze fixed on her younger brother. Experience told her he was likely to run at any time, even if it had been his idea to meet.

'You gave me a heart attack.' He massaged his chest, his eyes everywhere but on her.

'What's going on? Why did you want to meet me?' The Glenbriar May fair wasn't a place he was likely to be 'just passing', not when he lived in Dundee, forty miles away. And when did meeting up with him ever have a good result? She ran her hand over a little quiver in her tummy. It could be hunger, but she had a really bad feeling about this. Deep down, she wanted to love her family, believe that they could have normal relationships, meet up for coffees, go to each other's birthday parties and spend Christmases together. That hopeless wish somehow tricked her over and over. Why did she always think things would be different? The reality had never yet played out anywhere near her elusive dream. Maybe this time she'd be lucky.

'I need your help,' he said, moving closer and taking her by the arm.

'My help?' She raised an eyebrow and her stomach sank. Of course, this was why he was here. No chance of a 'hi, Lilah, I got a job and thought it would be lovely to meet my sister at the fair and buy you a cake.' No. He needed help, and when Jaxon needed help, it meant things were a mess. And she didn't want to be involved. Not this time. 'I doubt I can help you.'

'Sure you can. You've got a place. I need to use it to lie low for a bit.'

She shook her head and stared at him. He couldn't be serious, right? 'Are you having a laugh? My *place* is a cold caravan with barely enough space for me to lie down in. There's no room for anyone else.'

'Even your brother?'

'Sorry, Jax. It's got nothing to do with who you are. There's just no room.' And for that, she sent up a silent prayer. Much as she wanted to do anything that would bring her family together, she didn't need the kind of stress he brought. Having him lying low would only attract trouble.

'Money then. Can you lend me some so I can get away?'

'I have literally one pound and sixteen pence to my name. You can have it if you want, but it won't get you very far.'

'Thanks.' He held out his palm. Why had she offered? Of course he'd want it. With a sigh, she put her hand in her pocket and pulled out the only money she had left.

She dropped it into his outstretched palm and watched as his fingers swallowed it up. Bye-bye cash.

'I thought you had a job,' he said, pocketing the money.

'I do, but it doesn't exactly pay well.' She'd been turned down for so many 'real' jobs she'd almost given up hope. Someone was always better qualified or more suitable, even for the lowest paid, most menial positions. Now she was living in a draughty caravan in a local couple's garden, helping them to make fudge. *Yes, fudge!* A step-up from cleaning toilets, perhaps, as far as career satisfaction went, but it paid a pittance. The couple were a right pair of wheeler dealers. Having grown up with people like them all around her, Lilah could spot them a mile off. Since moving into the caravan, she'd heard all their sad tales of how one by one their previous enterprises had been thwarted – nothing to do with them, of course. Fudge was their latest thing, only neither of them could actually make it, so as business ventures went, it was basically a nonstarter. Or it had been until Lilah came along. She got a roof over her head in return for her baking skills, and that was it. If they occasionally gave her pocket money... bonus! But they rarely did.

'Look.' Jaxon took hold of her arm. His grip was tight to the point of painful. 'I need—'

'Jaxon!' a loud voice shouted through the crowd. He let go of Lilah and spun around.

'Shit.' He shoved her roughly out of the way and she stumbled back.

'What the—' Before she could register what was happening, two large men lunged for her brother.

'Leave him alone!' she screamed, staggering out of the way as one of the men muscled into her. She nudged against the table of the yellow stall beside her. Her hand flew out to stop herself from crashing and landed on the large log decorated with the badges and little bee pins.

The man grabbed Jaxon. He struggled wildly. 'Get off! Get off me!'

Lilah grabbed the log off the table, scattering the bee pins everywhere, and walloped the man on the back with it. He yelled and let go of Jaxon, who ran for it. Both men turned to glare at Lilah. She wasn't short, but she was a twig compared to these two thickset guys. She clung to the log, holding it in front of her like a sword, and stared at them.

'Hey, you thief,' a woman's voice said from behind the stall. 'Give that back.' Someone wrenched her arm and Lilah wrestled herself away.

'Leave me alone.'

'Maybe I should take that,' one of the guys said, groping toward Lilah. She swung the log out of his reach, ready to wallop him again if he got any closer, and felt its weight vanish from her hand.

'Break it up, lads,' a deep, commanding voice said.

'Hey,' Lilah snapped, spinning around. Her eyes levelled against a grey safari-style shirt, half open across a broad chest. She raised her gaze to catch a dark-haired, dark-eyed man with thick eyebrows drawn together forming a menacing expression on what was a ruggedly handsome face. He held the log across his body.

'Move along,' he said to the big guys. Beside him was a wolf-like husky dog. Its hackles were raised on the back of its thick grey coat and it bared its teeth at the men. 'Or I'll have the police on you,' the dark-haired man continued. 'Go on, get out of here.'

The guys lumbered off, ramming their fists into their hands and throwing Lilah a we'll-get-you-next-time stare.

'You can scram too,' he said to Lilah without looking at her. Her heart hammered as she tried to calm the wild thoughts and sensations attacking her from all directions. Where was Jaxon? Who were the men? What trouble was he in this time? Hopefully the men didn't know where she lived or how to find her.

Before she could make a move, a woman's voice spoke again. 'She's not going anywhere. She wrecked our stall.'

Lilah stared at her and her heart chilled. The woman was Scarlett Finch, an old schoolmate. *Will she recognise me?* Could Lilah get away before anything else happened? She could make a run for it.

'She?' the dark-haired man snapped his attention to Lilah. 'Christ, sorry. I thought you were a boy.'

What?

'Wait a minute,' Scarlett said, thrusting her fists into her hips. 'I know you. You're Delilah Clarke, aren't you?'

Lilah winced at the sound of her full name. No one really used it except her mum or people trying to take the piss – as Scarlett Finch had always liked to do at school.

'Well, that makes sense,' Scarlett went on. 'You were always a thieving mink.'

'Scarlett,' the man growled. Lilah was pretty sure she'd never heard anyone with a lower voice – so commanding, and a little frightening. 'Don't be so rude.'

'I'm not being rude. It's the truth.' Scarlett narrowed her eyes at Lilah. 'Now you can pay for the damage to our stall.'

Lilah shrugged; she couldn't pay for anything. Her pockets were empty. They could check if they wanted. The wolf-like dog prodded its nose under her hand and sniffed. With shaky fingers, she petted its thick, soft fur. Its blue eyes were kind of other-worldly and seemed to x-ray her, though not in an unfriendly way. Her chest lightened and through all the nagging unpleasant thoughts, she suddenly wanted to smile.

Scarlett edged out from behind the stall. 'Don't let her touch Maya,' she snapped. 'You don't know where she's been.'

'Don't be ridiculous,' the man said.

'Oh, I'm not.' Scarlett eyeballed her. Lilah knew exactly why she was so abrasive. She'd once accidentally hit Scarlett with a hockey stick during a P.E. lesson at High School and knocked her tooth out. There had been a lot of blood and, until she got a crown, she'd gone around with a scarf tied high over her mouth. Having a missing tooth wasn't a great look for a sixteen-year-old and Scarlett had blamed Lilah for doing it on purpose. The incident had cemented her place as the class scum. Who else would stoop so low but the girl with tatty clothes and messy hair who lived in the only 'rough area' of Glenbriar? Classmates, who'd always looked down on her because her mum did drugs and her older brothers were constantly in trouble with the law or behind bars, now blanked her or were openly rude to her. Ever-popular Scarlett was always at the core.

Nothing much had changed for the better in Lilah's life since then, so she could hardly assume Scarlett's attitude had improved either.

'I can't pay for anything.' She gave a little shrug and turned to walk away. 'I haven't got any money.'

'You so will.' Scarlett marched straight for her, gently moving the dog and blocking Lilah's way.

'Let her go,' the man said. 'She's not worth it.'

Wasn't that the truth? She didn't need anyone to tell her. She already knew. But his attitude irked her. Not only that… Saddened her, but she wasn't going to admit that. No way.

'Who asked you?' she said, turning to stare at him and narrowing her eyes.

He glowered back and she held her breath. His irises were so dark they were almost black. And he was tall and broad shouldered. He ran a hand around his unshaven jaw, like he was pondering what to do with her. She wasn't sure she'd ever seen anyone as handsome as this guy. Her heart rate intensified and heat soared in her cheeks. In her dreams, she had a man like him. The kind of man she liked to read about. He held her close every night and told her he loved her every day. They were partners in everything they did. Lilah was good at dreaming. She could fall into a book and live in a story for hours if she got the chance. Reality never measured up. Finding men who were even a tenth as nice as her dreams or her book boyfriends was impossible.

'I'm telling you, she's not getting away.' Scarlett stood her ground and Lilah turned back to her. If she could just edge past her. People were moving all around. If she timed it right, she could run for it like Jaxon and disappear into the crowd before Scarlett had a chance to come after her. Easy, huh?

But what about Jaxon? In the kerfuffle of the last few minutes, she'd forgotten him. And maybe that was for the best. Why waste her energy worrying about what trouble he'd got himself into this time? It wasn't the first time and it was unlikely to be the last. She probably wouldn't hear from him again until the next time he needed money or a place to hide. Such was their relationship. That was her normal, not the fantasy she'd wished for on her long walk here when she'd dreamed of a fun reunion with her little brother. Oh well. It had been an interesting afternoon, if not the one she'd hoped for. And it had got her out of the caravan and given her a change of scenery. Time to leave.

She pushed off to run, but before she'd gone one step, a hand with a powerful grip closed around her upper arm.

'Just hold it there one minute,' the deep voice said, and Lilah found herself unable to move a muscle.

Chapter Two

Aidan

Aidan gripped the arm of the young woman in the baseball cap and the oversized t-shirt. Maya sniffed at her tatty old trainers.

'Right,' Scarlett said, and for a pint-sized twenty-three-year-old, she bristled like a fearsome dragon with her ringed-up hands on her hips and her ferocious stare. Her short hair was spiked high like it was carrying an electric charge. Would she have gone for the manic pixie look, spunky outfit and piercings if their mum had called her Jane? She seemed to want to live up to a reputation her name brought her – whether or not it was appropriate. Right now, it was.

'Let me go, will you?' The young woman pleaded, staring at Aidan and wriggling in his grip. He didn't want to hurt her but something didn't feel right. Her pupils were wide and adrift in her slate blue-grey irises. Her expression cried out for help, or at least compassion.

'Remind me of your name,' he said, letting go of her but standing in a place where she couldn't run past him.

'None of your business.'

'Funny name that.'

She gave him the evils.

'Her name is Delilah Clarke.' Scarlett folded her arms. 'She's always been a little sneak.'

'No, I have not. And no one calls me Delilah.'

Aidan shook his head. Delilah, or whatever her name was, had to be at least three inches taller than Scarlett. She was hardly 'little' in that sense, but she was all skin and bone in her skimpy denim shorts and that shapeless baggy t-shirt. That, and the baseball cap, was his excuse for having mistaken her for a boy. Up close, her face wasn't boyish at all. In fact, it was pretty in a youthful kind of way: heart-shaped with tiny freckles covering her button nose. For a moment, the way they blended together in an intricate pattern preoccupied him. He tried to make sense of the random arrangement, though, of course, that wasn't possible. Her long eyelashes fluttered fast, and she glanced around as if searching for an escape route.

'I don't need to know the history,' he said gruffly. What he needed was to diffuse this situation and get the stall tidied up before his mum returned. Running stalls at a fair wasn't his thing, but once he'd committed to doing something, he liked to do it properly. So far, he was doing a seriously crap job. 'Nothing's damaged or stolen from the stall, but you've made a right mess of it. So the least you can do is help put it back together again.'

'Seriously?' Delilah glared at him. He locked eyes with her and something stirred inside him. It was short-lived and unidentifiable, but briefly, he considered it might be better to let her leave.

'That's a total copout.' Scarlett shook her head and glanced skyward. 'She should have to pay or maybe I should report her.'

'Whatever. Now, give me that.' Delilah snatched the log from Aidan. For a second, she looked like she might clobber him with it and do a runner. Then, with a sharp glance, she put it back on the table. He moved closer, ready to stop her if she bolted, but she scooped up a handful of the tiny bee pins she'd scattered across the table and started placing them hastily back on the log.

'What were you doing with this anyway? And who were the guys?'

She gave a little shrug, sweeping some more pins into her hand. 'Don't know. They were about to go for my... er, some kid. I was trying to stop them. I grabbed the first thing I saw.'

Aidan frowned, scanning about. Glenbriar wasn't the kind of place where criminals often lurked, but the world was a messed-up place, and anything was possible. The market now appeared the picture of innocence, with its bright stalls and bunting flapping in the gentle breeze. Maybe he shouldn't have let the guys go so easily. He'd thought they were just having a petty squabble and hadn't noticed a kid. 'What age of kid?'

'A teenager. He ran off.'

He should report that.

Music from a nearby street entertainer struck up, almost deafening him for a second, until they adjusted the volume on their sound system. A gentle folk melody played and a woman sang soulfully. It wiped Aidan's thoughts, momentarily whisking him back to a day similar to this when he was a child and his dad had brought him to this very fair. Dad had bought him ice creams and candyfloss and they'd gone home with a bag full of cheap rubbish he'd won at the tombola and lucky dips.

'I don't believe a word that comes out of your lying mouth,' Scarlett said, and her voice cut into the memory, shattering it. 'I didn't spot anyone else hanging around. Those thugs were probably after you for drug money or something.'

'I do not take—'

'Will the two of you quit it?' Aidan snapped. This was just one of the many problems of having a sister so much younger than him. Even at twenty-three, she was still such a child. His gaze drifted over the top of Delilah's baseball cap, past the leg of the gazebo wound with yellow ribbons, and landed on a couple walking his way. He balled his fists. *Not them. Please no.* His blood pressure rocketed at the sight.

The male half of the couple peered over a stall before turning to the woman and smiling. They looked perfect together, but that didn't help Aidan's mood. He and that man were cousins. Cousins who looked annoyingly alike. Aidan recognised the similarity in their height, their thick dark hair and their muscular build. They were the same age and had grown up together.

They'd been more like best friends for the longest time. Now, Finlay McBride was holding hands with Elise Reid, laughing and joking with her. Aidan wanted to crush them both. That was what love did. It made people go crazy. It hurt and caused nothing but pain. Never again. His jaw was rigid but inside his head shook like turbulence was locked in his skull. No. He would not succumb to love again. His heart had turned to stone and was caged in iron. There it would stay forever.

He buried his hand in Maya's fur and she rubbed her nose on his thigh as if understanding exactly how he felt and wanting nothing but for him to feel ok again. If only people were as unconditional and uncomplicated as this.

'Aidan.' Elise glanced up from the stall she was browsing and caught his eye. She was as immaculate as ever, her shoulder-length dark hair perfectly straight, her smile wide and white. With a little tug on Finlay's arm, she made her way over. Finlay followed. He ran his hand through his hair, blinking and not meeting Aidan's gaze.

'Hey,' Elise said. 'I heard you were back.'

'I've been back two months.' Two whole months. Perhaps it was a miracle he'd avoided her this long. Or not. She'd probably been avoiding him.

'Wow, time flies.'

Clearly.

She'd hopped beds quick enough. And of all the people she'd had to choose. Not that Finlay wasn't a good choice of partner, but why did she have to pick someone so close?

'You got a ring yet?' Scarlett asked.

'Not yet,' Elise replied.

Finlay threw her a look, then caught Aidan's eye. Aidan's urge to hurt his cousin burned strong and he hated himself for it. Finlay hadn't had things easy in his love life and this should be something they could all celebrate. But it was too fresh. Aidan turned away and picked up some of the bee pins, placing them in a space at the opposite end from where Delilah was still dotting them around. He had a sneaky suspicion she was eavesdropping. The sooner he got rid of her, the better. He didn't need any more people knowing the gossip about his sorry excuse for a love life. Another odd twinge niggled him like someone inside his head was trying to attract his attention. *Don't let her leave yet. Hold on to her for a moment.* It felt like she had some purpose in his life he was yet to discover. But that was insane.

'Well, we sort of had a ring,' Elise went on. 'Finlay gave me his grandmother's one, but it wasn't exactly my style, so we're going to look at new ones soon.'

'Ooh, nice,' Scarlett said.

Aidan wished he could block out this entire conversation. Finlay having their grandmother's ring was enough to trigger several unwanted thoughts. Finlay's father was the oldest son, so that was why it hadn't come to Aidan. The fact it was something that kind of belonged to them both, but Finlay was the one to give to Elise, ate at Aidan's insides. Elise's rejection of it both annoyed him and gave him savage satisfaction.

Delilah smiled down at Maya, then gave her a pat. She glanced up, caught Aidan's eye and instantly started picking up more pins. Her fingers were pale and thin, much like the rest of her. She arranged the pins on the log, adjusting some of the ones she'd slapped on to start with, so they were evenly spaced.

'Would you like a drink or anything?' Elise said. 'We can pick something up for you.'

'Yeah, thanks,' Scarlett said. 'I wouldn't mind a tea.'

Aidan tried not to grind his teeth. Could Elise and Finlay just leave? He wanted them gone. He side-eyed Delilah and found her doing the same. She blinked and quickly looked away.

'What about you, Aidan?' Elise said.

'What?'

'Do you want me to get you anything?'

'No thanks.'

Elise screwed up her nose at Delilah, but on catching Aidan looking her way, she cast a quizzical glance at Scarlett. The expression on Elise's face and her barely concealed nod in Delilah's direction asked, *who is she and should I offer her a drink too?*

'She's no one,' Scarlett said. 'And she's definitely not getting a free coffee. She's going to put these pins back, then never darken our doors again.'

Delilah's lips were set in a tight line, like she was barely holding back the urge to slap Scarlett. Aidan empathised completely. The anger he'd harboured since his dad died simmered constantly, forcing nasty thoughts into his brain, but a different sensation surged in his chest, an odd need to protect Delilah, though he wasn't sure why. He just knew none of this was fair and, although she'd shown a tough side, something about her appeared vulnerable. Taking on two thugs with a log was probably less painful than being subjected to Scarlett's verbal attack.

'That's it done,' Delilah said, glancing up at him.

'Thanks. Listen.' He took her by the arm again, gentler this time. She pulled a face at the place where his hand was holding her, but he didn't let go and led her around the side of the stall. She shrugged him off as soon as they were away from Scarlett, Elise, and Finlay, and he didn't force it. If she ran, so be it.

'Here.' He pulled out his wallet and took out twenty quid. 'Take this and go get me a burger, will you? Get something for yourself too.'

'What?' She gaped at him. Her expression was wide-eyed, like she was looking at a madman. And maybe she was. 'I can't do that.'

'Why not? There's a stall down there. Please. Oh, and no onions, but cheese and salad.'

'You're trusting me with this?' She held up the twenty-pound note.

'Yes. So don't lose it. And did you hear me? No onions—'

'Just cheese and salad. Yeah, I heard you.'

'Good.'

'How do you know I won't nick this?'

'I don't.' He locked eyes with her again. She still had that look like she couldn't make him out. Then, with a little shrug, she turned and headed towards the burger stall.

Aidan watched her walk away, staring at the money in her hand. He'd likely never get the burger, but as he'd spent the last thirteen months raising money for charity, he could hardly ignore such an obvious case this close to home.

'Did you just give her money?' Scarlett marched up to him.

He turned. Thankfully, Finlay and Elise had moved on. 'She's gone to get me a burger.'

'What the fuck? Are you insane? Why didn't you ask Elise to get it? She offered.'

'Because I'm not asking Elise to do anything for me ever again.'

'My god, Aidan. You're such a grouch. Get over yourself. You abandoned her for thirteen months and you hardly spoke to any of us. You can't expect her to hang about waiting for you.'

'That's not what happened.'

'Oh yeah?' Scarlett moved in behind the stall, shaking her head. 'You went off radar completely. She waited for you to message and say something but you didn't. What did you expect?'

Aidan shoved his hands in his back pockets and didn't answer. He'd made a mistake with Elise – a big one. Now he was paying the price. He surveyed the people milling around the stalls and sighed. For once, Scarlett was annoyingly accurate. He'd been in such a state when he left all those months ago. Dad had died after losing his battle with motor neuron disease. Aidan had resigned from his job, put his cottage in the care of his mum, bought a dog and gone off to Canada with one goal – raise money to help other souls suffering from that accursed disease. Elise had understood. She'd stood by his choice. Or so he'd thought. But he hadn't really spoken to her about it properly. It had seemed so clear in his mind he hadn't thought that others might not get it.

Now he was back and nothing was right. Why was he standing here, at this bright yellow stall in a market that meant nothing to him? And where was his mum? So much for helping her out for twenty minutes. It had been almost an hour.

He scanned the crowd again but saw no one familiar. Not his mother. Not Finlay or Elise. Not Delilah with his burger. He gave a wry shrug and returned behind the stall. He'd probably never see her or that twenty-pound note ever again. But if it helped her out for a day or two, then where was the harm?

CHAPTER THREE

Lilah

Lilah rolled the twenty-pound note into a tube and held it tight in her balled fist. Her eyes darted around. Wouldn't this be the moment for Jaxon to reappear and snatch it? But neither he nor the two men were anywhere in sight. How easy would it be to vanish in this crowd with the money?

She took a long, hard look at her hand. Her knuckles turned white as they clenched around the money.

She chanced a peek over her shoulder. The tall, handsome man was talking to Scarlett again. Who was he? *Why has he trusted me with this money?* He obviously had no idea who he was dealing with. No doubt Scarlett would enlighten him. Was he Scarlett's boyfriend? Lucky her. Lilah's heart squeezed like an icy fist had grabbed it. The kind of guys she attracted never looked as good as him and definitely wouldn't give her money. No, they'd be more likely to take her on a cheap date, expect her to pay, want to go home with her, then offer her drugs and sex. By the time she got up the next day, they'd be gone and so would any money she'd had on her.

Time to leg it?

No, I mustn't.

With a heavy sigh and a stomach rumble that could rival a thunderclap, she reluctantly joined the queue at the burger van. Had Jaxon managed to stay out of trouble this time? A tiny part of her ached to know he was safe. But hey, she couldn't spend her entire life worrying about him. If she did, she'd become a twitchy bundle of nerves and never do anything. Same thing went for her whole family. Shutting off to their dramas was the best coping mechanism she had. None of them were exactly pros at keeping in touch and it was simplest that way.

The rolled-up twenty-pound note clenched in her palm was causing her some serious sweat-inducing anxiety. Who was the man who'd given it to her? And was it really ok to splurge some of it on herself? Well, he did say she could, so it must be legit, right? Unless there was some hidden catch she hadn't figured out yet.

She was so famished she'd almost forgotten what it felt like to be anything else. She fidgeted with the money, her eyes scanning over the stalls. Behind a table selling handmade soap was the bright yellow canopy on the Crafty Bee stall. Once she had the burger, she'd have to go back there. That would mean seeing Scarlett again. Ugh. She almost groaned aloud. If anything was likely to put her off returning, it was that.

The noise and commotion were disorientating. She caught sight of someone she thought was Jaxon but no, he'd be long gone. Her mind seemed dead set on playing out worst-case scenarios. She took a deep breath. Had she done enough to help? She couldn't have said yes to him bunking in the caravan with her. The people she lived with wouldn't allow it. If those guys who were after him came searching for him, who knew what they might do to the caravan? Torch it? She just had to switch off the remaining worries and trust in Jaxon's miraculous powers of evasion. He'd always had a knack for finding himself knee-deep in some sort of trouble, yet somehow, he emerged unscathed, like he had a secret pact with the universe to make sure he kept getting away.

As she moved closer to the front of the line, the aroma of sizzling burgers filled the air. She glanced at the menu board. How could she decide? She wasn't even sure what some of the stuff was – like a jalapeño... She wasn't brave enough to find out.

Finally, it was her turn to step up to the opening.

'Two burgers, please. With cheese, salad and no onions.'

A young man about her age nodded and began assembling the burger on the grill. She could do that. How did people find jobs like this when she was turned down for everything?

'Can I get you anything else?' The man placed two boxes in front of her.

'Um, no thanks.'

'That's eight sixty then.'

She handed over the twenty-pound note that now wouldn't stay flat and lifted the burgers. The man scooped coins from the till and handed them to her along with a tenner. Lilah clutched the money tightly as she turned back to the stall. This was the moment when her mum, Jaxon, her older brothers and most of the people she'd grown up with would thrust the burger at Aidan and run with the change, assuming they hadn't run with the twenty in the first place. And that was highly unlikely.

She made her way through the throng of people perusing stalls and chattering. Someone handed her a leaflet for The Cosy Bean Café. Like she could afford to buy anything there.

As she approached the yellow stall, her eyes linked with those dark sombre ones. The man's grey shirt and black jeans were a solemn contrast to the bright gazebo and table. Everything about him was brooding and dark, but heart-stoppingly attractive: from his muscular shoulders and upper arms encased in the safari shirt to his trim waist – a feast for weary eyes.

Before she reached him, he strode towards her. 'Which one's mine?' he asked.

'They're both the same.' She handed him a box. With only a second's hesitation, she held out the change.

He took it and the slight brush of his skin against hers sent tingles spreading outwards from the contact point. Her hand twitched and she withdrew it quickly. He shoved the money in his back pocket without counting it or asking her how much she'd spent.

'Can I go now?'

'I'd like you to tell me more about those two men first. I really should report it. Was it you they were after?'

She shook her head. 'I told you already. They were after some guy. I've never seen them before.' Which was the truth, though she wasn't sure he believed her. No surprises there.

He opened his burger box, flipped up the top half of the roll and the corners of his lips quirked. Her brain had already established he was blindingly handsome but when he smiled... Oh my... Lilah liked reading old books in the library or swapping them in charity shops. This guy definitely had something of a Mr Darcy about him but he was way too rugged. Maybe more like Mr Rochester.

'Are you Scarlett's boyfriend?'

'No.' He pulled a disgusted face as he bit into his burger. Lilah thought for a moment he would spit it out and say it was gross, but he swallowed it and said, 'Scarlett's my sister. Half-sister. She has a different father.'

He said it like it was an important fact, but it didn't bother her. She had five siblings and none of them had the same combination of parents as her. It seemed quite normal from where she stood.

'What do you do?' he asked.

'How do you mean?'

'For a job.'

'Oh.' She prised open her burger box. 'I bake and... that kind of thing.' Which was as close to the truth as she could get without making something up. Would it even matter what she said? It wasn't like he really cared. He was just making small talk while eating his burger so fast it was like he'd swallowed it down.

'Scarlett is convinced you were trying to steal something off the stall.'

Lilah shook her head. 'She hates me. She always has. Why would I want to steal anything from it? I don't need any bee badges or bunting, thanks.'

His lips twitched again. 'Yeah. Listen.' He closed the empty burger box and ran his thumb across his mouth, removing the faintest trace of flour. 'If you're looking for a job, I've got just the thing.'

Her heart raced. No way. He better not ask her for anything inappropriate. She might look like trash but she wouldn't do it. Not that it was the first time a guy had asked for that kind of thing, but no way. She wouldn't stoop low enough to sell herself.

'What do you mean?' She held the burger box across her chest like a shield.

'I need a cleaner. And I don't mean someone who pops in once a week to do a bit of dusting. I've got a cottage that's in a bit of a state. In fact, it's in a terrible state.'

'And you want me to clean it?'

'That would be the general idea.'

'Where is the cottage?'

'At the top end of Glenbriar. It backs onto a field in front of the Lower Briar Woods.'

That was on her walk back to the caravan. She'd probably passed it hundreds of times. 'Is it near the place with the bee-hives?' She nibbled the edge of her burger.

'It *is* the place with the beehives, though all the bees are gone.'

'Oh.' She gazed into his eyes for a moment. Her chest hurt a bit, kind of like indigestion, even though she'd barely touched the burger yet. *It's not indigestion, you idiot. It's him.* 'I-I… Well, I don't think I can.'

'No?'

How could she? She didn't know this guy. He could be anyone and all she knew for a fact was that he was Scarlett Finch's brother, which didn't go in his favour. How did she know this wasn't a trick? When you'd been brought up on a doctrine of *never trust anyone*, it made you wary. She wasn't saying yes to anything.

'I don't even know your name.'

'Aidan McBride.'

She glanced around and saw Scarlett squinting her way with narrowed eyes and a murderous expression. 'I can't. Sorry.'

'Fair enough,' he said.

'Thanks anyway. But I better go.'

'Here.' He fished in his pocket and pulled out the tenner. 'Take that. Get yourself something for dinner or whatever else you need.'

Lilah didn't put out her hand to take the money; she clamped her fingers tightly to the burger box. 'I don't need—'

'Take it. I insist.' He put it on top of the box, whipped around, and marched back to the Crafty Bee stall.

Lilah stared at the money. No denying she needed it. She clutched it in her palm and kept it there as she nibbled her burger.

Being hungry didn't mean she had to eat fast. No. She had to make this last. She moved through the crowd to the edge of the square where it joined the street beyond. Glenbriar was a touristy town and, even out of the main hubbub, the street was busy. It was a long walk back to the tiny village where she lived.

Was this another wasted journey? On the way down she'd been buzzing with thoughts of catching up with Jaxon. Ha! How stupid could she get? Since when had her brother ever wanted a catch up? Now she had a two-mile uphill walk to Clachnabronnachan. At least she had a burger… and a tenner. Not a complete waste then.

Savouring each bite of what had to be the best food she'd had in weeks, maybe months, maybe ever, she considered the unexpected job offer. Thoughts swirled around like bees searching for the brightest plants, except she couldn't land on the one with the right answer. Any job was appealing, considering her financial situation. The jobs she did for her landlady earned her accommodation and occasionally food but barely any spending money. She wasn't complaining. A roof over her head was better than nothing. But something held her back from taking Aidan's offer. *Never trust anyone.* The nagging voice in her mind warned her to stay away from Scarlett's brother. Surely accepting a job from him was asking for trouble and she really didn't want any more of that.

She tossed the empty burger box in a bin and carried on up the hill, past the houses on the edge of town. These were all grand buildings: large, with spacious gardens and flashy cars. The kind of places Lilah hadn't even been inside. When she'd been at school here, the kids who lived in homes like that didn't invite girls like her round for playdates.

Up ahead was the cottage with the beehives. She'd passed it so often but never paid it much attention. The grass by the path had been strimmed back but on either side the garden was completely overgrown. Slates were missing from the roof and the beehives stood abandoned and neglected in an orchard area to the side. The cottage's weathered walls and a boarded-up window told a sad story of neglect and forgotten dreams. Yet, despite its dilapidated state, Lilah felt a strange connection to the place. It reminded her of something she'd once read about the Brontë sisters and how, on their travels, they'd seen interesting buildings and made up stories about who might live there. It was what started them writing novels.

She paused for a moment and leaned on the stonewall. A sign swung on a pole close to the gate. Woodend Cottage.

Who lived here and what would their story be? Perhaps Lilah Clarke would be swept off her feet by Aidan McBride? She almost laughed at the stupidity of the idea.

Wind whispered through the trees just coming into leaf in the orchard and disturbed the tall grass in the field behind the cottage. Aidan might own this place but surely he didn't live there, not in its current state. What would it be like living in a place like that? Once it was done up, it could be beautiful. But what a lot of work. He'd asked her to clean it, so did that mean it wasn't so bad he needed a pro? She had no formal training in cleaning... or anything. Her best skill was baking. At school, she'd enjoyed art but it was too expensive a hobby for her to do now. She slowly breathed in the soft earthy smell, dreaming a little more about how it might feel to lie in that long grass next to a man like him, then carried on towards the woods.

Birds twittered like mad in the trees surrounding the gate to the Lower Briar Woods, their sound interspersed with the heavy crash of wood pigeons making ungainly take-offs. Lilah took the main path. The thick tree cover cast dancing shadows across the ground, and she swung her arms. What to do? She didn't exactly have an army of family and friends to turn to for advice.

As she ventured deeper into the woods, a sense of peace washed over her. The worries and uncertainties temporarily faded. The path wound its way through the trees, a tapestry of greens and browns stretching out before her.

But it was a short-lived reprieve. When she left the woods at the far end, it was only a short walk to the tiny village of Clachnabronnachan, which was little more than a cluster of houses – mostly some boxy ex-council semis around a small green, a few older cottages, and some scattered farms. The place she lived was one of the ex-council semis and the ugliest house on the street. Its owners, Malcolm and Brenda McManus, were outraged by the slightest wrongdoing of anyone in the neighbourhood they didn't like, but conveniently blind to the state of their own lives. Their garden was completely taken over by old machinery, broken bits of metal, empty oil drums and mess. Just mess. So much mess. Lilah had grown up in chaotic homes but this was a whole new level. Almost unbearable. Inside wasn't much better.

Her 'job' of helping Brenda make fudge was laughable. If anyone buying it saw the conditions they made it in, they'd throw the box straight in the bin and call environmental health.

Lilah cleaned the area she was working in but it was a losing battle. Brenda knew very little about baking, though she liked to supervise and criticise.

As Lilah approached the messy garden, Malcolm ambled out of the house, rubbing a hand across his huge belly. 'Afternoon, lass,' he said, shoving a biscuit into his face. 'You've been away a long time. What you been up to?'

'I was at the fair.'

'Dear, dear,' he muttered, lifting a plant pot and shifting it to a tiny corner he'd cleared on the potting table. 'Bet it's not as good as when Brenda and me used to organise it. All these things have gone downhill since we moved on. Well, it's the punters who're suffering like we knew they would. But you know what it's like. Red tape and the like. It meant we had to leave after so many years. Pity, pity.'

'It was really busy.' She gave a little shrug. 'So whoever is organising it now seems to be doing ok.'

'Aye well, it's a nice day. Draws people out.' With difficulty, he heaved a large plant pot onto the table. 'Brenda's had a big fudge order. She's looking for you.'

'Ok. I'll go and see.'

Lilah entered the kitchen and cringed. Brenda was shoving boxes and detritus out of the way. 'There you are. I need you to make this by tomorrow. I don't have time. We've got my friends coming round later for vino in the back garden.' She fanned her large jowls, her skin very red.

Seriously? She could call that a garden. They barely had a square metre where they plonked their deckchairs. The rest of it was taken up by some cobbled together outbuildings and more junk. Apparently they sold the junk somewhere nearby in a place they called a salvage yard. Who bought it? Lilah sure didn't know.

'Ok.' She put on an apron and scrubbed her hands. Working for Aidan wouldn't get her out of here but it would give her a bit of extra money and a chance to escape for a few hours when she wasn't making fudge. She didn't exactly have much else she could do other than taking walks in the woods and reading in the cold damp caravan.

'Do you know someone called Aidan McBride?' she asked Brenda.

Brenda leaned her voluptuous bottom on a cabinet and crossed her arms. 'I don't know him exactly but I know who he is. I know his mum quite well. His dad was well-known around these parts. Tragic what happened to him.'

'What?'

'He had motor neuron disease. Awful to watch such a strong person fade like that. Aidan took his death hard. I heard from his mum that he went off to do some long-distance walk to raise money for charities, but she reckons he couldn't face living in that house without his dad. I doubt he'll ever come back.'

Lilah decided not to mention he was already back; she didn't want any questions, in case she blurted out that he'd given her money. Brenda didn't need to know about that.

'He lived at that Woodend Cottage,' Brenda went on. 'Then buggered off to do his walk and the place was abandoned. Looks like a right state these days.'

'Yeah.' Lilah poured sugar into the bowl, making sure she said no more. But really, Brenda hardly had the right to call anyone else's house a state, even though in this case she was right.

'Why do you want to know about Aidan?'

'I met his sister at the fair. We were at school together.'

'Scarlett?'

'Yup.'

'She's definitely her mother's daughter. Aidan's much more like his dad. He lived with him in the cottage even after his parents split. When he got his own place and his dad got sick, he was always back helping him and caring for him. He was shacked up with that Elise Reid for a bit. I heard she's run off with his cousin.'

Lilah frowned at the mixture in the bowl. She didn't know either of those people but her mind flew back to the stall and the beautiful woman that had offered to buy them a coffee. Was that his ex? And was the man she was with his cousin? Poor Aidan.

As she stirred the gloopy mixture, she couldn't ignore the thoughts rising to the surface. Was it too late to reconsider his offer? This might be an opportunity. A turning point and a chance to escape the cycle she'd been trapped in for so long. She had questions though. Like where would she live? Brenda wouldn't want her staying here if she was working elsewhere. But would she mind if it was only for a couple of weeks?

When all the fudge was made and crammed into any space she could find in the fridge, she headed out to the caravan which stood in an overcrowded corner of the McManus's driveway. She pulled on her thick bed socks and curled under her lumpy and completely pathetic duvet in the foldout bed. The caravan door didn't shut properly and a draught constantly streamed under it. Lilah huddled in, shivering. Maybe her dreams would take her to a better place. She quite liked the one she'd started earlier of lying in the sunny meadow with someone who looked a lot like Aidan McBride.

Chapter Four

Aidan

Aidan stepped out the back door of Woodend Cottage, the dewy morning grass damp under his bare feet. He took a sip from his mug of coffee, his gaze sweeping across the overgrown back garden and the neglected orchard area to the side. The weathered wooden hives stood in rows, waiting patiently for their new occupants. The field behind the cottage stretched to the woods beyond and some early mist hung over the tallest trees.

He'd started the clean-up operation inside, so the house stank of bleach, but it was either that or carry on camping in the back garden.

The boarded-up window in the front bedroom still needed fixing and so did some loose slates. Plus, there was the garden. This cottage was blessed with a great space around it and even had some disused outbuildings. Dad had often talked about further extensions. The one out the back he'd completed when Aidan was a teenager and it had made the place seem like a palace. It had gone from a cramped two-bedroom cottage to having three bedrooms, a larger kitchen and living area and even a study. Dad had always fancied a conservatory where he could sit and look out over the field towards the wood. Aidan imagined him sitting there with his binoculars as an old man, watching the squirrels climbing the trees and the deer sifting through the long grass. Except his dad would never be an old man.

Maya slumped down, chewing at a stick. Made a change from some of the stuff she'd gnawed on in Canada. Aidan padded across the long, damp grass and sat down beside her. She grumbled at the stick, then nuzzled her head into his leg.

'Beautiful girl,' he said, scratching behind her ears. 'I'm lucky to have found you.' If only he could say the same about the women in his life. He sipped his coffee and sighed. Thinking about Finlay and Elise made his blood pressure soar. How had he let this happen? Why had he been so blind?

Grief.

He supposed that was what it was anyway. But what about Finlay? Was he an innocent party caught in the crossfire? Even if Aidan was partly to blame, it didn't make their actions any less galling.

'Good morning,' a voice called from over the fence.

Aidan turned and looked across to the opposite side of the garden from the orchard where an old man was leaning on the fence that separated their properties. Getting to his feet, Aidan strolled towards the large barren area that had once been a driveway, though he no longer had a vehicle other than his bike. On the orchard side, there were no houses between Woodend

Cottage and the woods, but on this side was a row of old terraced houses. Aidan's feet quickly adjusted to the harsh stone of the old drive. It had cracked concrete with grass and weeds growing through it. If he ever got round to clearing it, it would give him another workable space. You could park at least four cars in here, maybe more. Not that he ever planned on having that many, but like everything else at Woodend, it had fallen into disrepair. He passed the large wooden garage that was more like a barn and headed towards the old man.

'Good morning, Jim,' he said. 'How are you?'

'Ah, not too bad. Arthritis playing up a bit, but it's to be expected at my age. And how are you?' His words were directed at Maya who'd jumped and placed her front paws on the fence.

'She's on good form,' Aidan said.

'She's a very lovely dog, yes, you are.' Jim chuckled as Maya licked his nose. 'And how is the work going?' He looked up at Aidan.

'Work?' Aidan had given up his job before he left for Canada and didn't want to go back to the daily grind. A flashy career had never been important to him. 'I haven't decided what I'll do in the long term.' He'd rather do some good in the world than worry about where his next pay check was coming from. 'I've lined up some motivational speaking jobs over the next few weeks. It's quite funny that people will actually pay to listen to me waffling on. And I'm going to do some dog walking.'

'Oh, that sounds marvellous,' Jim said. 'Though I actually meant the work on the cottage. I knew you'd have no difficulty finding a job. You've always been a hard worker.'

Maybe that was true but he also liked balance. Working hard was fine as long as it didn't take over his life. Maybe that was another reason Elise had chosen Finlay. The man with a steady job and a 'normal' lifestyle.

'Thanks, Jim. We're meeting the dogs today.' He patted Maya's head. 'We'll make this a good day with some new chums.'

'Good stuff.'

'And I'm getting new bees.'

'I'm very pleased to hear it,' Jim said. 'This place needs the bees. They're like the heart of it.'

Aidan smiled, leaning on the fence and looking back across the garden towards the orchard. 'Yes, they are.' He'd prepared the hives, ensuring they were clean and ready. The bees would bring life back to Woodend. 'And Dad would appreciate it. Bees were the love of his life.'

'He certainly adored them. But I think there was something he loved more.' Jim looked at him seriously. 'You.'

Aidan nodded, glancing skyward, trying to stop a lump in his throat. 'Yeah. I know.'

'He'd be very proud.' Jim gave Aidan a gentle cuff on the arm. 'Now, I'll let you get on. I think it's going to be a nice day. I'm off to put out some food for the birds. Hopefully the goldfinches will be back today. Beautiful, so they are.'

'Yes, they are. Enjoy your day.' Aidan returned to the house, left his mug in the kitchen and flung on his old trainers. Maya trotted after him as he busied himself with the final preparation of the hives.

It had been stupid leaving his mum in charge of this. She loved bees too, but not the practicalities. She liked making and selling bee crafts, but beekeeping was beyond her. His dad had taught Aidan how to care for the bees without a bee suit. Most people, including his mum, thought he was mad, but he wasn't. And it wasn't arrogance or cockiness. It was just naturally co-existing with beautiful living creatures. Bees were gentler and more accepting than most humans.

As he checked and arranged the frames, an engine rumbled up outside the cottage and Aidan turned his attention to it.

Was this the delivery van? Nice and early.

'I think this is the bees, Maya.'

A man jumped out of the van and opened the passenger door to take out a clipboard. 'Are you Aidan McBride?'

'I am.'

'Ok. I've got your nucs. I need you to sign some paperwork.'

Aidan signed the papers as the deliverer opened the back doors and carefully lifted out the packages. He set them down outside the gate. 'There you go.'

'Thanks,' Aidan said. The gentle hum of the bees was so familiar and comforting. He carried the packages to the hives, then carefully lifted the lid of one, revealing a mass of bees clinging to the frames. 'Welcome to Woodend,' he said. 'Let's settle you in.'

Eventually, he might make some money from them, but right now, he just wanted bees back in his life. His mum was already pestering him about honey for the Crafty Bee. If she'd been more diligent with his last colony, she could already have some. But they weren't for everyone.

With a groan, he realised just how many mistakes he'd made. People had said he needed counselling after his dad died, but bullishly he'd gone off thinking he could solve everything in his own way. Only now he was dealing with the fallout.

He stood for a few moments until the dark thoughts passed, then he spoke quietly about the weather as he scooped the bees into their new home. Dad had always insisted they understood him and he made a point of talking to them. Sometimes people thought he was mad but Aidan got it. The bees learned gentle words weren't threatening. It helped them to trust.

After he said goodbye, he returned to the house. Maya jumped up from her spot in the grass and followed him.

Picking up her lead, he jangled it, and she trotted up beside him. He fixed on her harness and left by the front door. Several people had already contacted him about dog walking since he'd let it be known he was available. Today, he'd be back and forward a few times to the Briar Woods with his four-legged companions. Maya, used to endurance walking, didn't object to accompanying him every time he went out.

Once he'd collected Bella, a golden retriever, Coco, a collie, and Max, who was a mishmash of breeds, and what his dad would have termed a Heinz fifty-seven, Aidan walked back up the road past his cottage towards the woods.

As soon as he got back, he needed to investigate getting someone to help him clean. That was something he'd happily outsource, so he could focus on his other causes. He passed the gate to the field behind the house. It had lain empty for some time and left a beautiful open vista behind the cottage. So much wildlife lived in it and it was like a wildflower meadow now. The lower part of it was a waste ground. Hopefully it wouldn't be sold to developers. Or at least if it was, then hopefully someone progressive. It would be an amazing site for a bird hide or an eco café.

With Bella leading the way, her golden fur shimmering in the sunlight, Aidan and the pack ventured along the path. It ran alongside the field for half a mile. A carpet of bluebells stretched out under the trees.

Magnificent.

Scents of earth and pine filled the air, mingling with the sweet fragrance of the bluebells. The dogs darted ahead on the long leads, their tongues wagging. Maya sniffed about off the lead. She wouldn't go anywhere without him but Aidan didn't know the others well enough to trust them not to run if he unclipped them.

The worries of the outside world faded, if only momentarily, replaced by the soothing whispers of the wind. This was exactly why he loved walking. Being alone with his thoughts indoors made him brood and get irritated. But something about the outdoors made it impossible to dwell on the bad.

He made a quick time check on his phone and saw a message from his cousin Hayley. He took a deep breath. Hayley was a sweet and loving person he'd always had a lot of time for, but she was also Finlay's sister and Elise's friend. Tension built in his chest, making him want to both check the message and delete it without opening. Part of him would like to cut off every tie he'd ever had to Finlay and Elise. But Hayley deserved better. She'd always been kind to him. He'd avoided seeing her since he got back but he couldn't do that indefinitely. She was the kind of person who would turn up on his doorstep eventually. And some days he kind of hoped she would; he could do with a human friend occasionally. But what if she'd sided with her brother and thought Aidan the enemy?

Open it and find out!

With a grunt, he flipped open the message.

HAYLEY: How's things, big cuz? I can guess pretty much how you're feeling right now. I wouldn't want to talk to me either if I was in your position. But seriously whatever happened between you and Elise and now Finlay, please don't count me as having anything to do with it. I love my brother and Elise is my friend, but I also love you and count you as a friend too. And I don't want to lose that. I'd love to come and see you sometime. Hope that's ok. XX

Aidan pocketed his phone with a smile. How could he refuse a plea like that? And truth be told, he wanted someone to talk to. Needed someone. No one else really understood.

The dogs' energy was contagious. Aidan watched them sniffing and panting. Bella belonged to an elderly couple who liked having a companion but found her walking needs beyond them. Coco's owner was a busy doctor, and Max's family had recently welcomed a new baby, making it difficult for them to give him the attention he deserved. Aidan was happy to take on the burden. Doing this didn't feel like work, not when he loved the outdoors so much.

A figure emerged from the winding path ahead, and Aidan squinted at it. His heart skipped a beat, like he'd missed a step going downstairs. Dappled sunlight highlighted a vision of long red hair. A young woman so glowing and lost in her own world she almost didn't seem real. She reminded him of one of the flower fairies his mum used to show him in a book when he was a kid. Her arms were swinging by her side and she was gazing around, humming a sweet and very delicate melody.

With a jolt of recognition, he almost tripped over one of the dogs, who'd stopped to sniff something on the path. It was Delilah. But how could it be? He'd taken her for a bit of a basket case in need of a good feed and a wash. But not now. His eyes widened at her transformation. No longer hidden beneath a cap, her red, wavy hair flowed around her, accentuating delicate features and an elegant neck. She sure didn't look like a boy anymore. Christ, no. She was striking. *Close your mouth, idiot.* Why was he gaping like a stupid teenager? Something stirred deep within him. A burning sensation, almost carnal. *Steady.*

A painful longing woke in his chest, pushing him towards her, almost daring him to approach her. And then what? His mind fast-forwarded through a number of inappropriate but deeply satisfying scenarios. What was he thinking? Fantasising about some poor unsuspecting young woman? With an effort, he re-focused on the dogs as they continued their cheerful exploration of the woodland.

All these scenarios were drifting into his mind because he was lonely. Pure and simple. He maybe didn't want to admit it out loud and, in all honesty, he didn't mind his own company, but deep down, something was missing. It left a gap. Elise had previously filled it and he, perhaps arrogantly, had believed she'd always be there. Now, it was safer to retreat into self-imposed isolation.

His eyes flickered back to Delilah; she was just a few metres away. The dogs, curious about the newcomer, tugged at their leads, urging him forward.

'Hello,' he said.

Delilah stared at him and for a moment he thought she might put her head down and walk on. Then she stopped and fingered the strap of her khaki top. 'Hi. I was on my way to see you.'

Completely blindsided, Aidan frowned. *On her way to see me?*

CHAPTER FIVE

Lilah

Lilah's breath caught in her throat as she stared at Aidan. It didn't wholly surprise her to see him. She believed in coincidence and fate, though she often wondered what had gone wrong with her destiny.

His presence was larger than life. He was so powerful looking and well built. Not to mention those penetrating eyes. She felt weak and insignificant next to him.

'You were on your way to see me?' Aidan repeated her words in that impossibly deep tone of his.

'Yes,' she replied. He stood like a pillar of power and it both impressed her and made her slightly nervous, though his vibe was nothing like the thugs in the market. Anyone who had four dogs either needed a lot of guarding or wanted a lot of friends who didn't talk back. Which was he?

'What did you want to see me about?'

'I... I was, um...' Her fingers toyed with the strap of her top while her focus roamed over his tight black t-shirt. His biceps were thick and toned. He raised his hand and ran his fingers through his lush dark hair. Everything about him screamed hot and sexy. If she was going to accept his job offer, she'd have to make sure she only worked when he was out, otherwise she'd get nothing done. She'd just want to gape at him all day long.

'You…?' He gave a little shrug, as if urging her to continue.

'I wanted to talk to you about the job you offered me.' She fidgeted with the worn fabric of her jeans. Whatever daydreaming she might have been doing about him, she could guarantee he wouldn't be returning the favour. Who would want a scummy piece of filth like her? She did everything she could to keep herself and her clothes clean but the bathroom at the McManus's was disgusting and she sometimes suspected her clothes came out the washer dirtier than when they went in. She glanced up at Aidan through downcast eyes. 'If… if you still need someone.'

Her words trailed off, her voice barely audible amidst the gentle rustle of leaves and the distant chirping of birds. Aidan would know all about her past and her family. No doubt Scarlett would have enlightened him. She couldn't bring herself to meet his gaze. So much for this big chance. Of course he didn't want her. Story of her pathetic life. *Time to move on.* She shouldn't have wasted the trip.

'Yeah. I do need someone to help with the cleaning. The cottage was damaged by a storm or possibly vandals while I was away and it's in bad shape. Lots of stuff got damp and needs going through. I just don't have the time.'

'Ok... I can do that. I can pretty much do anything.' She cinched her shoulders. 'Just say when. What are the wages?'

He let out a short rumbling laugh. 'Whatever the going rate is. I'll investigate, unless you already know.'

She shook her head. The minimum wage didn't seem to apply to the job she had. 'How long do you want me to do it?'

'We can discuss that, but wouldn't you like to see the cottage first? Maybe you should see what you're agreeing to before we talk about the details.'

It was unlikely to be any worse than the McManus's house, but she wasn't about to turn down the chance to see inside Woodend Cottage. 'I'd like to see it, yeah.' She put her hands in her pockets.

'Ok. If you want to walk back with me, I can show you now.' On his words, the husky trotted forward, sniffing Lilah and wagging her tail.

Lilah patted her and giggled as her wet nose nuzzled her wrist. 'Are these all your dogs?'

'No. Only Maya. I'm walking these dogs for people.'

'Like people are paying you, you mean?'

'Yeah.'

'So, is that your job?' She remembered what Brenda had told her about him disappearing abroad for over a year.

'It is for now.'

'For now?'

'Yeah. I do different things. I'm not tied to a career and I make money where I can. Soon, I'll be growing things so I can be as self-sufficient as possible. I'm not big on stuff and I try to live frugally. My one indulgence is going to be hiring a cleaner.'

Lilah half-smiled, glancing up at him. It was hard not to. He drew her focus. She kept in step with him back to the cottage, her heart beating fast. He walked at some pace but it wasn't keeping up with him that was causing the problem. Just being beside a man of this stature was something she wasn't used to. Having grown up among people who smoked, took drugs and drank their health away, this was so new. So often when she was in men's company, she felt on edge and wary, like she had to watch her back, but Aidan had a different kind of presence. He seemed more likely to protect her from harm than to cause it.

The dogs trotted alongside them, their paws crunching on the forest path. Maya stayed close, occasionally nudging Lilah's hand again with her wet nose. Lilah smiled at her and gave her a pat. Just like her owner, she had a comforting presence.

'She likes you,' Aidan said, with a half glance and Lilah's chest swelled.

They exited the wood through a gate that joined a pavement and approached Woodend Cottage. Lilah rubbed her sternum at a twinge of something... Could it be excitement? She was finally going to see inside the house that had so often drawn her eye.

'You're allowed to say no after you've seen it,' Aidan said. 'I wouldn't blame you if you did.'

'I bet it's not that bad compared to some of the places I've lived.' Heat bloomed in her cheeks. Why had she said that? It was just adding to her already dented image.

'Don't bet on it.' He threw her a dark look. 'I'll put the dogs in the back garden before we go in. Maya's allowed in but I don't take the others into my house.'

Lilah followed him through the side gate, past another gate into the orchard area. The grass was still partially overgrown at the back, though some of it appeared newly trimmed. Aidan filled some water bowls at an outside tap and put them down on a small patio area.

'Right. Let's go in.' He unlocked the side door, and they stepped into the dimly lit kitchen. The air was musty, and the wallpaper was peeling and bubbling around some damp patches. Lilah's eyes darted around, taking in the old-fashioned units and uneven lino. She and Aidan progressed into a small hallway with original floorboards.

'So, here we have it. I've done the really noticeable bits with bleach, but there's still loads I've missed and ...' He pushed open the door to the living area. 'This is one of the worse bits. It's dusty and... Well, see for yourself.'

Lilah peered in, and though she could see what he meant, it was like a palace compared to the caravan she was living in. The house she'd grown up in had been ten times worse, possibly more.

She turned to Aidan. 'I'm happy to give it a go.'

Aidan nodded, his gaze meeting hers and for a split second a tremor of something passed between them but it was quickly lost. 'Great.'

'Do you want me to do like a week of intensive stuff or like one day every week or what?'

'How about I engage you for two weeks of intensive cleaning, and we'll see how things progress from there? If you're ok with that and your work's good, then we can think about extending it to a couple of hours a week or whatever suits you.'

'When can I start?'

He let out a dry laugh. 'I need to find out how much to pay you first.'

'Ok. So, should I come back tomorrow? Or when?'

He checked his phone. 'I have to get the dogs back to their owners. So, yes, tomorrow would be great.'

'Ok. I'll do that.' Hopefully Brenda wouldn't get any big orders in for fudge. Much as Lilah loved baking, she was so over fudge.

'Tomorrow at eleven o'clock then.'

'Ok.'

'And Delilah, do you want my number in case anything happens?'

Never in a million years would she have expected to be swapping numbers with someone like him, though, of course, this was business. She tried to hide her phone as she got it out. It was an utterly ancient thing that only held a charge for about an hour and she had to keep it switched off most of the time. The screen was cracked and it was probably out of credit. He said his number and she typed it in, not looking at him. What must he think of her?

'By the way, my, um... my name is Delilah but no one calls me that. Lilah is fine.'

'Fine. Lilah it is.' He gave her a brief smile and opened the door for her. As she passed him, she got a lungful of some kind of body spray. Its woody freshness was manly and very him. But it reminded her of something else. Something that made her cringe. A memory from years ago, when she'd taken the bus into Perth with one of her older brothers, Blake. They'd gone into Boots the chemist and Blake had covered himself in something that smelled not dissimilar to whatever Aidan had on. After deciding he liked it, he'd stuffed two bottles of it into his coat and walked out. It had seemed so normal at the time.

'See you tomorrow,' Aidan said.

'See you.'

She walked quickly up the pavement to the gate into the woods and, as soon as she reached it, she broke into a run. To-morrow couldn't come soon enough. Who cared about any-thing else? What was it exactly she was looking forward to? She couldn't be sure. But she would see Aidan again. And she really wanted to. Her heart skipped along the path with her.

Once back at the caravan however, the rest of the afternoon dragged. So did the evening. So did the next morning. When it was finally time, she left early, walked quickly and arrived at the door of Woodend half an hour before she was supposed to be there. Should she knock? Or go back to the woods and hang about there for a bit? A voice somewhere nearby caught her attention and she glanced towards the orchard area. Among the trees, overgrown grass and wildflowers, Aidan stood bending over one of the beehives and talking softly. His deep voice vibrated almost like he was chanting. Lilah closed her eyes, letting the sound soothe her like a warm breeze massaging the tension from her neck and forehead.

As she opened her eyelids, Aidan seemed to sense her and turned to face her. He raised his hand in a brief wave, then made his way towards her. Should she speak? Or would it disturb the bees? Any sound might sever the bond her gaze had made with his and she didn't want that.

'Sorry, I'm early,' she said, her voice barely above a whisper. 'I don't want to disturb the bees.'

'You won't. Not from this distance. Just don't scream or shout if you're close to the hives.'

'I'll stay away from them. Bees scare me.'

'Do they? I'll need to introduce you to these bees. They're not scary at all. Bees are beautiful creatures and very important to humans.'

'Don't you wear a big white suit when you go in there?'

He shook his head and his lip curled into a small smile, pushing a dimple into his lightly bearded cheek. 'I never wear a bee suit.'

'But don't you get stung?'

'No. I've very rarely been stung. Bees are gentle by and large.'

'Wow. You must be really brave.' He looked it.

'It's not being brave or stupid. I just know bees well and I understand their behaviour. Now, come in. I've done some research on payments and I'd like to see what you think.'

Lilah followed him along the corridor. The cottage had obviously been extended, making it a bit of an odd shape with corridors off corridors, almost too many for what wasn't a particularly large building. The new rooms had carpets and plastered walls while the original ones had wooden floorboards and dated wallpaper, though it wasn't completely terrible apart from the damp patches. Once it was scrubbed up and tidied a bit, it could be tasteful.

It was much larger than anywhere Lilah had lived, that was for sure. Aidan opened a door to a small and very tidy room with an old-fashioned desk and a solid wood bookcase. This room had an austere air and Lilah thought it resembled a Victorian gentleman's study, like the ones she'd read about in Charles Dickens' books. It probably wasn't actually that old but she imagined a top-hatted gentleman sitting there organising his affairs.

'Take a seat,' Aidan said, indicating a wood and leather chair that might once have belonged to a dining set but was now by itself. He took the swivel chair on the other side of the desk. 'This is what I found online about the going rate for cleaners.' He handed her a printed piece of paper. 'Is that ok?'

Lilah took it and read. Should she tell him it was more than she'd ever been paid for anything? For a few hours a day, she could earn that much? It would be like being a millionaire. 'That looks... good.'

'And is cash in hand ok to start with?'

'Yeah.' She gave a little shrug. It would have to be. She didn't have a bank account; she'd never even been in a bank. 'Do I start today?'

Aidan sniffed out what might have been a scoff or a laugh, opened his mouth as if to say something, seemed to change his mind, and frowned. 'Well, if you really want to. I suppose you could. Don't you want to wait until I can write out a contract?'

'Um... I don't think I've ever had one before. I don't mind starting as like a trial or something.' It was such a long walk and she wasn't ready to leave him yet. She was developing a hefty crush and being in his company sent pleasurable little tingles through her veins.

'Well, ok. I'll write something up while you're doing the trial. Let me show you exactly what I'd like you to do. If you stick to the hallway, the living room and the kitchen. The other rooms aren't as big a problem.' He led her back through the house, explaining what he wanted cleaned, places he wanted things sorted or boxed up and where she could find the cleaning supplies. 'I've got to go and collect the dogs in an hour, so you'll have to finish up then.'

'That's fine.'

'Good. I'll write up a contract.'

As soon as the door clicked shut, she let out a sigh and rubbed her hands together. Where to even start? It was like being thrown into a room full of straw and being told to spin it into gold, like in Rumpelstiltskin, one of the old fairy tales she loved, though that one also creeped her out a bit.

She returned to the kitchen and found the cleaning products and cloths. If she did it bit by bit, she'd get there.

She tossed off her hoody and got to work, starting in the living room. First, she sorted through the piles of books and papers that Aidan wanted boxed up. Anything she deemed too badly damaged was to be put in a separate box, so he could decide if he wanted to salvage it or not. The soft thud of books landing in the boxes was the only sound in the still house. Through the French doors, the grass fluttered in the breeze and the trees in the wood swayed against a grey sky. After the pleasant heat of the day before, it was overcast and cool. She pressed on, occasionally diverted by the headlines on the old magazines, then she'd flip through them to read the articles.

Aidan came in with a printed piece of paper and surveyed the scene with a half smile, half frown. 'Do you want to read this through and see if you agree or if there's anything you want to change?'

Lilah took the paper and read it. She had no idea what to judge it by but it all sounded very official. The dates started with the following day and carried on for two weeks with suggested hours of nine until four o'clock.

'After the two weeks, we'll do another one if we want to continue.'

'Yeah... That's all good.' Lilah handed back the bit of paper. 'Should I sign it?'

'If you want. Or if you want someone independent to read it, that's fine too.'

'No. It's ok.' She couldn't imagine asking Brenda or Malcolm's opinion.

'Let's get a pen then.' Aidan opened a drawer on the sideboard and pulled one out.

Lilah wasn't sure she had an official signature, so she wrote her name neatly on the line. Aidan signed his below with something of a flourish. A weird sense of belonging fluttered through her. That bit of paper meant she had somewhere to go, somewhere to be, and something important to do.

The following morning she arrived at eight-thirty. It felt like she was late rather than half an hour early but she'd hardly slept a wink all night, thinking about coming back to Woodend.

'You're early,' Aidan said as Maya greeted her with a waggy tail.

'It's hard to judge when I'm walking.'

'I'm not complaining. Come in. You don't have to start until nine or feel free to leave early. I won't be clock-watching as long as the work gets done.'

'I'll just start. May as well.'

'Great.' He gave her a little smile. 'I'll be in and out all day walking the dogs and seeing to the bees. If I'm going out, I'll let you know.'

'Ok, but...' She frowned at him. Was he trusting her to be here alone when she could steal anything and run with it?

Her heart slipped into her stomach. Why did she always have to think like that? And what was there to steal from here anyway?

'But what?' He raised an eyebrow.

'If you're ok with me being here alone.'

'Is there a reason I shouldn't be?'

'No.' She shook her head.

'Well then. I'm fine with it.'

Lilah got to work on the magazines again. She heard Aidan moving about the house and doors closing every now and then. From the window, she spotted him crossing the garden, heading for the orchard, with Maya following him. A while later, he returned to the house. He poked his head around to tell Lilah he was going to fetch the dogs.

She'd moved on from the magazines to the next dusty book-shelf and was midway pulling out an armful of old books, when a knock on the front door startled her. Who was it? Did Aidan expect her to answer it? Maybe it was the postie. She hadn't expected any interruptions and Aidan hadn't said what to do if someone came looking for him. Her heart quickened. She remembered hiding under her bed as a child when people came to the door, and she didn't know where her mum or her siblings were. The steady beat of urgency came to a head with another knock. Should she hide now or just answer it? Maybe Aidan would be annoyed if she left it.

With a deep breath, she headed for the front door and pulled it open. A young woman with long dark glossy hair glanced up from a phone. She had a warm smile, bright, lively eyes and a stylish – probably expensive – outfit.

'Oh, hi,' she said. 'I didn't think anyone was here. I was about to message Aidan. Is he about?'

'He's not here at the moment. He went to walk the dogs, but he'll be back soon.'

The woman's eyes flickered with curiosity as they raked over Lilah. 'And who are you?'

'Oh... I'm the cleaner.'

'Ah, I see.' The woman smiled again and Lilah tried to smile back. Was this Aidan's girlfriend? She'd heard from Brenda about his ex-girlfriend running off with his cousin. This wasn't the same woman she'd seen at the fair but Aidan was so very handsome it wouldn't be surprising if he had other admirers.

'I love your hair,' the woman said. 'What a stunning colour.'

Lilah's cheeks burned. 'Um, thank you.'

The woman grinned. 'I'm a hairdresser. If you ever want it styled, come my way. It really is beautiful.'

What a kind offer, but presumably this woman didn't know she was talking to someone with zero money. No way could Lilah afford a hairdresser. 'Er, thanks.'

'Can I come in and wait for Aidan?'

'I guess.'

'Sorry, how thick of me. I haven't even said who I am. I'm Hayley, his cousin.'

'His cousin?' A tremor of relief coursed through Lilah, which was silly because she had no claim on him. 'Oh... I'm sure he won't mind.'

'What's your name?'

'Lilah.'

'That's a lovely name.'

'Thanks.' Lilah swallowed and tossed her hair over her shoulder.

'So, what's Aidan getting you to clean?'

'The living room and the kitchen mostly.'

'It's in a right state, isn't it?' Hayley scanned around. 'No wonder he wants someone to help him out. I would have helped him, even though I don't have a lot of time. But I'm not sure he's talking to me.' She flopped onto the sofa.

'Oh. Why?' Lilah went back to sorting the books. Hopefully she hadn't let in somebody who Aidan didn't actually want to talk to.

Hayley sighed. 'Because my brother is now engaged to one of my best friends and that best friend happens to be Aidan's ex. I'm stuck in the middle of it all and it's so awkward. Technically, Finlay – that's my brother – hasn't done anything wrong. Aidan and Elise hadn't been together for several months when Elise started dating Finlay. But when Aidan left, he convinced himself that Elise would wait. And now it's just a mess. I can't stand conflict and I love all three of them. It's horrible seeing them all upset and awkward.'

'Sounds awful.' Lilah wasn't sure she could relate. She'd never had friends or family to look out for. She grew up looking out for number one. Suddenly that seemed like the easy option compared to what Hayley was going through. A lonely option too.

Something clunked in the kitchen and both Lilah and Hayley glanced towards the living room door. 'This cottage is cute,' Hayley said, 'but it's a bit creepy sometimes. And poor Aidan being here all alone. I really wish he could find someone else. I'd love to set him up. Matchmaking is always fun, but I don't think he'd like that.'

'Too right, I wouldn't,' he said from the doorway and the two of them leapt a mile as his deep resounding voice filled the air.

'Aidan!' Hayley screamed. She jumped up from the sofa and flung herself at him, throwing her arms around his neck. With a low, rumbling laugh, he hugged her back.

'What are you doing here?' he asked.

'Coming to find out why you don't reply to my messages.'

'Touché.'

Lilah watched them from the corner of her eye. What must it be like having someone who greeted her like that? She couldn't imagine anyone ever hugging her with that much meaning or being that pleased to see her.

Hayley backed away from Aidan a little, still smiling at him. He returned it but an edge of melancholy seemed to linger in his eyes. Then he turned and his gaze connected with Lilah's before she could look away. Caught in the act of staring at her new crush... The most intense one she could remember.

'I should leave the two of you to talk.' Lilah put down a pile of books and got to her feet.

'Stay if you want,' Hayley said. 'I don't mind and I'm sure Aidan won't.'

He shook his head like it didn't bother him, but Lilah didn't want to intrude. None of this was her business and it would be awkward hanging around while they chatted about stuff she knew nothing about.

'It's ok. I've got things to do in the kitchen. I need to stretch because I've been sat on this floor so long.' Lilah wished she could stay and be part of his world but it wasn't her place and she didn't want to be a spare part. Who needed some girl with a crush hanging around? Better she kept out of the way.

'Ok,' Hayley said. 'It was nice to meet you.'

'This all looks great,' Aidan said, peering into the boxes of magazines. Aidan and Hayley's chat drifted faintly into the hallway as Lilah made her way to the kitchen. Alone again.

CHAPTER SIX

Aidan

Aidan leaned on the old sideboard, his eyes lingering on the door Lilah had exited. His mind remained on her a moment longer than it should. There was something about her. He'd felt it at the fair and, when his gaze connected with hers, he caught it again, though he couldn't quite place what it was.

Hayley rapped her fingertips together and the sound brought Aidan back to the room. Turning his attention to her, he sighed and rubbed his temples.

'I guess I should apologise,' he said. 'For not answering your messages.'

'I don't need an apology, Aidan.' She sat on the sofa and patted it.

Taking the seat next to her, he didn't relax but leaned forward with his wrists on his knees.

'Where's Maya?' Hayley asked.

'Gone into the garden. She only really comes in at night. She loves being outside.'

'A bit like her owner.'

'Exactly like me.'

Hayley beamed at him and his heart softened. She was always so kind and full of love. The thought of not talking to her gnawed at his bones and hurt him deep. Why had he distanced himself from her since he came back? It wasn't worthy of him.

'You know, Hayley, I can't deny I'm upset about the whole situation with Finlay and Elise but I shouldn't have dragged you into it. I should have visited before now or at least answered your messages.'

'It's ok. I understand. And I'm in the equation whether I want to be or not. It concerns so many people I'm close to. That's the problem. I understand how all three of you feel. I just can't do anything about it.'

'And I suppose you think I'm in the wrong?'

Hayley shifted on the sofa, her eyes wide and glassy. 'Not entirely. Some of what you did wasn't the smartest and I think expecting Elise to wait for you was completely unrealistic but you had your reasons. After your dad died, I know how awful it was and I understand your need to get away.'

'But?'

'No buts. You did what was right for you and what felt right at the time.'

He groaned and put his head in his hands. 'I had no right to expect Elise to wait for me. I guess I completely misunderstood the level of feeling we had for each other.'

'Maybe. But I think it's more the case that you didn't really communicate your expectations to her. She felt abandoned and it was almost impossible to get in touch with you. She didn't know how you really felt because you never told her, so she gave up.'

'Is that what she said?' Hadn't he told her?

'She's said a lot about you. None of this was easy for her either. At one point, she thought you'd disappeared as an excuse to dump her. It was confusing for her.'

'I've been such an idiot.'

Hayley rubbed her hand along his arm. 'You were suffering terrible grief, Aidan. You weren't stupid, you just weren't thinking straight.'

'You're always so kind. I don't deserve it.'

'Of course you do. You're a good guy who made a choice. It maybe wasn't the best choice but we've all made mistakes.'

He let out a snort. 'This was a pretty big one.'

'Yup.' She sighed.

'Do you know how they got together? Why would they? I'm struggling to understand Finlay's motive in all this.' He looked up. 'What's his problem? How does he think it's remotely ok for him to behave like that?'

Hayley reached out and placed a hand on his arm. 'I guess they must really care about each other. Finlay wouldn't do anything to hurt you. You know he had a nightmare breakup before and he's not the type to rush into anything. I admit I was pretty shocked at how quickly they got engaged but sometimes you can't help where your heart leads.'

'It feels like he's betrayed me. I can't help wonder if they always had feelings for each other. Was I blind to something that had already started?'

'No, I don't think so. Elise has been my friend for a long time and I never got that feeling. Finlay's had a tough relationship history and I never saw him interested in Elise until after you'd gone. I was as surprised as anyone.'

'Hmm.' Aidan shook his head. Was it wrong to wonder if this was an attempt by Elise to get back at him for abandoning her?

'You chose to follow your own path, and it was something you had to do for you. It's okay to feel hurt and angry, but don't let it consume you.'

He gave her a half-hearted smile. 'I'll try. But, please, lay off the matchmaking for a bit. I heard what you said before and I'll tell you now I'm not ready to jump back into the dating game yet.' Not when a candle in his heart still burned for Elise.

'I get it. But don't close yourself off completely. You deserve happiness too.'

'Do I? Maybe I'm better on my own. Look at our relatives. It's not like we come from a gene pool of people who've aced it at relationships.' Both his and Hayley's parents were divorced. His mum twice. Hayley's parents both had new partners. 'Sometimes you have to ask if settling down and all that is really worth it. Is that the point of life? I wonder if I'd be happier going away with Maya and doing another walk or something like that. I'm not sure a life here is really what I want.' And if this was love, it definitely wasn't for him. He couldn't put himself through this again. Not any time soon.

Hayley smiled and nodded. 'If that's what makes you happy, then do it. Do what you have to do, and remember I'm here for you, no matter what.' She leaned over and pulled him into a hug. He yielded. It was easier than resisting, and really, he craved the comfort of something like this.

'Thank you. And I am truly sorry I didn't reply to your messages or come and see you before now. It was a stupid thing to do.'

'It's ok.' She patted his back. 'But let it be a lesson for the future. Talking isn't bad, ok?'

'Ok.' He released her from the hug and sat back at a knock on the door. 'Come in.'

Lilah peeked around the door. 'Hi.' Her cheeks were pink and she wore an uncertain smile. Her hair tumbled wildly out of a messy updo, twisting around her shoulders. She resembled an earth spirit who should be running barefoot through the woods. As she ran, flowers would bloom in her wake and trails of light would follow.

'Are you ok?' Aidan blinked, ridding his mind of such utter nonsense. 'Do you need to go?'

'No. I'm still cleaning. I opened the door for some air and found this letter stuck in the letterbox. It was kind of folded in.

It might have been there for a while. I hope it's nothing urgent. Where should I leave it?'

'I'll take it, thanks.'

She edged into the room with a brief glance at Hayley. The poor girl looked as uncertain as a baby deer taking its first steps. She hadn't seemed this nervy when they first met. In fact she'd been feisty and ready to take him on with the log. This was so obviously out of her comfort zone. She held out the letter and he took it. His eyes lingered on her strappy vest top. The skin across her chest was dappled with hundreds of tiny freckles. She tugged a band from her hair and wound up the loose tresses behind her head, exposing her slender neck and well-defined cheeks and chin. She fastened her hair back in place. For someone with such an unkempt air, she was actually beautiful. Very natural.

Screw this silly nonsense.

Why was he looking at her like that?

'Would you like me to get you a drink? Either of you?' she asked.

Aidan glanced at the letter and shook his head. 'No thanks, I'm good, but Hayley might.'

'Yeah, I could murder a cup of tea, if you don't mind. Thank you.'

Lilah smiled and nodded. 'Sure, I'll make one.'

'Great. Just milk and no sugar, please.'

'Have one yourself,' he said. 'Take a break. You're entitled to it.'

'I... er, ok.'

As she turned to leave, Aidan's gaze involuntarily followed her. A few loose strands of hair still tumbled over her shoulders, coiling down her back. Her top was low cut and tapered into a thin waist. Her tight jeans accentuated her narrow hips. Why the hell was he noticing shit like that?

He glanced back at Hayley.

'She's a sweetie, isn't she?' Hayley raised an eyebrow and smirked.

'Is she?'

'Yeah. She looks like she could do with a good meal or two but she seems nice. Where did you find her? Was she from an agency?'

'Ha.' He grunted. 'No. She knocked over part of Mum's stall at the fair on Saturday and I felt sorry for her. Scarlett told me she was a horror at school, but hey... You know me.'

Hayley's eyes widened and she shook her head.

'Oh my god, Aidan. You are unbelievable. I mean, it's really kind but... Oh my goodness. You and your charity cases.'

'Don't I know it!'

'I mean, she could be anyone. And' – Hayley glanced towards the door and lowered her voice – 'do you believe what Scarlett said?'

'Nope. You know what a drama queen she is.'

Hayley pulled a side pout. 'Yeah. She's got a lot of growing up to do.' She peered at him with an uncharacteristically stern look. 'This is all above board, right?'

Aidan shifted in his seat, his neck heating slightly. 'Meaning what?'

'Oh, come on, Aidan. She's an attractive young woman, you're an attractive man. She's also some random you picked up at the fair. I get your reason was primarily charity, but nothing else?'

'No.' He put up his hand. 'I forbid you to even go there.'

'Ok. Fine. You'll hear no more about it from me. But take care.'

Aidan raised his eyebrows. Like he believed for a second that she'd never mention this again.

Lilah returned with a cup of tea for Hayley. She placed it on the coffee table, her eyes briefly meeting Aidan's before she turned away. He ground his teeth to stop himself speaking, breathing or doing anything that might give Hayley the wrong idea.

'Thanks so much,' Hayley said.

'No probs.'

'Didn't you get one for yourself?' Hayley smiled innocently.

'I'll have it in the kitchen and let you two chat.' Lilah gave them both a brief look, then left.

Hayley lifted her tea and smirked but said nothing. Her silence was possibly more irritating than her speculation. At least when she gossiped, Aidan could deny everything. When she was silent, she was probably letting her mind form conclusions that were completely wrong and he could do nothing about it.

To stop himself from wondering what the hell she was thinking about, he ripped open the letter and read it. His hands clenched it tightly. What the actual...?

'What's wrong?' Hayley asked. 'You've gone white.'

'I don't believe this.' He shook his head, his chest contracting like someone was crushing it with a brick. 'The council are proposing to build housing on the field.'

'What field?'

'That one.' He pointed through the French doors to the beautiful field between the cottage and the forest. 'How can they? That field is a sanctuary for wildlife, and...' He jumped to his feet. It was a place Dad had loved. Aidan did too. They'd watched the wildflowers take over, reclaiming the land and making it a special place. Boiling blood surged through his veins. How could anyone consider destroying such a precious and sacred space?

He exhaled sharply. Why had he ever believed people would treat it with the same reverence and respect he did? It had always been a distant worry but now it was a devastating reality about to bulldoze over everything that held meaning for him.

'I can't believe it,' he muttered.

'Can I read it?'

He passed the letter to her. 'Don't they understand the significance of this place and the wildlife that calls it home? Why can't they leave it? Or at least build something small and in keeping with nature.'

Hayley's eyes widened as she read. 'That's terrible. I can understand why you're upset.'

He nodded, his jaw set. 'I can't stand by and watch it be destroyed. I bloody won't.'

'What are you going to do?'

'Even if I have to lie down in front of the bulldozers or chain myself to the gate, I'll do it. They are not getting to build on that field.'

'Let's hope you don't have to do anything quite so dramatic. How about trying to drum up community support first?'

'Yeah. Good idea. My friend Gabe might be able to help.'

'As in Gabriel Wilder, Glenbriar's local celebrity?'

'The very same.'

'That's two celebs we have now, what with him and Marcus Bowman. You could ask him to help too. I know him pretty well these days, as he's dating my wee cousin Willow.'

'Who? Not Willow.' Obviously he knew who Willow was, even though she was a cousin from Hayley's mother's side. His relationship to Hayley was through their fathers. 'Marcus Bowman? The TV presenter?' he asked.

'The very same. He presents *Destination Forecast*. I can speak to him if you like?'

'The more the merrier.'

'I could also ask my friend, Genevieve Harrington. She's an influencer and has a big following. Her dad's also big in the eco sector.'

'No, leave her out of it. She's Elise's best friend. I doubt she'll help me.'

'Gabriel sounds like your best bet anyway.'

Aidan hoped so. He was kind of the Joe Wicks of eco blogging and had a way of getting people onboard. It was he who'd inspired Aidan's own journey of discovery.

'I'll get in touch with him and see if he can do anything. You don't happen to know anyone who's a lawyer, do you?'

'Only Finlay's mate, Oliver, but he's a divorce lawyer, so I don't think that'll be much use.'

'No.' Aidan let out a sigh and clapped his knees. 'Do you want to go see Maya? I'll tell her about the field, though I won't tell the bees. They'll be sad.'

'Are you serious? The bees will be sad?'

'In my mind they will be. They're very sensitive... or maybe that's just me.'

They headed outside and Maya bolted to Hayley, wagging her tail and snuffling excitedly. 'Aw, you are the cutest dog ever,' Hayley said.

Aidan pulled some long grass away from the side of the house. 'This garden is such a mess.'

'At least you've got a cleaner now. You'll have more time to spend out here.'

'Yes. That's true. But I can't imagine what this would be like with a bunch of houses squashed in there between me and the wood. It's unbearable.'

'I know, but you might be able to stop it. Channel your energy into that and sorting this garden.'

'You're right, yes.' He rubbed his forehead.

'Once you're doing something, you'll feel better.'

Aidan nodded, his mind racing with ideas. 'Yup. I need to call Gabriel.'

'Keep me posted, ok?'

'I will.'

'Right. I'll head off and I'll let you know if I can persuade Marcus Bowman to do anything. I'll just stick my head in the kitchen door and say bye to Lilah before I go.' She gave Maya another cuddle, then headed round to the side of the house. Aidan followed her. 'Bye, bye, bye, Li-Lilah,' she called and Aidan smirked as she attempted to sing it like Tom Jones.

'Bye,' came Lilah's voice.

Aidan watched Hayley leave, then entered the kitchen. Even in the short time she'd been working, Lilah seemed to have made inroads. 'This is looking better already.'

'That's good,' she said.

He sighed and sank back, leaning on the worktop.

'Is everything ok?'

'Not really.'

'Have I done something wrong?'

'Of course not. It's just stuff. Stuff that's out of my control.'

'Oh.' She scrubbed away at the surface next to the sink.

'I'm sorry this house is such a tip.'

'Don't be. If it was clean and tidy, you wouldn't need a cleaner. And actually, it isn't that bad.'

'Are you being funny?'

'No.' She put down the cleaning cloth. 'Compared to where I'm staying, this place feels like a palace.'

'What? Where are you staying?' He remembered what Scarlett had told her about Lilah's impoverished living conditions growing up.

She sighed. 'I'm in a tiny caravan in someone's garden. It's cramped, run-down, and all round gross. But it's the best I can afford for now and at least I have my own space.'

'Where is this caravan?'

'In Clachnabronnachan. It's owned by Malcolm and Brenda McManus. You might know them.'

'Yeah. I know who they are. Most people around here do. So, when you told me you baked for a living. Where do you do that?'

She shrugged. 'I just help Brenda make fudge, mostly. She's trying to run an online business, but she doesn't get that many orders.'

'And she pays you?'

'They let me have the caravan and they give me food... sometimes.'

'Sometimes?'

'It's no big deal. And it's better than nothing.' She picked up the cloth again.

'Sounds utterly outrageous to me.'

'It's fine.'

He raised an eyebrow. Scarlett might think this was someone coming from a scummy background or whatever she called it but Aidan thought it a bloody crime. How in this day and age was anyone living like that? What a disgrace. And for someone so young. What future did she have? 'We'll talk later,' he said. 'You've made me think. I'm not sure what to do but... Leave it with me. I need to call someone.'

He went straight to his office and with a deep breath, dialled Gabriel's number. After a few rings, his friend answered.

'Hey, Aidan! Long time no speak. How's it going?'

'Hey, Gabe. I wish it were under better circumstances, but I need your help with something.'

'Of course, mate. What's going on?'

'I got a letter from the council today, and they're proposing to build housing on the field behind Woodend.'

'No shit, man. That's the pits. What can I do to help?'

'I was hoping you could use your influence to raise awareness about the importance of preserving this area. Maybe even help rally support or provide guidance on how to fight against this proposal.'

There was a brief pause before Gabriel responded. 'I'll do everything I can. You can count on me.'

'Thank you. I knew I could.'

'No problem at all. Let's schedule a meeting and we can make a plan.'

'Sounds good. Just let me check my calendar.' He was no longer alone in his fight to save the field, and that, in itself, lessened the weight on his shoulders.

'How's it going otherwise?'

'Ah, you know.'

'You happy to be back?'

'Not particularly.' Aidan glanced around the room that had been his father's pride and joy. The cottage would never be the same again without Dad. 'Things feel a bit flat, you know. When Dad was ill, I let things slip because I was more interested in taking care of him. When I went away, Mum didn't bother with it.' Again, his own stupidity. His mum had never liked it here and she didn't want to be back somewhere that reminded her of her failed marriage. 'Now it's a mess and it's overwhelming at times.'

'Aw, that's shit, mate. This field business will be making it ten times worse too.'

'It is.'

'Would you be better selling up?'

'I don't want to do that.' It was all he had left of his dad. 'I've hired someone to clean it and that might help.'

'Good plan.'

'I hope so. She seems good but she's really young and from a shit background. I took her on because I felt sorry for her and now, well...'

'Give her a chance. You're good at that. And it sounds like she needs it.'

'Yeah. That's exactly what I'm going to do.'

CHAPTER SEVEN

Lilah

Lilah stood frozen outside Aidan's office door. So that was what he really thought – she was just a young person from a shit background that he felt sorry for. Where did that leave her? And what did 'That's exactly what I'm going to do' mean? Like she couldn't guess? Throw her out, of course. Now he'd realised what he'd taken on, it was obvious. Why had she told him about the caravan? Maybe it was a miracle he'd allowed her into his house, even for a day.

A lump formed in her throat and she swallowed it back. Why so sentimental? By now, she should be used to this kind of thing, but it was different when she was crushing so hard on this guy. Oh well. No point hanging around where she wasn't wanted. Just as well it was three o'clock, and she'd finished cleaning for the day. She'd only gone to tell Aidan she'd be back tomorrow but now she wouldn't.

She found a scrap of paper and a pen in the cluttered corner of the kitchen she hadn't tackled yet and scribbled a quick note.

Done what I can. I heard what you said about me, and I guess that means goodbye. Save you the need to sack me. No need to pay me. I already owe you for the tenner you gave me before.

Lilah

Determined not to let Aidan see her again, she marched out of the side door and straight into the garden. Maya bounded up, wagging her tail.

'Hey,' Lilah said, stroking her wonderfully soft fur. 'It was nice knowing you, but I have to go. Bye, Maya.' Her voice choked. She hastened to open the gate and leave. Maya watched and her tail dropped as Lilah turned onto the path. Putting her head down, Lilah sped up, running towards the entrance to the wood but it wasn't a joyful run like the day before. Now she wanted to put as much distance as possible between her and the cottage.

As she got further away from it, she slowed to a jog. *It'll be ok. You've survived worse.* Since leaving her mum's home, she'd done what she needed to survive and she'd get through this. She wiped away her tears, determined to start over. Aidan was a blip. Someone she barely knew. His kindness had seen her through a few days but it would be soon forgotten. If she'd crushed on him too hard, so what? Was it any different from crushing on actors or celebrities? People she didn't have a real chance with anyway. And she definitely didn't have a chance for anything with Aidan McBride.

Her feet pounded against the pinecone covered path in a desperate attempt to get home – at least the place she was calling home. The looming trees closed in around her, casting eerie shadows across the forest floor. Every crack of a twig or whisper of wind made her jump. Why was she so on edge? This was stupid. She'd walked here hundreds of times and never been bothered by anything. And why couldn't she stop thinking about Aidan?

A stupid, childish infatuation.

Get a grip.

As she jogged, another sound caught up with her. Padding footsteps. What the...? Her gut twisted and she dared a quick glance over her shoulder. A shadowy wolf-like figure was chasing after her. Her chest spasmed and her legs weakened, but she had to keep on running.

As the shape drew nearer, her racing heart slowed, and she took a breath that burst from her like a cry.

'Maya? Oh my god. You scared me,' she panted. Maya closed the remaining distance between them and nuzzled against Lilah's leg as if to reassure her. 'But what are you doing here? Have you run away?' Surely she wouldn't. She was too well-behaved to do that.

Another sound on the path made Lilah whip around. Whirring through the woods came Aidan, standing to pedal a bike up the track. He spun the bike to a stop and steadied it, blocking the forward path, his thick forearms tight on the handlebars as he balanced it. What was he doing? Why the hell had he followed her? Was he even following her? Could this be a coincidence?

'There you are,' he said, his deep voice resonating around the woodland path.

Uh-oh.

Lilah's mum had a habit of getting caught up with controlling and cruel men. Was he just as bad? Did he think he had a right to make her go back, even if she didn't want to? Would she have to fight him? How could she? He looked so powerful. She wouldn't stand a chance... and he had a dog.

'I'm going home.' She made to sidestep him but he dismounted his bike, his expression wary.

'Home?'

'Yes. Home.'

'To the caravan?'

'Yes. That freezing cold caravan with the hanging off door.' She marched past him and he didn't stop her. Turning around, she added over her shoulder, 'I know it's shit but it's where I live, ok?'

'Uh-huh. And what about the cleaning?' He dropped his bike on the path and caught up with her on foot.

'I've done what I can.'

'Have you forgotten the contract? This was meant to be for two weeks.'

She stopped and glared at him. 'I quit.'

'On what grounds?'

'There's no point in me staying where I'm not wanted.'

He turned away and rubbed his chin. 'What's brought this on?'

'I heard what you said about feeling sorry for me and all that.'

'I was on the phone, so you couldn't possibly hear both sides of the conversation.'

'I heard enough.'

'Look, if me saying I felt sorry for you offended you, then I apologise.'

She tossed her head and looked away. 'It wasn't just that. You said you were going to sack me.'

'I didn't say that.'

'Well, something like that. You said you "would do exactly that", or whatever. Doesn't take a brain surgeon to work out what you meant. I might come from a "shit background", your words, but I'm not totally thick.'

'I know that. And you'll never hear me say so. But you've got it wrong. I wasn't going to fire you. I was going to offer you a place to stay – if you want it.'

'What?' Her heart skipped a beat and her eyes snapped back to him. The thought of having a place in his cottage, of not being alone in her dilapidated caravan, was beyond anything, but how could it be true? People didn't do things like that for other people... Not without wanting something in return. 'Why?'

'Why not?'

'Because you feel sorry for me?'

'Yes, I do. And is that wrong? Why shouldn't I feel compassion towards someone in your position? I think it's a crime in this day and age that anyone is living like you. And I feel sorry for every single person who is. I can't help everyone, but I can help you.'

She stared at him, hardly believing. In the past, men had offered her arrangements like this that she'd run from.

'So, what are you saying? You'd offer me a room in the cottage?'

'If you want, then yes. It might be slightly better than a caravan. And I'd make sure you got food not just "sometimes".'

She shook her head. 'And what do you want in return?' She wasn't green around the edges. You didn't get something for nothing. But she so wanted to trust him. If he was really bad, he could have dragged her back with him already, or worse. She shuddered to think what a man of his strength could have done to her out here alone in the woods. But a sense of security and of being completely safe in his presence swept away any lingering fear. He wouldn't hurt her; she was sure.

His gaze was intense and he drew his brows together. 'In return?' he said slowly.

'Well, yes. I can't pay rent. The only money I have will be from cleaning.'

'I understand that. Well, perhaps you might help me out with other things.'

'Such as?' She folded her arms and narrowed her eyes.

'Admin jobs, maybe some cooking, shopping and that kind of thing. Also, you'd be nearer the town if you wanted to apply for jobs. It would be easier than coming all the way from Clachnabronnachan.'

Was he really this kind? He didn't want anything sordid from the arrangement? 'Ok,' she said quietly. 'If you really mean it.'

'I do. There's a spare room and it'll be your own space.'

Maya, sensing the change in the atmosphere, wagged her tail and ran her nose up Aidan's muscular thigh, before leaping towards Lilah.

Lilah smiled and ruffled her fur. 'When will this start?'

'Whenever you like.'

'Now?'

He quirked a grin. 'If you really want. But don't you have belongings? And don't you want to say goodbye to the McManuses?'

'I guess. Well... ok.'

'If you're dead set on coming now, hop onto the back of the bike and I'll give you a ride to the caravan to get your things.'

Lilah's lips parted and her chest swooped. Get on the back of his bike? And what the hell would she hold on to? Him? He wanted her to put her arms around that hot wall of muscle. Her heart hammered in her chest more than it had done when she'd thought Maya was a wolf chasing her up the path.

'Of course, you don't have to. If you'd prefer to walk to Clachnabronnachan, then back, that's perfectly fine by me.' His dark eyes held hers.

'No. The bike would be great.'

'Jump on then. It might not be the comfiest ride, but it'll be quicker.'

On the back of the bike was a metal rack with paniers suspended from it.

'Side saddle will probably be easiest,' he said. 'If you have a lot of stuff to get, we'll have to go back another day. I'm sure Hayley would help out with a car.'

'I don't have anything much. Just some clothes.'

'Really?'

'Yeah.' She shuffled onto the uncomfy seat and swallowed. Should she grab hold of him? Or try to balance?

'Clothes might fit in the paniers. They're empty. I've never taken them off since I did a long ride two summers ago. Feels like a very long time ago now.' He glanced over his shoulder. 'You better hold on.'

'Oh. Ok.' She held her breath and slipped her hands around his waist. It was just as firm and warm as she'd imagined. Possibly more so. He kicked off, seemingly oblivious to having an extra weight clamped to his back. Maya darted off ahead. Lilah kept her fingers as still as she could. She didn't want him thinking she was groping him. If she closed her eyes, she could lean on his back and relax as the world flew by. But she didn't dare.

When they reached Clachnabronnachan, Aidan parked his bike near the caravan, and Lilah hopped off, her thighs and her bum slightly achy.

'I'll wait here,' he said, steadying the bike on the road outside the carnage that was the McManus's garden, and clipping a lead to Maya's harness. She sat obediently by his side and Lilah smiled. If doggy cuddles were part of her new life, she couldn't wait.

'Ok.' She darted into the caravan and gathered her belongings, which consisted of a small duffel bag containing her limited wardrobe and a toiletry bag. She didn't even take a second look at the place. No way would she miss it.

Back outside, she handed the bag to Aidan.

'Is that it?'

She nodded. 'I better say bye. Give me a minute.'

'Sure.'

Lilah made her way up the short path and knocked. She glanced back at Aidan as she waited. He was shoving her bag into an empty panier and Maya was sniffing it.

After a moment, the door creaked open, revealing a dishevelled Malcolm.

'What do you want, lass?' he grumbled, barely looking at her. 'We've already eaten.'

Lilah forced a smile and kept her voice steady. 'I just wanted to say goodbye. I'm moving out.'

'Eh? Haven't you just arrived?'

'I've been here six months.' Six cold months that had included a very lonely Christmas and a January so cold she'd thought she might die of hypothermia. 'Could I speak to Brenda?'

'Aye, sure. Brenda!'

Lilah drew back as he shouted. His oral hygiene left a lot to be desired.

'What?' Brenda's perpetually scowling face appeared behind him.

'The girl's leaving.'

'Eh? Leaving where?'

'Leaving us. She's moving out.'

Brenda muscled onto the doorstep and folded her arms across her ample bosom. 'Where are you off to?'

'I've got new lodgings, but I'd like to thank you for letting me use the caravan. And I'm sorry I won't be able to help you with the fudge anymore.'

Brenda's scowl deepened. 'Well, that's just great, isn't it? Who's going to help me now?'

'I'm sorry. I don't know.' Lilah focused on her feet. 'If you really need help, I could come back and help out for one-off big orders and the like.' She almost pitied her... and the customers. Brenda couldn't make the fudge on her own but she hadn't exactly paid Lilah properly for the work so she shouldn't feel bad. If Brenda wanted to start a business, she should choose something she could actually do, not just something where she enjoyed tasting the end product.

Brenda's forced smile didn't reach her eyes. 'Oh, don't worry about it. We'll manage somehow.' She frowned, gawping over Lilah's shoulder. 'Who's that with the bike?'

'Um... Just someone giving me a lift.'

'On a bike?'

'Yes.'

'I see.' Brenda raised an eyebrow. 'Is this you running off to live with some bloke? What's he getting from the arrangement? Don't suppose it's fudge he wants you to make.'

Lilah threw her a dirty look. 'It's nothing like that.'

'I hope not. I wouldn't like to think he was taking advantage of a vulnerable wee lassie like you.'

Lilah held her tongue. Wee lassie? And who was Brenda to talk? It wasn't like she'd treated Lilah that well herself. 'Well, take care of yourselves,' she said after an awkward pause. It was what they did best, after all.

Malcolm grumbled something inaudible and closed the door. Lilah didn't waste another second before returning to Aidan and Maya.

'Everything alright?' Aidan said.

Lilah nodded. 'Yeah. Let's go.'

Aidan mounted his bike, and Lilah took her place behind him once again. She wrapped her arms around his waist, finding comfort in the solid warmth of his body. With a gentle kick, they set off, leaving the caravan and the McManus's behind. Maya trotted beside them as they moved along the short street, down a little hill and onto the main road. They followed it for a hundred metres or so before cutting into the woods. Aidan stopped and let Maya off the lead.

The clothes packed in the panier padded it out, making it a little comfier. Lilah clung to Aidan as they whizzed down the forest track. A new chapter of her life was about to start. She could almost feel it in the air as it touched her face. Sunlight streamed through the trees, casting a warm glow upon them, as if nature itself was rejoicing at this new beginning. The wind whipped through her hair, carrying away the remnants of her old life and ushering in a glimmer of hope for the future. Bluebells danced along the side of the path and the rhythmic motion of the bike beneath her was calming. If only she could stay like this for a long time. She inhaled the scent of pine trees and tightened her grip around Aidan's waist. Her head inched slowly sideways until she finally gave into her resistance and allowed it to rest on his back. Here was safety, strength and a chance to start over.

CHAPTER EIGHT

Aidan

What was another word for endurance? Aidan had used it way too many times already in this document. Lounging back in the seat at the desk in his study, he rubbed his fingers together. The words the thesaurus offered him didn't really work. Did it even matter? These were just notes, after all. When he was making the motivational speech, would anyone be counting the number of times he used a word?

The scent of freshly brewed coffee filled the room, fuelling his focus. He ran a hand through his thick hair and reviewed the key points of his speech. His walk across Canada and Alaska had given him so much inspiration. Memories rolled back, transporting him to breathtaking landscapes and unforgettable moments.

He sipped his coffee, recalling the awe-inspiring beauty of the Rockies, their majestic peaks piercing high into the clear blue sky. He could almost taste the crisp mountain air in his lungs as he navigated treacherous trails, challenging himself to go further and higher. The sight of snow-capped mountains reflected in crystalline lakes had left an indelible impression on his soul. If he could just find the words to do them justice.

Lost in his thoughts, he was interrupted by a knock on the study door.

'Come in.'

Lilah peered around the door with an uncertain expression, similar to the one she wore when Aidan suggested she visited the bees. One day, hopefully, her courage would extend to that. She'd been here just over a week and, so far, things were going well. She did her cleaning work, helped with the cooking and had even done some weeding. Most of the time, she kept out of his way, and that suited him fine.

'Aidan... Your, em...'

'Excuse me,' another voice said, and Aidan groaned.

'Your mum's here,' Lilah finished, stepping aside.

His mother, Patricia, swooped in. Perfectly coiffed silver hair framed her face. She marched to the seat opposite Aidan and sat with a dramatic sigh.

Lilah backed out and closed the door. At the sound of it snapping shut, Patricia leaned forward and muttered, 'What is *she* doing here?' She rested her hand on her bright pink floral shirt as if shocked.

'Hello to you too.'

'Yes, hello,' Patricia said. 'But why is she here? Isn't she Delilah Clarke? The one who knocked Scarlett's tooth out at school?

'Yes, she is.'

'It cost us a fortune to get that tooth sorted and poor Scarlett was mortified for weeks while she waited for the dental work. Why on earth is she in your house answering the door?'

'She's my lodger,' Aidan answered. 'And she's doing some work here while she looks for employment.'

Patricia's eyebrows shot up. 'Your lodger? She's living *here*? What kind of work is she doing? I dread to think.'

'Cleaning the house.' He folded his arms. 'So, keep a lid on your imagination.'

'Cleaning? You think she'll be any good at that? Her family lived in one of those dreadful houses on Rowan Way. After they moved out, environmental health and pest control were called in to blitz it. I heard it was almost uninhabitable. I used to see her mum outside the school, still in her pyjamas, swigging straight from a bottle. She sometimes asked the kids for lights for her cigarettes. And Delilah wasn't any better, always looked filthy, constantly had the nits. Her brothers would get suspended regularly for attacking other children. One of them put a chair through a window, you know.'

'I'm well aware of Lilah's past. But she deserves a chance to turn her life around, like anyone else.'

'Lilah? Is that what you call her?' Patricia drew back and narrowed her eyes.

'That's what she likes to be called.'

'Well, I find it hard to believe she has no other motives for being here. I'd make sure you lock up the valuables.'

Aidan let out a long, slow breath. 'I'm giving her a chance and I'd like you to do the same.'

Patricia studied him, her eyes searching. 'I worry about you, Aidan. You've always had a heart of gold under that scowl, but sometimes you're that blind to reality.'

'What's that supposed to mean?'

'Look what happened with Elise. You bugger off to Canada and expect her to wait for you. Unrealistic. You leave me in charge of your bees when I haven't the first idea what to do with them. Unrealistic. And now you're trying to reform this girl, who for all you know is trying to diddle you right under your nose. Do you see the pattern?'

Aidan clenched his teeth. Even if his mum had a point, he wasn't ready to acknowledge it. 'I understand your concerns, but I won't let you dictate how I choose to help someone. I'm giving Lilah the benefit of my trust in her and while you're under this roof, I'd like you to do the same. While you're my visitor here, I expect you to treat her like an equal.'

Patricia pouted. 'I would never be rude to anyone, but I hope you're right. I'm only looking out for you.'

'I'm perfectly capable of looking after myself.'

His mum raised an unconvinced eyebrow, then glanced out the window. 'If you say so. Just remember, you'll always be one of my babies and I'll never stop worrying about you. I'm so glad you're back. It was torture when you were away and we didn't know how you were for weeks.'

'Yeah.' He leaned across the table and took her hands in his. 'Sorry, Mum. I've been selfish.' How had he managed to switch off from the concerns of others for so long? No man was an island, but he'd made himself one without thinking about how his actions had affected others. In his attempt to do good and find peace, he'd hurt so many people. Had any of it been worth it? Now he was back, memories of his dad were as acute as ever. Realistically, nothing could take away the pain, but being in this house made it worse. Or it had done until Lilah had moved in. She was a welcome distraction, breathing new life and spirit into the place.

'It's your life, son, but just because you're thirty-three doesn't mean I'll stop worrying or wanting what's best for you.'

'Thanks.' He gave her hands a squeeze, then let go. 'Why are you actually here? Is everything ok?' She couldn't have come just to talk about Lilah; she hadn't known she was here before she turned up.

'Everything is fine, but I have a problem with the Crafty Bee and I wonder if you could help me.'

'I'll try. Do you want me to look after a stall again?' It wasn't exactly his favourite thing to do, but if he had to, he would.

'No, not that. It's just that I'm running out of space for my stock at the house.' His mum spoke with her hands as much as her mouth; her fingers waved around, rings and bracelets glinting in the sunlight streaming through the window. 'I fancied setting up a studio with a wee shop. Something I could open up to passing trade as well as doing mail order and the fairs.'

'It sounds like a great idea to me and hardly a problem.'

'That isn't the problem. It's *where* I can do it. And that set me wondering. Would you mind me using that old garage of yours?'

Aidan raised an eyebrow. It wasn't like he had any great need of the place. He just wasn't sure he wanted his mum hanging around all the time. But how could he turn away his own family? 'I'm sure that would be fine. You go right ahead.'

'Can I have a look at it?'

'Sure. But it'll need some work. It's a mess and I can't guarantee how stable it is. You should probably get a builder to look at it.'

'Hmm. Yes. I know a builder from the village who might do it.'

'What's his name? I need someone to sort the window in the back room.'

'Brann Duthie. I'll find his number.' She scrolled through her phone.

'I can help you with some of the easy stuff, though I've got a lot of other things to do.' He glanced towards the orchard area. 'Seems quite fitting for you to have the Crafty Bee here, what with the real bees.'

Patricia's smile widened. 'Aw, son. You're such a good boy. And I love you so much.' She moved around the desk, clamped her hands on both of his cheeks and leaned in to kiss him on the forehead.

'Thanks, mum.' He wiped what he assumed was the residue of her lipstick off his face as she straightened up. 'The only issue I can see is the proposal to build new houses on the field.'

'What proposal? Are you joking?' She stepped back, looking scandalised.

'No. I had a letter about it the other day. It's not gone through planning or anything yet. It won't stop you using the shed but having a whole bunch of houses out there won't be as appealing as a meadow full of wildlife.'

'What a bloody disgrace. Who's building them? A developer?'

'The council.'

'Oh great. Just what we need. Well, there will be no changing their mind, I suspect. Those councillors do whatever they want. That's a right pain. I just—'

A knock on the door stopped Patricia speaking. Aidan threw her a warning glance as he got up to open it.

'Is everything ok?' he asked Lilah, standing in the door frame and putting a block between her and his mother.

'Yeah, all fine. I just put the kettle on and wondered if you wanted another coffee... Or maybe your mum wants something.'

'Another coffee would be great, thanks,' Aidan said. What about you, Mum?'

Patricia craned her neck to look around at Lilah. Aidan had the sense she was sussing her out. 'That's very kind. I'd love a sweet tea, please.'

'Sure. No probs.' Lilah flicked a little look at Aidan, her lips curling into a brief smile and a pinkish blush spreading across her freckly cheeks. He kept his expression flat, but something stirred in him when she smiled like that. Something he had to keep squashed.

'Thank you.' He closed the door again.

Patricia drummed her fingertips on the windowsill.

'Mum? What's wrong?'

'Well, it's not the valuables you need to lock away. I'd be locking my door at night if I were you.'

'That's ridiculous. She's my lodger.' A lodger who was Scarlett's age. Her boyfriends would all be younger and interested in the same stuff as her. And he certainly wasn't interested in her. His thoughts drifted to Elise. Always Elise. 'I assure you, nothing's ever going to happen there.'

His mum's eyes searched his. 'I just don't want to see you get hurt again. Speaking of which, are you going to Finlay's birthday party? I expect Hayley told you about it. Elise is organising it for him as a surprise. Scarlett wants to go, but I'm not sure she'll get an invitation.'

The connection between Aidan and Finlay was through their fathers, so Scarlett technically wasn't related to Finlay, neither was his mum. They both loved parties however and were so nosey, they wouldn't want to miss an opportunity for gossip. 'She can go in my place. I don't mind in the slightest. I think Hayley did mention it but I'm not going. It's too fresh.' He couldn't handle seeing them together. And celebrating anything with Finlay was the last thing he wanted to do, especially when Elise had never done anything as extravagant as throwing a party for him. Obviously Finlay was a lot more special.

Patricia reached out and gently placed a hand on his arm. 'I understand it's not easy, but maybe attending the party will help clear the air between you two. It's time to move away from Elise and find some closure.'

'Maybe. But I can't promise I'll stay for long.'

Aidan pedalled up the lochside path to the Loch View Hotel, known locally as the pink hotel. It was obvious why. Its pink exterior was famous. He chained up his bike in the car park and nipped inside with a small bag from the paniers. He located a bathroom near the entrance and nipped in. It was private enough for him to get out of his cycling gear, give himself a rinse and quick blast of body spray before changing into smart jeans and a white shirt – only slightly crinkled from being folded. If he was going to make a living from motivational speaking, he'd have to get used to wearing clothes like these, though they were hardly made for comfort.

He returned to his bike and reattached the bag to the paniers before heading back to the foyer. Taking a deep breath, he pushed open the door to the bar where Elise's surprise party for Finlay was in full flow. Other guests milled around, chatting and laughing. Soft jazz music floated through the air. The room was adorned with twinkling string lights, casting a warm and intimate glow on the polished wooden tables. She'd really gone to town on this, which struck Aidan as odd because Finlay wasn't a party animal. Aidan didn't remember him ever liking so much attention. He wasn't exactly shy, but he'd always put practicality over frivolity. This didn't fit.

Aidan made his way through the crowd, adjusting his cuffs, his eyes scanning the room for Hayley. She was the only person he really wanted to see tonight. Spotting her by the bar, he weaved through the guests. Not far off, he saw Finlay and Elise talking to Aunty Lisa, Finlay and Hayley's mum. His blood simmered when he saw Finlay's face, a face that had the same kind features as his sister but the sight now left a bitter taste. Aidan turned away, thankful none of them had noticed him – or if they had, they weren't acknowledging him.

Hayley's eyes lit up as Aidan approached, a warm smile spreading across her lips. 'Hey.' She embraced him. 'I'm so glad you came.'

'Yeah, but I'm not staying long.' Why had he ever thought this a good idea? It was a waking nightmare. He ordered a drink, keeping his eyes fixed behind the bar and not looking over his shoulder. He was convinced Elise was watching him. If he looked at her, she'd ensnare him. He knew it and he couldn't stand it.

'Come with me.' Hayley pulled him into a corner of the function room, away from the bustling crowd.

'Is it just me or is this party completely un-Finlay-like?'

'It is, but it's Elise-like. I kind of get the feeling it's more for her than him.'

'Hmm.'

'How are the bees?' she said brightly.

'Why are you asking me that?'

'Just talk to me about normal stuff.'

'Fine.' He gave a dry laugh. 'The bees are thriving.'

'Aw, that's brilliant. And is Maya home alone?'

'No, she's with Lilah.'

'Ah, yes. And how's that working out?'

'Fine, so far. She does what she's supposed to and keeps out of my way when she's not working.'

'Aw, bless her. I'll come and see her again soon, in case she's feeling lonely. I like her and it seems to me she could do with a friend.'

'Good idea. She'll like that.'

He chanced a look around and somehow his focus landed on Elise. She locked eyes with him for a second, then slid her hand around Finlay's neck and pulled him in for a kiss.

Aidan downed his drink. 'You know what? I appreciate your company but I can't stay. This was a mistake.'

'I understand.' Hayley patted his arm, her gaze also on Finlay and Elise. 'If you need to leave, then go. If anyone asks, I'll make something up.'

'Thanks, cuz. I shouldn't have wasted my time coming.' He pulled her into a one-armed hug and gave her a peck on the forehead, then made his way back through the crowd. Before he reached the door, his aunty Lisa caught his arm. She was like an older version of Hayley, all smiles and warmth.

'Nice to see you again. I've heard all about your travels. Canada sounds wonderful.'

'Yeah. It's a beautiful place.'

She carried on talking to him and he answered all her questions with half an eye on Elise. She and Finlay had broken apart and she was heading towards the foyer. Finlay was laughing with some friends. Aidan's chest filled with lead. Once upon a time, he'd have been right there, joining in, but his friendship with Finlay had hit rock bottom and he didn't see how it could ever be recovered.

Eventually, Aunty Lisa moved on, chatting with other people, and Aidan backed out the door into the foyer. Just as he emerged, he came face to face with Elise nipping out of the ladies.

'Aidan.' Her hand jumped to the base of her neck and she blinked.

Their eyes met, and ice crept into Aidan's veins. The world faded into the background, leaving only the echo of their shared history.

Aidan cleared his throat. 'Elise.'

'I—'

'I should explain,' he said before she could speak. 'It was unreasonable of me to expect you to wait for me.' Though deep down, a part of him had assumed she would. Such thoughtless arrogance. His mum was right. It wasn't realistic. But he'd truly believed their love was strong enough. If only he'd communicated that to her better. Or maybe it wasn't love at all.

He squashed all the questions he had about why she'd chosen Finlay. How they'd even got together. If he needed to know at some point in the future, Hayley would tell him.

Elise's eyes glistened. She reached out, gently placing her hand on Aidan's, her touch bittersweet. 'Aidan, I tried to wait, but I was angry. It felt like you'd abandoned me. You hardly ever called or messaged. You just disappeared.'

His jaw set and he didn't reply. How could he? It was true and she wasn't likely to accept his reasons as being anything but poor excuses. He should have tried harder. His dad wouldn't be proud. The endurance walk was meant to be in his honour but Dad would be devastated that Aidan had thrown away his own chance of happiness. 'Truly, Elise. I hope you and Finlay are very happy together.'

'Thank you.' She gave him a brief smile and flicked her perfectly straight dark hair over her shoulder. 'We both deserve happiness, even if it means finding it on different paths.'

'Yeah. Sure,' he said with a final glance.

This had to stop *now*! He'd made his peace and this was the end.

The door to the bar clicked shut and she was gone.

Aidan strode out of the Loch View Hotel and into the car park. He clipped on his helmet and mounted his bike, leaving his cycling gear in the paniers. What was the point of changing?

Solar lanterns, starting to glow in the twilight, lit the track towards the path around the loch. He followed it for a few moments before veering off on the track that led back to Glenbriar. It was quite a way to Woodend Cottage from here. The cottage was at the top of the town, while the hotel was to the west. Streetlights popped on as Aidan whizzed down the main street of Glenbriar. Some shops were lit up with security lights, offices were closed, and a few rowdy people chatted outside of the chip shop. He passed them all without a second glance, stopping only at the off-license and grabbing a bottle of cheap whisky. He needed it. After shoving it into the panier, he started the uphill climb to the cottage, standing up and working his leg muscles as he powered up. By the time he reached Woodend Cottage at the top of the town, he was ready to neck the whole bottle. He shoved his bike into the garage, then uncorked the bottle and took a swig.

It was fully dark now. He opened the door expecting Maya to greet him but she didn't. Odd. Flicking on the light on his phone, he moved into the living room. The beam caught on two bright, glowing eyes. From the sofa, Maya's tail thumped against it.

'Hey, girl. I wondered where you were.'

The tail thuds increased. Aidan moved the torch along and realised Maya wasn't alone. Curled up and fast asleep beside her was Lilah. For a second, Aidan stood still. Should he go straight to bed? If Lilah woke up, he didn't want to explain why he was back so soon and why he must reek of whisky. Sure, he'd been at a party, but how the guilt mites clawed. Maya already seemed to wear a look of judgement.

Ah, to hell with it. He reached the sideboard and shone his torch across the top. It was so tidy. Lilah had even placed a bunch of flowers in a vase. The cottage was breathing again. He opened a cabinet door, lifted a glass, and poured himself another whisky.

'Aidan, is that you?'

He froze, hand hovering over the glass. 'Yeah. It's me.'

'What time is it?'

'No idea. You should go to bed.' He replaced the whisky on the cabinet, hearing her shifting around behind him.

'You ok?' she asked.

He lifted his drink and settled down beside her, a heavy sigh escaping his lips. Maya shifted so her head was on his thigh.

'Sure. I'm ok.' He downed half the glass in one.

'Yeah, right.'

'What's that supposed to mean?' he muttered, taking another swig.

'I grew up with people who had a love affair with the bottle.'

'What are you suggesting? I'm not a frigging alcoholic. In fact, I hardly ever drink.'

'Exactly. So when you do, something's up. Also, I thought you weren't going to drink as you had the bike.'

'Ah, Christ.' He stared at the glass. The amber liquid shimmered in the dim light.

'You don't have to tell me if you don't want to, but sometimes it helps to talk. Or so I've heard.'

'So you've heard? What does that mean?'

She gave a little shrug. 'I don't exactly have a big circle of friends. It's everyone for themselves where I come from.'

He sighed again and put down his glass. 'My life is a fucked-up mess.' He rubbed at his cheeks with the heels of his hands.

'Because of your girlfriend and your cousin?'

'How do you know about that?'

'Brenda mentioned it, then Hayley told me.'

'Of course she did. She doesn't know when to stop talking sometimes.'

'So, did you see your ex tonight?'

'Yeah. I saw her.'

'I bet that hurt.'

'It did.'

Lilah gazed at him. Even in the dim light, her eyes pierced him. 'It can't be easy to let go.'

'I've been an idiot,' he murmured, his voice barely above a whisper, and he rubbed at a pain on his forehead.

She reached out, placing a trembling hand on his arm. 'You weren't the one who ran off with someone else.'

'No. But I was the one who left. I went to Canada to do my walk. I believed Elise understood. She didn't. I was so blinded by grief and anger after my dad died I lost sight of the here and now.'

'I can't even kid on that I get it. I've never been close enough to anyone to be sad about losing them.'

'Really? Christ, that's sad in itself.' He took another sip.

'It's just my life. If you don't know anything else, there's no point being sad about it.'

'I should go to bed. I'm going to regret this in the morning.'

'Stay there a minute.' She got to her feet.

Aidan closed his eyes, too drained to argue or do anything else. He absently stroked Maya's head.

'Here.' Something thumped on the table beside him. 'It's water,' Lilah said. 'Drink it. Drink as much as you can. It'll help.'

He opened his eyes. Lilah stood beside him, and his gaze met hers. 'Thanks,' he said.

'I'll leave you to it then. I better go to bed.'

'Wait.' Aidan grabbed her hand and held it.

'What... What is it?'

'Just thanks. Not just for the water, but for what you've done in the house. I want you to know I appreciate it.' For a few moments, he watched her, then released her hand. 'Goodnight. See you in the morning.'

CHAPTER NINE

Lilah sat cross-legged on the living room floor, surrounded by an array of forgotten trinkets and treasures she'd discovered while tidying the old sideboard. The top was now cleared and tidy but inside every drawer and door was an Aladdin's cave of old bits and bobs. Her fingers raked through the bizarre mix of beads, charms, buttons, and colourful threads.

Aidan hadn't been bothered about keeping most of the things she'd found so far, but she made sure she showed him everything, in case something was of sentimental value.

Aidan.

Her mind was consumed by him. She picked up some of the beads and threaded them together, enjoying the patterns but not giving them too much thought. Memories of her conversation with him the previous night replayed in her mind. He'd needed her and she'd been there. His heart was in pain. The love he had for Elise was powerful. Lilah got it. Oh yes, she got unrequited love now. The burn in her soul every time she saw Aiden thrilled and gutted her all at once. Even the smallest glance from him was like a hot knife slicing into her, reminding her she couldn't have him. Then he would speak with his deep voice and soothe her back together again. That voice seemed to promise impossible things. If she just kept listening to it, she'd be fine.

She held up the necklace she'd strung. With a better string, it would look quite good, but it was really nothing but a pointless diversion. If she had money and time, she'd enjoy doing this kind of thing as a hobby.

At night, she was sleeping better than she ever had. The cottage felt safe and impenetrable. With Aidan and Maya close by, nothing bad could happen. She didn't have to sleep with one eye open and a rolling pin under her pillow anymore.

She hadn't seen much of Aidan today. Between bees and dog walking, he was hardly ever in the house. When he'd returned from the party last night dressed in that shirt, he'd looked incredible, like a men's fragrance model. No doubt the party was filled with other glamorous people – a scene she could only imagine. She didn't remember ever attending a fancy do like that. Someone her mum knew had once got married at the social club in Dundee and Lilah had gone along. But after sitting for hours watching her mum filling up on free alcohol, she'd had enough and left before everyone else.

Back at school, she'd never been invited to parties. She didn't have friends. Breaks and lunches were spent hanging around the grounds, walking the streets or sitting on a swing in the park close to the school. Why would she want to socialise with people who called her *that little mink, scuzzbag* or *skank*? Even the teachers didn't care, sometimes turning away to pretend they couldn't hear the blatant verbal abuse or to cover their sniggers.

Lost in her thoughts, she wove another thread through the beads, forming an intricate pattern.

'There you are.' Aidan entered the room, his footsteps and his voice interrupting her daydreams.

She spun around and dropped the string of beads. 'Yes.' Shit. She should be working not faffing about with the contents of his cupboards.

'Are you ok?' A flicker of a smile played at the corner of his mouth.

'Oh. Yes. I was... um...'

'What's that you've found?'

'Some old beads and buttons.'

'Very pretty.' He eyed over the necklace she'd strung up. 'Did you make it?'

'Yup. I thought it looked like the bluebells or maybe the sea. But it would be better with black string.'

'You're a surprising talent, aren't you?'

'Not really. Kids can do this kind of thing.' She looked away, heat creeping into her cheeks.

'They can string up beads, sure. But really, Lilah, I'm not talking about that. You make amazing food. That soup that's sitting in the kitchen smells delicious. You can bake. What you've done in here and the garden is... Well, beyond helpful.'

She let out a little laugh. None of it felt like a talent. Just stuff she'd learned to do to survive.

He crouched beside her, resting his wrists on his knees. 'I'm glad you took the chance,' he said.

'You were the one who took a chance.'

'Maybe. And I don't regret it.'

'Me neither. I'm sorry I haven't looked for jobs yet. I've been so busy here.' Working... And indulging her crushy feelings.

'You don't have to do anything in the house outside your working hours.'

'I know, but I'm not paying rent. It feels like the best way to earn my keep.'

His eyes met hers, and a flicker of something sparked in his deep chestnut irises. 'Well, I appreciate it, but don't let it get in the way of job hunting. If you're finding it hard, then I can give you a hand. I know people in the town, so does Hayley, and she'd be happy to help. She was saying at the party how she'd like to get to know you better.'

'That's kind...' Lilah sucked on her lip. But was it a good idea? Didn't outside help lead to being indebted to people? She didn't want that. But then, maybe Aidan and Hayley wouldn't see it like that.

'But?'

'No buts,' she said. 'I'm just not used to people helping me for nothing.'

'Even though you help people for nothing.'

'Do I?'

'You're helping me, even if you think it's to pay for your lodgings. It's still help.'

She gave a little shrug. 'I guess. Ok then, if you or Hayley can find me something, I'll try it. Nothing to lose, have I?'

'Everything to gain.' He gave her a gentle pat on the arm and jumped to his feet. Her heart swelled at the touch and the positive electricity that passed between them. 'Fancy meeting the bees?' he asked.

Much as the thought terrified her, she really would do anything for him. Crush or not, she liked him and trusted him. The bees would be fine as long as he was there too. 'Sure.'

'Great. You'll soon find there's nothing to be scared of.'

She gave a little shrug. They couldn't be any worse than what she'd faced in her life so far. 'Feel the fear and do it anyway.'

He barked a little laugh. 'That's a good motto. It's what I thought I was doing when I went to Canada, but actually it was the opposite.'

'Really?'

'I made a mistake going away. I should have stayed here and faced reality.'

'Everybody makes mistakes. Just let it go.'

'You sound like Hayley. The two of you will get on like a house on fire.' He checked the clock on the wall above the sofa. 'Mum's coming round in a bit. She wants to start clearing the shed for her studio.'

'Oh.' Lilah got to her feet. That wasn't something she was looking forward to. How could she avoid seeing her? Patricia would want to see her son and Lilah would have to get used to her being about.

The sun cast a golden glow over the orchard as Aidan led her through the rows of fruit trees, their branches dotted with pretty white blossom. The gentle hum of bees filled the air.

'Welcome to my world.' Aidan gestured around the hives. 'And say hello to the bees.'

Lilah chewed on a cuticle. Aidan had already warned her not to flap or scream but the temptation to do both burned strong.

'Here.' He opened a small potting shed. 'You might feel happier with this on.' He handed her a hat with a net hanging from it. 'I bought them for my mum when I thought she might look after the bees.'

'I can't believe you don't wear anything.'

'Well, I don't run in there starkers.'

'I meant protective stuff.' Lilah put on the hat and pulled down the net. Hopefully it would cover her blushes. What must he be thinking?

'I know what you meant. I was joking.' Aidan put his hand close to a bush covered in bees. 'Hello, friends.'

Lilah admired their delicate wings fluttering as they went from flower to flower.

'You see how beautiful they are? Look. Don't be scared. Bees are gentle creatures.' He stood tall, holding out his arm to let her come closer. How could she refuse? It was like being welcomed into the safest place in the world. 'They do no harm,' he continued as she stood close. 'In fact, they're an essential part of our ecosystem. They're nature's pollinators, and they're responsible for the reproduction of countless plant species. Without them, the world as we know it would crumble.'

'Is that why there are flyers all around about saving bees?'

'Yup. Look here.' He pointed to the opening in one of the hives. 'Inside these hives, each colony functions as a superorganism. There's the queen bee, who lays eggs and maintains the colony's population. The worker bees, all female, collect nectar and pollen, pollinating flowers in the process. And then there are the male drones, whose sole purpose is to mate with a new queen.'

'Why do men always get the easy jobs?'

Aidan chuckled and it was a low rumbling sound that tickled Lilah deep inside.

He carefully lifted the lid of a hive, revealing a bustling community of bees within. 'Hello, beauties. Look how they work together and selflessly for the good of their hive. Each individual plays a vital role.'

'You should do talks on this too.' People would pay to listen to his beautiful voice.

'That's not a bad idea.' He gently brushed his finger over the honeycomb. 'And check out this honey. So clever. A gift of nature.'

Lilah stood close, so close she was almost touching him. His magical voice calmed her enough to see beauty in these incredible creatures. His passion for the bees seeped into her and awakened something new. 'Thanks for showing me them,' she said softly. 'I'd never have dared do anything like this before.'

Aidan smiled. 'It's not me. It's the bees. Who wouldn't love them?'

Who wouldn't love *you*? He was beautiful and so warm. When she stood this close to him, he didn't recoil, screw up his nose or snigger, as so many before him had. Her crush was getting out of control.

She scanned around the buzzing orchard, the chorus of bees serenading them. Her eyes fell on someone walking towards the house.

'Isn't that Scarlett?' she said quietly.

'What?' Aidan spun around. 'Oh. Mum probably sent her here to start tidying the shed.'

'Nice of Scarlett to agree to it.' It was hard to imagine her ever doing anything pleasant for someone else. She'd been one of the worst bullies at school and Lilah's insides squirmed at the sight of her.

'She doesn't have a job, so she's at a loose end. Mum probably wanted to get her out of the house.'

'Really?' So, she hadn't done any better for herself than Lilah, though she had more respectable connections. 'Maybe I should... You know, make myself scarce. Your sister really doesn't like me.'

'I don't think she likes me much either most of the time. Mum always says she went through an angry phase as a teenager. Personally, I don't think she ever left it.'

Lilah shook her head. 'It would be better if I kept out of her way. She thinks I knocked her tooth out on purpose when we were at school. But it was an accident. I swung the hockey stick too fast to stop and it hit her as she dived in to get the ball. I tried to tell her at the time but she was screaming so hard and no one would listen.' Scarlett had made it her mission to exact revenge on Lilah after that – or so it had seemed.

Aidan cocked his head and frowned. 'Yeah, I think she mentioned that. Ok, you go in the kitchen door and I'll meet her at the front.'

Lilah did as he said but as soon as she was in the kitchen, she hastened to the other side to close the door between the kitchen and the hallway, in case Scarlett chose to nosey in. With a sigh, she pulled some Tupperware boxes from a drawer and poured in the soup she'd made that morning. Aidan might call it talent but it wasn't really. She'd learned to cook early on. If she hadn't, she wouldn't have had anything to eat. No one else in her family bothered.

Aidan's deep voice intermingled with Scarlett's sharper tones. Lilah was gripped by a sudden desire to know what they were saying. She'd grown a thick skin when she was at school and ignored Scarlett as much as possible back then. What other option did she have? Collapsing into a pit of despair every time they crossed paths wasn't her style, and she didn't want to give any-one the satisfaction of knowing they'd broken her. If she heard torturous words coming from Aidan's lips, she'd leave and never come back. How could she stand it? She pressed her ear to the door.

'I thought mum was messing with me when she said she was living here. I can't believe you're allowing it,' Scarlett said.

'I've been through this with Mum already. Lilah has as much right to a home as you do, so leave her alone.'

'Don't worry. I won't be going near her.' Scarlett's voice grew sharper. 'She bloody attacked me at school.'

'Grow up, Scarlett. That was years ago and it was also an accident.'

'Bloody wasn't. She knocked my tooth out. You can't do that by accident with a hockey stick. She took a swing at me 'cause she was jealous that I was going out with Jamie Farrell and she fancied him.'

Lilah balled her fists as more memories came flooding back. It was nothing to do with Jamie Farrell. *When did I ever fancy him!* Like never. This was ridiculous. Taking a deep breath, she steadied herself. *Must not let this affect me. Be strong.*

'Scarlett, stop,' Aidan said. He should be on the stage with that voice. 'I told Mum and now I'll tell you too. You're both welcome in my house. Mum can use my shed for her studio. I won't ever turn away my family, but I will not allow you to carry on this hate campaign against Lilah. She's also a guest in my house. Drop the resentment and move on.'

'Hark who's talking,' Scarlett said with the echo of a laugh. 'This from the man who won't even look at his cousin these days.'

'That's entirely different.'

'No, it isn't. You just don't like it thrown back at you. Always like to be the one dishing it out, don't you?'

With a determined resolve, Lilah opened the door and stepped into the hallway. Aidan's eyebrows were grooved in an impressive V on his forehead and his lips were tightly sealed, like he was barely holding back everything he wanted to say. Scarlett looked nothing like him facially, but her stance was equally poised for a fight.

'Is everything ok?' Lilah smiled sweetly, first at Scarlett then at Aidan.

With what appeared to be an immense effort, Aidan met her gaze. 'Yes. Everything's fine.'

'No, it isn't.' Scarlett glowered at Lilah and, for a second, the resemblance to her brother was apparent, but it was quickly lost. An ugly expression spoiled what should have been an attractive face. Her spiky hair seemed to crackle into angry spears. She folded her arms and narrowed her eyes. 'Why don't you go and sponge off someone else?'

'Scarlett,' Aidan growled. 'That is enough.'

'Shut up. God knows what hold she has over you, but we all know her game. I was talking to Brenda McManus yesterday and she told me you've been scrounging off her for months. Now you're doing the same to my brother. You always were pathetic.'

'Scarlett—'

'You need to listen to me, Aidan, or you'll have your heart broken all over again. And not just your heart. You'll find yourself cleaned out. It's time to quit being so bowled over by a sob story and actually see the truth.'

'Stop right there.' Aidan held up his hand. 'If you want to clear the shed, go and do it, but get out of my sight.'

'You're not my dad.' Scarlett eyed him. 'I'm just looking out for you.'

'I don't want to break up this family,' Lilah said. 'Me being here is always going to cause problems. I should just go.' She couldn't go through this every time Scarlett or Aidan's mum came around, and that would be a lot if they were setting up a studio here.

'No—' Aidan began.

'Sensible.' Scarlett butted in. 'The kindest thing you could do.'

Lilah muscled past them and into her room. In a few days, her two weeks would be up anyway. She still hadn't found a job. What was new? She'd survived this long and she could keep on doing it. Aidan and Scarlett's voices had stopped. Lilah stood at the end of her bed with its old-fashioned floral bedspread. This room was small and probably hadn't been decorated in at least twenty years, but it was cosy and homely. At least she'd felt safer and more at home in here than she ever had anywhere else. She lifted her duffle bag and sighed. It wasn't like she had a whole lot of stuff to pack. Her chest hurt. She didn't want to leave Aidan. His family was another matter.

A knock on her door. She ignored it.

'Lilah. Can I come in?' Aidan's low voice spoke from the hall.

'If you must.'

The door clicked open and he came in. 'What are you doing?'

'Packing up.'

'You're free to go if you want to, but I'd prefer it if you didn't. Not yet anyway.'

'Why?'

'I'm heading to Perth this afternoon. I could do with some company.'

'Me?'

'Yeah. You're an organised-type person and I have a list of things to do. It would be quicker if there were two of us. We could get you set up with a proper bank account while we're there, then when you get a job, you'll have somewhere for the money to go.'

That made sense; she'd been putting it off as she wasn't sure how to go about doing it. But the thought of going somewhere alone with him sent her crushy feelings into overdrive.

'What do you say?'

'I suppose I need a bank account. But what about Scarlett?'

'Never mind her. I'll sort her out. Now, you better get your coat. It's raining.'

She shrugged. 'I haven't got one.'

'Seriously?'

'Yup.'

As they passed the shed on the way out, Scarlett scowled and shook her head. Aidan let out a low, rumbling growl. 'She is so very irritating and she always thinks she's right.'

Lilah half-smirked. A trait that obviously ran in the family.

'If you turn on the Bluetooth on your phone, I can send the list of things to do,' he said. 'I took a picture of it.'

She glanced up at him, swiping a damp strand of hair from her face, and gave him a sad smile.

'What?' he said with a frown.

'Have you seen my phone?' She pulled out her ancient Nokia from her pocket. 'It barely holds a charge for more than half an hour and I'm pretty sure it thinks Bluetooth is something Scarlett needs to replace the one I whacked out in fourth year.'

Aidan chuckled, coming to a halt at the bus stop. 'Ok. Well, I hope you've got a really good memory then.'

'I do.' A grin spread across her face and Aidan returned it. Her head and chest filled with fluff and bubbles at the sight. If she had to remember his face for a test, she'd be a top-grade student. Every faint line on his forehead, dimple on his cheek and hair on his closely trimmed beard was ingrained in her mind, but she'd never tire of looking.

She raked in her pockets as the bus approached. 'I don't think I've got enough change,' she muttered, pulling out some loose coins.

'Put that away,' Aidan said. 'You can put this trip on expenses.'

'What does that mean?'

'It means it's all on your employer. i.e., me.'

They boarded the bus and settled into their seats. The engine rumbled in the background along with the clack of pins from an older lady who appeared to be knitting a very bright sock as she chatted to a friend.

'So, what's on the list of things we need to do?' Lilah asked.

Aidan took out his phone and pulled up the picture of the list. 'Take a look and you can decide what you'd like to do. I'll do the rest.'

'I could post the parcels. Is that what's in the bag?'

'Yup.' He patted the large shopper at his feet. 'I'll give you some cash to do that. I'll go pick up the other things. There'll possibly be a queue for the post office. I could do this in Glenbriar but the queue there can be even worse and I need to speak to a man in the planning department. I feel like he can't evade my questions if we're face to face.'

She wasn't sure why he needed to speak to someone in planning. Perhaps he was considering more building work on the house, but she didn't think it was her place to ask. She was so caught up with how trusting he was of her that her mind couldn't focus properly on anything else. She had to let him know she was worth it and she wouldn't 'clean him out' like Scarlett had suggested.

As they reached the bus stop in the centre of Perth, the heavens opened. 'Run,' Aidan said, bolting off the bus and under a shelter. Lilah followed. 'Can you find your way to the post office ok?'

'Yeah, no bother.'

'Ok. I'll go and speak to the man at the planning department. Let's meet in the shopping centre in an hour.' He handed her the bag of parcels and some notes. 'Don't lose them.'

She rolled them up tight and slipped them into the cuff of her hoody.

Raindrops fell softer now, dotting the pavement and slowly soaking Lilah. The top layer of parcels was slightly damp but nothing to cause concern. Everything she did felt like she was on a mission to help Aidan. Seriously? If she could hear herself! She was a lovesick little puppy dog.

Once all the parcels were safely dispatched, she made her way to the shopping centre. She was early but it was dry in here and she sat on a bench wiggling her ankles and checking out the window displays of the nearby shops. More painful memories surfaced. In times gone by if she needed a coat, one of her brothers and their mates would have nicked her one. Blake had once laden himself down in a department store with all the items he wanted, then cool as you like set off the fire alarm, walked out carrying everything and disappeared into the crowd.

She shuddered. Thank goodness Aidan didn't know any of that.

'Hey.'

Speak of the devil. She got to her feet and instantly pulled out the change from the parcels and handed it to him.

With a rueful smirk, he took it and put it in his wallet. 'All ok?'

'Fine,' she said. 'You?'

'Nothing. He was already in a meeting and I got sent to someone else who couldn't tell me anything about what I wanted to know. Anyway, it's hammering down out there again. Which reminds me, I've added a couple of things to the list.'

'What things?'

'Number one. Let's get you a coat.'

'No. I can't—'

'On expenses.'

'Are you being funny?'

'Am I ever?' He gave her a half smile.

'Sometimes, though I don't think you mean to be.'

His deep laugh rumbled, and he steered her into a clothing store. 'Come on. Let's try in here.'

'How do you have so much money?' she asked. 'I don't want to waste it on this.'

'It's not being wasted. This is an essential. And as for where I get my money, I have investments. But mostly it's money I inherited from my dad.'

'Well, I don't need anything too expensive.'

'Just choose something you like and something practical. Don't look at the price tag. Ok?'

She peered up at him and shook her head. 'I'm not sure I can do that.'

'Try.'

With shaky hands, she flicked through the rails. Why did she feel like every store assistant's eye was on her? Could they see right through her? It didn't matter if she was with Aidan, she still looked like a potential shoplifter.

She pulled out an olive-green trench coat with an asymmetrical zip and a belt. Its lightweight fabric made it ideal for spring, while the slightly oversized collar added a touch of sophistication. And it felt waterproof.

'This one looks nice.' She held it up. 'Pockets too. Multiple pockets. Who doesn't love a pocket?'

Aidan smirked as she ran her fingers over the soft fabric. 'Try it on and if it feels right, it's yours.'

As she slipped it on, the hood caught. Aidan took hold of it and gently adjusted it over her shoulder. Lilah held her breath until he let go. 'Does it look ok?' The length hit just above her knees and it felt warm but not over-warm.

'Nice.' Aidan skimmed his eyes over her, and Lilah swallowed. She didn't need him examining her like that. Why had she asked? In her fantasies, he'd like what he saw. She wasn't stupid enough to think that would actually happen. Like he'd look twice at her in real life.

'I think it's practical and... I like it,' she said.

'Then hand it over.'

Lilah shrugged it off and passed it to Aidan. He went straight to the till with it. When he returned, he handed it to her.

'You can wear it. I got them to take the tags off.'

'Thanks.' She took it from him but waited until they were outside the shop before putting it on. 'What's the other mission?'

'We need to go to the bank still, but before that, I need my staff to have proper working phones.'

'Oh, no way, Aidan. That's far too much.'

He stopped and looked at her. 'If you weren't cooking for me, I'd have beans on toast every night. This is my thank you for keeping me well fed. Consider my debt paid.'

'You owe me nothing.'

'I insist.'

She shook her head, resigned to the fact he wouldn't take no for an answer. And while she felt the need to resist, she couldn't shake the joy underneath. She didn't want him to feel obliged to take care of her, but she couldn't deny that she liked it. It was nice not having to carry the mental load for a while. Why shouldn't she enjoy it while it lasted? And life didn't come with a guarantee, did it? She knew that only too well. This could be over tomorrow and there would be zilch she could do about it.

As they got back on the bus later in the afternoon, Lilah had on her new coat, a shiny new phone in her hands and a brand new bank account, ready for her first real pay cheque... as soon as she found a proper job. The way she felt now, she was sure it wouldn't be long. She could conquer the world in this mood. A surge of warmth enveloped her and she smiled at Aidan, hardly daring to believe the afternoon had really happened. He returned her smile and they held eye contact for a fraction longer than she expected. She would have kept it going but he turned and focused out the window.

'How can I thank you?' she asked.

'Don't. Just keep being you.'

Keep being you.

The words kept repeating in her head over and over. She smiled when she thought about them. He wanted her to be herself. For once, she was enough. Maybe not enough to win his heart, but enough to make him happy in small ways.

He had an important meeting the next day and Lilah got straight to making dinner when they got home. Aidan gave her a look that she interpreted as 'you don't have to do this' but all he said was, 'I have a lot of work to get through before tomorrow and you should chill for a bit. Have some fun with your new phone.'

She left him to it, still grinning at the memory of his words. Chilling wasn't something she was good at. Cooking was fun and much more her thing. She could set up the new phone at the same time.

By the time he got through to eat, it was late and he looked weary.

'Everything ok?' Lilah asked, putting food on a plate.

'I'm just trying to get all my ducks in a row before my meeting tomorrow morning. It's important I have as many ecological facts as possible.'

Lilah assumed it was something to do with the bees. He took his plate from her. 'Thank you,' he said. 'This looks great. I don't expect you to cook every day, but I'm grateful for this. Just don't feel obliged to do it, ok?'

'I don't. I enjoy cooking.'

'Aren't you eating too?'

'I had some earlier. I wasn't sure when you'd be done.'

He cocked his head. 'Then, really, you shouldn't be here waiting on me. Go and relax. As soon as I've eaten, I'm going to bed.'

Lilah tidied away the remaining dishes. 'I'll see you tomorrow then.'

'Yeah. Night-night,' he said. 'And thanks again for doing this.'

'I should be the one thanking you for the coat and the phone. It's too much.'

'No, really, it's not, so don't worry about it. Enjoy it.'

With a smile, she headed for her little bedroom. Once she was under the covers, she closed her eyes, enjoying the warmth and security of the duvet. Aidan was somewhere nearby and that meant everything was going to be ok and she could sleep without worrying about a thing. Today, life was good.

CHAPTER TEN

Aidan

Aidan embraced the man on his doorstep. 'Gabe. It's great to see you.'

Gabriel Wilder stepped back, his face breaking into a grin. 'Always a pleasure, mate. It's been too long.'

'Well, you've been busy making a name for yourself.'

'I'm not the only one. Your Canada walk has got you quite a following yourself. Hey, Maya.' He bent down and gave her an enthusiastic ruffle. She wagged her tail and nuzzled his leg. 'Gorgeous girl, this one.'

They headed through the house towards the garden that backed onto the field. Gabriel glanced around the living area. Now a renowned eco blogger, environmental activist and something of a local celebrity in Glenbriar, where people liked to claim him as their own, Gabriel, like Aidan, had taken an unconventional path. They also shared a similar build and height, occasionally being mistaken for brothers when they were out together, though that rarely happened these days, as Gabriel was always busy.

'You've got the place looking great. Very homely.' Gabe cast his eye over an arrangement of wildflowers on the sideboard.

Lilah really had done an amazing job, no denying it. Her presence in the house brought light and cheer.

'Yeah. I have a lodger and she helps out with the cleaning and cooking. It's all her doing, not mine.'

Gabriel's eyebrows shot up. 'A lodger, huh? Female, aye?'

Aidan nodded. 'Yeah. The cleaner I told you about on the phone. It's all above board.' And that was how it would stay. He wondered about the things Lilah did for him, like she was going over and above to please him, but he wasn't on the market and surely she didn't want anything from him. If he admired her a little from afar, so what? It kind of felt like she was looking at him in the same way at times. As long as they kept it to looking, there was no harm done. He had no plans to act on it. She was nice to talk to and pleasant to be around, but that was all.

Gabriel clapped Aidan on the shoulder. 'It's cool, man. Now, let's get down to business. We should get some pictures of the field so we can put together an action plan.'

'We need to play heavily on the ecological importance of the area because the councillors don't care about whether it'll be an eyesore or spoil the view. You see some of the planning applications they grant? But if we can prove it'll be an environmentally disastrous move, then we might get somewhere.'

'Absolutely. We'll get the community onboard, raise awareness, and make our voices heard. I'll use my platform to spread the word and gather support.'

'That would be great.'

'We can get you on local radio too and we can do some podcasts. People love that voice of yours, Aidan.' Gabe smirked.

'Funny.' Though even from a very young age, his voice had been deep and low. At school, it had been a joke when it broke before anyone else's.

'You leave it to me. I'll organise some live chats and we'll get this campaign up and running.'

'Thanks, mate.'

Aidan poked his head into the kitchen. Where was Lilah? It wasn't like her not to be about. She was free to come and go but he couldn't imagine her going anywhere without telling him first. Not that she had to... it just wasn't her way. She'd never gone out without telling him except that one time when he'd gone after her. In fact, she didn't really go anywhere without him. She sometimes walked the dogs with him. If they needed shopping, he could trust her to do it. Scarlett would go insane if she knew, but that didn't bother him. So what if Scarlett didn't like Lilah? Lilah was one of the kindest, most helpful people he'd ever met. Cooking that meal for him yesterday had been completely unnecessary but he couldn't deny how welcome it had been; he hoped she didn't think he expected it and that she really did enjoy it as much as she claimed.

Normally she'd be up at the same time as him, but he'd been out and walked the dogs and when he got back, the door of her room was open, and she didn't seem to be in the house. Maybe she'd nipped to the shops.

'Not sure where Lilah is. I'll message her.' He pulled out his phone.

'Pity. I'd like to meet the wonder woman who's got your house looking so good. Looks like she could be a permanent fixture.'

'In what way?'

'You know. Starts off as your housekeeper and ends up as your wife.' He winked. 'Tale as old as the hills.'

'Hardly. She's the same age as Scarlett and she's got her own life. Plus... Well, there's Elise.'

'Let her go,' Gabriel said with a shake of his head.

'I have, but she's left a scar.' He punched his fist into his chest.

'Yeah, well, just keep away from her. You don't wanna go there again. I'm not saying she should have waited for you or you should have expected it, but if she's going to take up with your cousin, then nope. Just no. Maybe if it was a cousin in a different country you never see, then fine, but not one who's been your friend for years. That's not on. From Elise or Finlay.'

'You're not wrong.' But he didn't want to think about that. 'Let me get you a drink. What do you fancy? Tea, coffee, Coke?'

'I wouldn't say no to a coke.'

'You sit then and I'll fix it up.' Aidan pulled open the fridge, took out two cans, and decanted them into tall glasses. He peered through the kitchen window into the side garden. The trees in the orchard were now so leafy it was hard to see the hives.

He returned with a coke in each hand, and he and Gabriel reminisced about their younger days. Everything was so simple back then. Kind of. The situation between Aidan's mum and dad wasn't always the best. But his dad had been Aidan's top supporter and champion. Aidan had stayed at Woodend Cottage after the split, when his mum had started a new relationship. This was his true home. He'd visited his mum at weekends but when Scarlett came along, she was the priority and Aidan was fine with that because he had his dad. They were a team. The best team. He slugged back his coke. No one could ever replace him. Since he'd lost Dad, he was emotionally unstable. How could he begin to get back on track? Maybe Elise had recognised the fact and that contributed to her reasons for jumping ship. She wanted someone who could provide stability and Finlay was the one with a safe job, a steady income and an uncomplicated lifestyle.

Gabriel sipped his coke, a pensive expression on his face. 'Happy times, eh? But we can't always be mourning what's past. What we have now is important and so is the future.'

'True.' Aidan sucked in a breath. They could make a better future for the town by preserving the greenbelt and stopping the proposed housing development. If he channelled his energy into that, it would give him a purpose. Something to fight for.

Gabriel raised his glass in a toast. 'To old friends and new battles.'

Aidan clinked his glass against Gabriel's.

'It's been great catching up,' Gabriel said as he downed his last mouthful. 'I should get on, but I'll keep you in the loop about where we should go next.'

'Great.' Aidan walked him to the front door. 'Thanks for this.'

Gabriel clapped him on the shoulder. 'No bother, man. It's what friends are for.'

Aidan watched his friend's car disappear down the road before closing the front door. He returned to the front garden and sat down in the grass beside Maya, gazing out over the field.

'Where's Lilah?' He frowned. 'This is not like her.' And she hadn't replied to his message.

The soft hum of the bees was always soothing music to his ears but another sound blended with it. Was that someone singing?

He got to his feet, trying to pinpoint the source of the soft melody. It was definitely coming from the orchard. Maya stood watching. Good girl. She knew to stay away from the bees. They weren't always as friendly to prodding doggy noses as they were to gentle human hands.

As he approached, his eyes widened. Lilah stood peering into one of the hives, her voice carrying a sweet and captivating tune. The bees seemed almost to be working in harmony with it. Aidan knew why. It was alluring, like a siren. Her long red curls tangled in the breeze. He leaned on a tree and watched. She was a free spirit now, not the chained and beaten soul she'd been when he first saw her. This was where she belonged. In nature.

He couldn't tear his gaze away and a deep longing stirred within him, moving his soul – almost painfully. With a slight wince, he closed his eyes. What was going on? Why was she affecting him like this?

Shaking off an unexpected heart tremor, he approached her, unable to resist the pull of the music. Her voice was natural and would have been spoiled by instruments accompanying it. The wild outdoors was enough. The song had a rustic feel, like she was a young girl of old, working on the family farm singing a lament for a long-lost love.

A twig snapped beneath his feet, alerting her to his presence. She turned with a start, her hand leaping to her chest. 'You gave me a fright.'

'Sorry,' he said. 'I've been wondering where you were. My friend came round to talk about the field. I was going to introduce you, but I couldn't find you.'

'Oh. I didn't realise. I was round at Jim's. He's struggling with his arthritis and asked if I could help him open a tin.'

'You know Jim?' Aidan raised his eyebrows. He didn't remember ever introducing Lilah to his neighbour.

'He potters in his garden quite a lot and I started chatting to him. I hope you don't mind me helping him. Once I opened the tin, I helped him clean up and made him a cup of tea. He's a sweet man.'

'Of course I don't mind. Jim's a good guy. I need to pop around and see him myself. He'll appreciate your help.'

She smiled and her cheeks turned slightly pink. Why did she suddenly look so pretty? More than pretty. Irresistible. It made him hot, twitchy, not himself. Was she doing so much for him because she liked him? Maybe a bit more than was good for her... or him? He'd dismissed his mum's insinuations that Lilah might be interested in him, but maybe she was. When he looked at her, it would be easy to forget she was someone working for him and not a woman he was allowed to be attracted to.

'Thanks.' He cleared his throat. 'Gabriel's in town doing a radio show and we arranged to meet while he was here. I have to catch him when I can. He's a busy man.'

'I didn't realise anyone was here. When I got back from Jim's, I came out to read. It's such a beautiful day and I thought you were busy in your study.' She glanced away. 'I shouldn't be playing around out here. My two weeks are up and I haven't found a job yet. I don't even know what kind of thing to look for.'

'Maybe you should be a performer; you have a beautiful singing voice,' he said.

'Er, no. I don't fancy that at all.' The colour in her cheeks intensified and spread down her neck and onto her chest. He flexed his fingers, trying to expel their sudden desire to trace a line down her exposed skin. She was so freckly it made her appear fresh and youthful... *Which she is! Don't go messing with someone this young and innocent.* She might have had a tough innings and hard upbringing, but that gave him no right to look at her as anything more than his cleaner and his lodger. In fact, the opposite. He should protect her and make sure she was in a safe environment.

'What was the song?'

'I dunno.' She pulled a little shrug. 'Just a mix of some Scottish folk songs. Before we moved to the council house in Glenbriar, we lived above the Stagger Inn Bar and there were Scot's karaoke nights every summer. I used to listen to the songs in my bed and some of them stuck, though I don't really remember the words. I kind of make them up.'

'Well, it sounded good to me. And the bees liked it too.'

She blinked, then gave him a little smile. He returned it and patted her on the shoulder. It momentarily appeased the carnal need to touch her that had risen inside him. She wasn't tiny, but she was so thin, she might break if he put too much pressure on her, so he let go. He should let go anyway.

She sighed softly. 'I like living here but I hate that I'm not paying rent.'

'You more than earn it with the cooking and cleaning you do.' He plonked himself down on the grass beside where Lilah had put her book. He picked it up and peered at it. *Jane Eyre* by Charlotte Brontë,' he read aloud. 'Is it any good?'

'Yeah. I've read it before lots of times. It's my favourite Brontë novel.'

'Where did you get this?'

'The library.'

He put it down with a smile. 'I don't know why, but I didn't have you down as a library girl.'

'Why not?' She sat down beside him, crossed her legs like a pixie, and rested her hands on the torn knees of her jeans.

'Deep-rooted biases I guess.'

'What does that even mean?' Her smile was too cute.

'It means I've been conditioned to think in a certain way.'

'To think that I'm scum.'

'Not exactly but definitely to believe certain lies about people in your position or from your background.'

She nodded and picked at the grass. 'Yup. Which brings me back to what I was saying. I can't stay here. I feel like a scrounger.'

'You shouldn't because you're not.' A pang tugged at his chest, and he let out an involuntary grunt. He'd grown accustomed to having her around. Maybe a selfish part of him liked the way she cared for him. The lonely part of him liked her company.

'I need to get a proper job.'

'Doing what?'

'I don't know.' She tugged at some more blades of grass. 'I don't have any qualifications or skills or anything.'

He cocked his head. 'You definitely have skills. You can cook, bake, and sing like an angel. There are jobs out there for people like you. I think you just need more confidence in yourself. If you think people are going to look down on you, they will.'

'But that's just it. They do.'

'Yeah, I get that. But let's approach this methodically.'

'How?'

'Firstly, I brought you here and took you away from lodgings. I know I said two weeks but that was only for the cleaning. You can still stay here while you hunt for jobs. I won't throw you out.'

'What if it takes weeks or months to find something? Even if I do, I have no references. Will that matter?'

'I can give you a reference now. You've officially worked for me. I'm going to give Hayley a call. I messaged her and asked her to look out for you. Let's see if she's had any luck.'

'Ok.'

Aidan checked the time. She might be working but it was worth a try given that it was lunchtime.

The call connected.

'Hey,' Hayley said. 'Everything ok?'

'Yeah. I just wondered if you'd had any luck sourcing any jobs for Lilah.'

'I did actually have an idea. You remember my cousin, Willow, was working at the Old Schoolhouse Residential Centre before she left to film *Destination Forecast* with Marcus Bowman?'

'Kind of.' He tried to keep up with Hayley's stories, but often forgot the details.

'I'm not sure if they've filled her post yet or even advertised for it.'

'What kind of job is it? Like a carer?' He could imagine Lilah being good at that.

'It was more admin work but there would be no harm in approaching the people who run it.'

'Do you know their names?'

'Marion and Barry Corbett. The only thing I would say against them is that they're friendly with Malcolm and Brenda McManus.'

'Hmm,' Aidan said. A lot of people in the town were friends with that couple and either turned a blind eye to their dodgy activity or were unaware of it.

'Still, Willow always sang their praises and I reckon they're fair. They have a good reputation.'

'Well, it's worth a try. Thank you.'

They said their goodbyes and he ended the call.

Lilah looked on, her eyes wide and expectant. 'Has she found something?'

'Just an idea. Her cousin – one on the other side of the family to me – used to work at the Old Schoolhouse in Clachnabron-nachan.'

'I know that place. It's not far from Brenda's house.'

'Yeah, well, there might be a job up for grabs there.' Though it wasn't exactly next door to Woodend. Hopefully if Lilah got it, she wouldn't feel the need to move back in with Brenda to be closer. Surely she'd never prefer that to living here? He wanted her to find a job and be independent but part of him didn't want her to leave. A protective, almost possessive surge fired through him.

'Should I phone them?' she said.

'You can do. Or we could go and visit. I'll come with you if you like.'

She nodded. 'I don't mind going in myself but if you walked with me, that would be great.'

'Ok. Call them and find out when would be a good time. We can walk up with the dogs if it's during the day.'

'Thanks so much.' She beamed at him and for a moment, he thought she might hug him. He stood very still, not certain if he wanted her to or not. Part of him craved it so hard it made him ache, but the other part warned him against physical contact. Because who knew where a hug might lead? Especially if he'd read her looks correctly. The attraction was there, but they shouldn't encourage it.

The moment passed and Aidan let out a breath. A strange sensation burned in his chest, reminding him of something he couldn't quite place. Whatever it was it felt kind of nice but also a bit unsettling. He needed to dismiss it and get on with his day. Giving Lilah another brief pat on the arm, he headed back to the house.

CHAPTER ELEVEN

Lilah

Sun shone in the kitchen window, highlighting a stream of dust motes. Lilah put away the dishes on the drainer, then flipped through a recipe book. She'd spotted a tasty-looking egg and cheese dish. Aidan would like it. Snapping the book shut, she groaned, and Maya glanced up from her bed in the corner.

'Sorry,' Lilah said. 'But why am I such an idiot when it comes to Aidan?' The crush was quite ridiculous and she wished she could stop it, but she wasn't sure it was just a crush anymore. It had grown into something bigger. She flicked on the kettle and it started bubbling, much like the nerves in her tummy.

She half wanted to do a runner but she had to see this through and finding breakfast recipes was keeping her mind off the scary thoughts of visiting the Old Schoolhouse and the possibility – albeit small one – of a job there. When she'd phoned to make an appointment, the owner sounded nice, but they hadn't seen her yet.

She pulled out a pot and searched the fridge for ingredients. 'Oh, Maya.' She sighed as she pulled out crème fraiche and spinach. 'You're so lucky.' Not only did Maya not have to worry about fruitlessly trying to impress anyone, but she also had unconditional love from Aidan. What Lilah wouldn't give for that.

As she cracked an egg into a bowl, she gazed into the garden. Aidan was out there somewhere, hidden by the leafy trees, talking to the bees. He'd been kind to her and she, in her naivety, had grown attached to him. Far too attached. He was the first person to have shown her kindness and concern. *I'm reading too much into it, letting my mind wander into places it has no right to go.* Moving on from this would be harsh but she had to do it. No way could it be permanent. One day, Aidan would get over his breakup with Elise, realise he was a young and very attractive man and find someone to be with. And how many women would want to be with him? Lilah cracked another egg. Not only would they get a devoted man, but a beautiful house and a wonderful dog.

Not for me.

Sure, she knew that but it didn't strip away the desire to do what she could while she was here. Her chest burned constantly, like she had chronic heartburn but it was nothing Gaviscon could cure. A permanent desperation had moved in, pushing her to better herself and show him she was more than her past and the person Scarlett remembered from school. Could she do that today? Would these people care about where she came from and grew up? Would they even want to speak to her? Aidan had told her they were friendly with Brenda and that might be something else against her. This might be completely pointless.

A shudder rippled up her arms like a chilling breeze as she tossed the eggshells into the compost. What if she walked in and they screwed up their faces? She was used to that kind of reaction. A crawling sense of being dirty, pathetic and worthless swept in.

She sighed and whisked together the ingredients for the sauce, then poured them into a glass dish. Maya tilted her head, as if sensing Lilah's discomfort. 'You're such a good dog,' Lilah murmured, dropping the eggs into the mixture.

She grated the cheese over the top and put it in the oven. Crouching down, she patted Maya.

If she got a job, it would take her away from the house more and that had to be good because soon Patricia and possibly Scarlett would be at the barn every day and Lilah wanted to avoid them as much as possible. 'I wish we could keep it like this. Just the three of us. It's not too bad, is it?' Maya rolled over, opening her underbelly for Lilah to rub.

Not that Aidan would ever see her as anything more than a lodger or someone he was 'helping' anyway.

Taking a deep breath, she pulled plates and glasses from the cupboard, her hands trembling slightly. 'I've got to get a grip. I can do this.'

She pushed open the kitchen door and was immediately serenaded by an orchestra of twittering birds. Maya leapt to her feet and followed her into the side garden. As they approached the orchard, the hum of bees intensified. Lilah opened the gate and Maya lay down outside the fence.

'Aidan,' Lilah called.

He emerged through the trees, his tight t-shirt clinging to his muscular frame. Lilah swallowed. His arms and hands were tanned and weatherworn. His outdoor lifestyle had bronzed his face and neck. He was so rugged and sexy. Swarthy even, almost pirate-like – the handsome kind, not the one-eyed, toothless, scurvy-ridden variety.

'Morning.' He dusted his hands together. 'Everything ok?'

'I've made breakfast. It's something I've never tried before with eggs, spinach and a creamy cheese sauce.' She smiled, and he shook his head. Her heart flickered. Was he cross? He had a deep V on his forehead, highlighted by his thick eyebrows. Had she overstepped? She stood still until his lips curled and his face lit up. He wasn't a big smiler but when he did... Wow.

'Really, Lilah, you don't have to make me breakfast. I'd be happy making a slice of toast.'

'Oh.' Her heart slumped against her ribcage.

'I'm not complaining. I appreciate it. Just don't go thinking I expect it.' He put his hand on her bare shoulder, next to the strap of her vest top.

She inhaled sharply at the skin-on-skin contact. Had she covered it, or was it obvious how much he affected her? Her breathing was rough and she couldn't do a thing about it.

'I hope you've made it for yourself too.' He let go as if the touch had also burned him. 'You'll need energy for today.'

'There's enough for both of us.'

'Good.'

She led the way out of the orchard, giving Maya a wink as she passed.

Aidan scrubbed his hands as Lilah took her creation from the oven and plated it up.

'This looks amazing.' He took his seat and raised his knife and fork. 'I've got some good news.'

'Oh?' Lilah sat across from him.

'Hayley messaged me. She wants to come with us today. I hope that's ok.'

'Um... Yeah.' She kind of wished it could be just the two of them, though admitting that would open her up to too much speculation.

Aidan took a mouthful and chewed with an appreciative smile. 'This is really good. You're an amazing cook.'

'Thanks.' The heat in Lilah's cheeks and neck rose again.

'Hayley is very talented with people. She'll make sure everything goes smoothly and she knows the owners.'

Lilah nodded. 'Sounds sensible.'

'She is sensible, though she manages to be sensible and fun. Her brother's the same.'

'Finlay?'

'Yup.'

'You can say that even though he stole your girlfriend and got engaged to her after just a few weeks?'

Aidan huffed out a laugh. 'Yeah. I'm trying to get past that. But Elise wasn't actually my girlfriend at that point. She'd split up with me in her mind by then.'

He was talking about it much more evenly than he had before. 'I understand why it made you mad.'

'Yeah. I've always been quick to anger. Finlay and Hayley were good friends to me growing up. They were good at keeping me level and not letting me get too hot tempered.'

'That's good. We wouldn't want you getting too hot.' She almost choked on her eggs. 'Too hot-headed.' He was already too hot. So hot it distracted her every second of every day.

'Definitely not something you'd want to see.'

Her heart raced. She might... Depending on which bit they were talking about. She hated shouting and angry moods, but she was insanely in love with the idea of him being in a hot passion, especially if it happened to be with her.

They finished off their breakfast and cleaned up the kitchen together. Even moments like this made her nerve ends tingle. Her fantasies kicked in, making her believe they were a couple and this was domestic bliss rather than innocent cohabitation.

Lilah had paid close attention to her clothes and was dressed as smartly as she could in her limited wardrobe. She'd just grabbed her coat when there came a knock on the door. Expecting to see Hayley, she pulled it open. Her eyes widened at the sight of Patricia Finch.

'Hello,' Patricia said. 'Where's Aidan?'

'He's about somewhere.'

'I need to speak to him.' She headed down the corridor and peered into the living room. 'Aidan!'

Lilah let her go. She wasn't sure exactly where Aidan was but his mum could locate him herself.

'Hello, hello,' a voice said from the now half-open door and Lilah turned to see Hayley. Her long, dark hair tumbled down her back in effortless waves.

'Hi,' Lilah said.

Hayley smiled, then pulled her into a hug. 'It's so good to see you again.'

Help... What to do? Hug her back? Lilah wasn't used to people being so friendly. And she hardly knew Hayley. Plus, Hayley was close to Elise. Finlay was her brother. Those two had caused Aidan so much trouble. Could Hayley really be trusted? If it came to the crunch, wouldn't she side with her brother? These dramas were new and alien.

Eventually Lilah returned her hug briefly before Hayley let go.

'So, all ready?' Hayley looked around.

'I am, but I'm not sure where Aidan is and his mum's just arrived.'

'Oh, Aunty Tricia is here too. Is she through here? I'll go say hi.'

Lilah watched her go, standing alone like a loose part. Just seconds later, Hayley reemerged with Patricia and Aidan.

Patricia didn't look at Lilah as she approached but Hayley smiled. She moved up beside Lilah and popped her arm around her shoulder. 'You'll be fine.'

Hayley's protective arm gave Lilah a glimmer of hope. Maybe, just maybe, Hayley could be a genuine friend. Or was that as stupid as thinking Aidan could ever be anything more than a man she had a chronic crush on?

'Fine with what?' Patricia said.

'We've got a little project,' Aidan said, glancing at his phone. 'And we should be leaving.'

'So nobody can help me with The Crafty Bee Barn?' Patricia said.

'That's a good name,' Hayley said. 'I hope you're planning to paint it yellow.'

'Eventually, though goodness knows when I'll find the time.'

'I can help you move boxes later,' Aidan said. 'But not until we get back. Can't Scarlett do it?'

'No.' Patricia let out a sigh. 'She's taken up with a new man and is working with him.'

'What man?' Aidan frowned.

'A new boyfriend. He works on some local estate and Scarlett's been going out with him quite a lot.'

Lilah remembered what Aidan had said about Scarlett being babied. Judging by the expression on Patricia's face, she wasn't best pleased at her daughter's latest move. Maybe she felt shut out.

'I'll do it when I come back then,' Aidan said.

'I don't mind helping either,' Lilah said. 'If you want me too.'

Patricia looked at her for a second, then blinked. 'That's very kind. Thank you.' She seemed genuinely surprised.

'Let's go,' Aidan said. Lilah left first and made her way towards the woods. Hayley walked alongside her and Aidan collected the dogs from the garden before joining them.

'I'm glad you arranged this for a Monday,' Hayley said. 'I don't work on Monday or Tuesday and it's such a lovely day today. It's nice to get out for a walk.'

She was quite right, but Lilah wasn't in the right frame of mind to admire the scenery. All she could think of was how she could make a good impression.

'Just be yourself,' Hayley said. 'Marion and Barry are really nice people. They like everyone. Willow loved working for them. Even if they don't give you a job today, just look at it as experience.'

All good advice but Hayley didn't know how 'being herself' hadn't exactly worked well in the past.

They left the woods at Clachnabronnachan but didn't go towards Malcolm and Brenda's house. Instead, they doubled back along the road a short distance, where it ran parallel to the path they'd just walked. The Old Schoolhouse was a quaint building set close to the woods. The fence surrounding it still looked like a school but the playground had been converted into a garden and car park.

'I'll wait out here with the dogs,' Aidan said, standing by the gate.

'And I'll do the introductions, then leave you to it.' Hayley gave Lilah another bracing shoulder hug.

Lilah's stomach was in knots as Hayley knocked on the front door.

An older woman with very long silver hair opened it. 'Ah, hello, Hayley. And you must be Lilah Clarke.'

'Yes.' Lilah nodded. Her mouth had gone dry.

'Lovely to meet you. I'm Marion Corbett. Now, in you come.'

'I'll wait outside if you want,' Hayley said.'

'Not at all,' Marion said. 'Nothing so formal.' She led them through the building that still resembled a school in places, though it had been furnished in a homely style. Lilah spotted some old coat pegs in the hallway. The lounge area Marion led them to was cosy and she gestured for Lilah and Hayley to take a chair each. 'Tea? Coffee?'

Once Marion had made them drinks and settled in a chair, she smiled at Lilah. 'So, you're looking for a job?'

'Yes.'

'Do you have any experience working in a care centre or doing any kind of admin?'

Lilah's cheeks burned. Of course she didn't. She had no experience doing anything. 'Not really. I've mostly done cooking and baking.'

'Ah.' Marion nodded and sipped her tea. 'Well, the admin job has already been filled, but I am looking for someone to do a few hours a day as a carer. We struggle to find people to do bitty jobs as we're a bit out of the way and people don't always think it's worth the travel time. We can't condense the hours as we need someone every day. Perhaps this would interest you?'

'It sounds interesting,' Lilah said.

'Do you know about the work of this centre?'

'Yes.' She'd done her homework. 'I've read all about it and I know how you work with young people who've left school but aren't able to live alone.'

'Exactly. Cooking and baking skills would be a very useful place to start. We like to teach our residents life skills and cooking is a very important one. This job would cover the lunch period and hopefully get the residents you're working with into the habit of making their own lunch and cleaning up each day.'

'I could definitely do that.'

'Super. Now, there will be a lot to learn, so if you wouldn't mind, I'd like to start with a couple of weeks of training and induction. You'll get paid, of course.'

'Really? You want me to do it?' Lilah beamed at Hayley, who was nodding encouragingly.

'Yes. I think you can help us and we can help you. Win-win, wouldn't you say?'

'Totally. That's amazing. Thank you.'

Lilah's mind spun with dizzy excitement as she tried to concentrate on the details of the arrangement.

They'd barely got out the front door before Hayley squealed and grabbed hold of her. 'You did it!'

'I can't believe it.' Lilah returned her hug. 'I hardly did anything.'

'You were just yourself. You were natural and Marion could see that you're a sensible person.'

Aidan was across the road in a field, walking the dogs around. He gathered them all onto short leads and hastened over when he spotted Lilah and Hayley. 'Well?' he said.

'I didn't get the admin job,' Lilah said, and his shoulders sank slightly. 'But she's letting me work as a part-time carer, from ten until two every day.'

Aidan's smile filled his face. 'That's great.'

'Wow.' Lilah fanned her face. 'What a relief.'

'We have to celebrate this,' Hayley said. 'How about we go for a drink later?'

'Perfect,' Aidan said. 'As long as you promise not to set me up with anyone.'

'I won't.' Hayley laughed. 'Let's go to the Cross Keys. It's lovely there.'

They started the walk back through the woods. 'If you're going to be doing this every day, we'll need to find you a better way of getting here,' Aidan said. 'This walk is fine at this time of year and when the weather's nice, but it'll be a different story when it rains and in the winter.'

'I can't drive,' Lilah said. 'And no way can I afford a car.'

'I might get a car again,' Aidan said. 'I'd like to do without one but it's not practical when you live in rural parts.'

'But you couldn't give me a lift every day,' Lilah said. 'That wouldn't be practical either.'

'How about a bike?' Hayley suggested. 'Not that it'll keep you dry, but it'll be quicker. You can come up the road if the path is too icy.'

'You could borrow my bike,' Aidan said.

'Ok. That might work.' Lilah wasn't sure her bike riding skills were good enough to cycle up here but she'd never know unless she tried and right now she felt like she could do anything.

The idea of going somewhere with Aidan and Hayley later should make her jump with excitement but she cringed. *What should I wear?* How would they feel about being seen with her if she turned up dressed in one of the same old outfits? Memories of being taunted at school for her shabby, unwashed clothes resurfaced and pummelled her head.

She couldn't go. It made no sense to put herself through it.

'Listen,' she said. 'I don't think I can go out tonight.'

'Why?' Aidan frowned. 'And don't say you can't afford it. You know I'll buy you a drink.'

'I've saved some money so I can afford a drink. It's just... Well, I'll look so scabby next to the two of you.'

'What are you talking about? I'm sure no one will notice what you're wearing.'

Easy for him to say. He hadn't grown up with people telling him how dirty he looked or that he stank. When had he ever had people refuse to sit next to him in case they caught something? Even when Lilah scrubbed herself clean, nothing could fully wash away the smell of poverty.

'Hey, don't worry about that,' Hayley said. 'I've got tons of clothes and you can borrow something. I might even have stuff you can keep. You're super-skinny, so some of it might be loose on you, but it'll still be ok.'

'I don't mind that.' Hayley had a beautiful figure and always dressed nicely.

Would new clothes really make it any better? Could they really mask who she was inside? Even if she was dressed like a royal, she'd probably still do something to betray her status as a pauper. But she needed to ditch that attitude and get out and conquer the world. Twenty minutes ago, she'd felt like she could do anything, and going to the Cross Keys was definitely something.

Look out world! I'm on my way.

Chapter Twelve

Lilah

Lilah opened the door of Woodend Cottage late in the afternoon to a smiling Hayley.

'Hey,' Hayley said, handing a large red shopping bag to her. 'Take a peek in here. I've got lots of goodies for you.' She perched a pair of large sunglasses on her head, to hold back her long shining tresses, and beamed.

Lilah hesitated for a moment before peering into the bag. What a regular Cinderella she was. And Hayley was her fairy godmother. If only she could magic Aidan into Prince Charming... Well, as far as looks were concerned, you didn't get much more handsome than him. Same went for his physique; he was a chiselled Adonis. And really, he'd been so kind too. Who else would have gone the extra mile and given her a chance? Maybe Hayley could work a spell to make him fall madly in love with her. Lilah mustered a weak smile and whispered, 'Thank you.'

Hayley squeezed her shoulder gently. 'No problem at all. It's stuff I don't wear anymore. You're welcome to keep everything or choose some things you like. Or get rid of them all if you don't like them.'

'I'm sure I'll like everything.' It was bound to be a hundred times better than anything she already had.

'How about I fix your hair up too?' Hayley's eyes were all over her hair, like she was already imagining the perfect style.

'Um, ok.'

'Great. Where's Aidan? I hope he's not chickened out.'

'He's in the shower… I think,' she added. No need to make her stalkerish tendencies too obvious. The sound of rushing water in the bathroom when Aidan was in there always set her brain whirring into X-rated fantasies of him, all tanned and muscular, covered in droplets of hot water. Steam on the glass door. The air fresh with the heady scent of body wash.

Her eyes landed back on Hayley, who smirked and said, 'Ooh, taking things very seriously, is he? Getting all spruced up to celebrate.'

'Yeah.' Lilah made her way down the corridor and opened the door to her room. 'But he's been working in the garden this afternoon, so it's more likely to be that.'

'Typical Aidan. Even when we were little, he was always outside. In the summer holidays, our parents shared childcare, so they didn't have to take too long off work. When it was our turn to have Aidan, we couldn't get him to come in for dinner, even when it was raining. He was always wanting picnics or to go on long rides on his bike.' Hayley pulled a couple of items from the bag and held them up against Lilah, giving them an appraising glance. 'This green top will look really lovely with your pale skin colour and the way the neckline drops will show off your neck, especially if I pull your hair back.'

'Um... Ok.'

'Try it on, see if it fits.' Hayley handed it to her.

Feeling completely exposed, Lilah took off her top. Hayley didn't seem in the least bothered as she raked about in the bag and pulled out another item, chattering about everything and anything as she did. Lilah's skin prickled with memories. All those times at school when she'd been changing for P.E. and the other girls would spray deodorant at her while holding their noses. Sometimes they made retching noises or faked vomiting. Often they'd snigger and point if she had on tatty underwear or hadn't shaved her legs. She always tried to but how could she afford new razors when her mum nicked them?

These days, she had neatly shaven legs, was cleaner than clean and usually had pants without holes in them, but the agonising memories wouldn't leave her alone.

When the top was on, she turned a couple of times in front of the mirror.

'It's beautiful on you,' Hayley said, putting her hands on her hips and nodding. Her expression became appraising, and she indicated for Lilah to sit on the end of the bed. 'Now, let's see.'

Lilah sat and Hayley knelt behind her, lifting her hair and teasing it out gently. 'People pay hundreds of pounds to get hair like this. You're so lucky.'

'Am I?' Lilah raised an eyebrow. 'One of my stepdads used to say it made me look like an Irish tinker.'

'Silly man was probably jealous. Was he bald by any chance?'

'Actually, yes.'

Hayley chuckled and Lilah joined her. How funny when she thought about it like that.

Once her hair was up, Hayley showed her some simple make-up techniques. 'This will keep you looking natural, while enhancing your features, because you're already very pretty. We don't want to cake you or cover your freckles. Just pat a little bit of this on. Never rub it.'

The warmth of Hayley's compliments was affecting her more than the intense heat of the styling brush Hayley had put on the dresser. *Please don't let me blush.*

When Hayley was done, she switched off the brush, and Lilah stood before the mirror, hardly recognising herself. Her hair was styled beautifully to one side. The usual frizz was tamed into wider, slicker curls that hung elegantly over one shoulder. The green satin top looked stunning even with her old jeans.

'You look amazing.' Hayley smiled.

'Thank you. I feel like someone else.'

'You still look like yourself, just a bit more styled. You'd have been fine as you were, but this will give you more confidence.

Everyone likes looking their best for a night out. Now, let's see if Aidan's ready.' Hayley opened the door, but Lilah turned herself in front of the mirror a few more times. Her arms were pale and skinny but that was just the way she was. The rest of her looked incredible. She'd never dreamed she could look this good. No one seeing her now would guess her shitty background.

Hayley and Aidan were talking somewhere in the house and Lilah caught brief words and the happy sound of Hayley laughing. Opening the drawer beside her bed, Lilah pulled out the cash she'd saved and thrust it into a little bag Hayley had put in with the clothes.

In the hall, she closed the door behind her quietly. Hayley and Aidan were both at the other end, near the entrance to the living area. They turned at the sound of Lilah's door. Aidan instantly seized Lilah in his gaze. He blinked a few times with his long dark lashes, then adjusted his shirt collar. She stood stock-still. What was he thinking? Did he like what he saw?

'Looking good,' he said. A flash in his eyes told her he meant it and it wasn't just a flyaway comment.

Lilah blinked and gave him her best smile, though the pulse thumping in her ears was off-putting.

'Doesn't she?' Hayley beamed and linked arms with her. 'Come on then, beautiful people. Let's hit the town.'

Lilah teetered down the path, relieved to discover Hayley was taking them in her car because it was quite a walk to the Cross Keys Inn. The Inn sat on the edge of the River Briar, surrounded by trees and greenery. A riverside path wound past it and a few people strolled along it. A small hill rose behind and close by was a footbridge nicknamed 'the wobbly bridge' – because it did just that when people crossed it. Lilah had occasionally come down here before but she'd never set foot in the Cross Keys. Hayley parked in the car park, which was quite small and seemed to have been made by gouging out a section of the small hill. They crossed the path to the inn. Planters with fairy lights flanked the main doors and it looked very pretty... But expensive. The loose change in Lilah's bag wouldn't buy much in here. This was the kind of place she couldn't normally afford to even look in the window. Perhaps it showed on her face because Aidan gave her a little smile.

'Why don't the two of you go and get a seat? I'll get the drinks. My treat,' he added.

Hayley led them through the lounge with its beamed ceilings decorated in more fairy lights, then out of the French doors to a table on the decking with a view over the river. Aidan went to order. Close by, people were chatting with friends and following the progress of some kayakers navigating the rapids below. The last time Lilah had been in a pub, it was a lot seedier than this.

From her chair with its back to the railing, Lilah peered inside, watching Aidan as he approached the bar. Bartenders bustled around, pulling pints and popping open bottles.

Some kind of soft music played, but it was a mere whisper behind the sounds of the river and birdsong.

'How do you like the bees?' Hayley asked, leaning back and smiling. Her purple maxi dress was summery and fitted into this location like she was modelling for a magazine. 'They used to freak me out completely but Aidan has such a way with them.'

'Yeah, he really does,' Lilah replied.

'I'm glad he's got them. It's something to keep his mind off... Well, my brother and Elise.'

'Yeah.'

'Honestly.' Hayley leaned forward, bringing her closer to Lilah. 'It is such a nightmare. I get three different sides to the story. None of them has been perfect and I feel pulled in all directions. Sometimes, I think that Elise only agreed to marry Finlay to get back at Aidan. Some of the stuff she's said makes me worry for my brother. He's had his share of problems already and he doesn't need any more. He was engaged a few years ago, and it ended in a bad split. Ever since, I think he's felt cheated. Like he should be further forward in his life, if that makes sense. I just hope he hasn't jumped into this engagement to fast forward things.'

Lilah frowned, not wanting to react in a way that might give away her feelings for Aidan. 'So... Do you think Elise wants to get back together with Aidan?'

'Oh no,' Hayley said, and her eyes were now focused inside. Her face had turned white.

'What?' Lilah stared at her for a second before she realised she hadn't spoken in reply to her question, but something she'd seen.

'Speak of the devil.' Hayley let out a low grown.

Lilah followed her sightline. 'You mean...'

Hayley waved to a couple heading through the French doors and coming their way. With a swoop in her tummy, Lilah recognised them as the couple she'd seen at the fair. Would they remember her? Unlikely. But if they did, she'd have to go through the same palaver as she always did to prove she wasn't scum.

She let out a sigh 'Is that Elise?' she whispered, half-hoping it wasn't, though it was pretty obvious.

Hayley nodded, still smiling at the approaching couple.

'Hello.' Elise reached their table, leaned over and hugged Hayley. 'This is a happy chance.'

'Isn't it?' Hayley said, her smile seeming a little forced.

'Hey.' The man Lilah assumed was Finlay raised his eyebrows at her, then looked at his sister. Like Hayley and Aidan, Finlay was blessed with good looks. Nothing like as swarthy or defined as Aidan, but then no one was as handsome as Aidan as far as Lilah was concerned. She smiled inwardly. She couldn't imagine Aidan wearing a rugby shirt like that, but Finlay wore his navy one well. Maybe he liked sport. He looked like someone who did. His build was athletic.

'Hi,' Lilah said. The word drew Elise's gaze and she screwed up her perfectly straight nose. Everything about her was utterly immaculate – except for her current expression.

'Do we know you?' she asked, smoothing the front of her short green jumpsuit. It was very chic with her high heeled white pumps and matching clutch bag.

'This is my friend Lilah,' Hayley said. 'We're celebrating her getting a new job.'

'Oh, congrats. Can we sit?'

'I...er, yes,' Hayley said.

Elise and Finlay took seats at the table.

'So, um...' Hayley's eyes darted to the bar.

'We're thinking about having our engagement party here but I wanted to see what the function rooms are like,' Elise said before sitting down. 'Hang on, I'm bursting for the loo. Watch my bag, will you?' She plonked her handbag in Finlay's lap and darted off.

Hayley gave him a nervous smile.

'Wait a sec,' Finlay said, a frown darkening his otherwise pleasant features. 'Is that Aidan in there?'

'Yeah,' Hayley said.

'Oh man, I don't believe this.' Finlay dumped the bag on an empty chair and ran his hand over his neatly trimmed beard.

Lilah watched, knowing exactly why Finlay's face was now wearing a deep scowl. Elise hadn't got as far as the loo. She'd stopped at the bar and was talking to Aidan. Not just talking, but standing a little too close. They looked like the perfect couple, both gorgeous, well-matched in height and appearance.

Hayley gave Lilah a look that begged for an alien spaceship to zoom overhead and beam them out of this awkward mess.

'This is ridiculous.' Finlay shook his head and leaned his chin on his hand. 'Just ridiculous.'

'Hey. It's ok.' Hayley put her hand on his arm.

'Is it? If she'd rather go back to him, then why doesn't she just do it?' he mumbled, more to himself than anyone else.

Lilah almost held her breath, understanding now why Hayley felt like a pig in the middle. Her insides were writhing. Were Finlay's doing the same? She wanted to burst in and push Elise and Aidan apart. They weren't together anymore, so why were they standing so close? Why were they torturing another man...? *And me*. Because seeing Aidan with Elise made Lilah feel sick.

'Finlay,' Hayley said quietly. 'She chose you, but Aidan exists. You have to deal with it.'

'I know he exists. But what are they playing at?'

'Nothing. They're just talking. It's better than her walking past and ignoring him. At least she's making an effort.'

'And I'm not? Is that what you mean?'

'Of course not. But unless the two of you leave the town or the country, you have to accept you might see him and it'll be painful. You must have known when you and Elise got together that he wasn't going to disappear forever.'

'Oh yeah? Considering his disappearance was part of the reason we got together in the first place, I don't see why not.'

Lilah's thoughts spiralled out of the conversation. She liked Hayley and the way she always tried to keep the peace, but this time, Lilah was with Finlay. Elise should back off. She'd chosen Finlay and that was where she could stay.

Lilah stared at her. With her fashionable clothes and expensive style, Elise was the embodiment of perfection. How could Aidan resist? Maybe he didn't want to. What if he wanted Elise back? Lilah shrank into the seat, her heart shrivelling at the thought. How could she ever measure up to someone like Elise?

Chapter Thirteen

Aidan

Aidan leaned on the bar. The upbeat music, the clink of glasses and laughter, clashed with the dark mood that had descended on him with the appearance of Elise. This was all Hayley's fault. Why had she brought them here? Had she maybe engineered this? Her love of matchmaking was no secret. Maybe she thought he and Elise could get back together. They could have celebrated Lilah's success anywhere. It didn't have to be at a favourite haunt of Finlay and Elise.

He groaned internally. Why was he thinking like that? Hayley would never do that to her brother and, curse his grumpy mind, she wouldn't do it to him either. Or her friend. It was no one's fault. Just fate shoving itself in where it wasn't wanted.

The bartender added the last drink to the tray and Aidan slapped his card on the machine.

'You're probably not the right person to say this to,' Elise said. 'But I feel like I have to tell someone.'

'And what's that?'

'Finlay can be so closed off about things sometimes. He won't tell me much about who he dated before me. What's the story?'

Aidan shrugged. 'It's not for me to tell.' Finlay had suffered an embarrassing end to an engagement some years ago and, as far as Aidan knew, hadn't dated much since then but it wasn't his place to speculate.

'Do you think...' She took a deep breath. 'Why do you think he proposed so fast? It was quite a shock. Do you think he's trying to get revenge on an ex or something?'

Aidan shrugged, then knocked back some of his drink. Why was she asking him? Could she hear herself? She thought Finlay was trying to get revenge on someone. Wasn't it just as likely that was what she was doing? *To me!*

He glanced outside. Lilah was beaming at Hayley and Finlay and looked like she was laughing at something or telling them a funny story. The way Hayley had done her hair made her look older and so sophisticated. She was like a fairy-tale princess with her curls swept high; a few loose ones tumbled down her long slender neck and over her pale angular shoulders. That smile suckered Aidan in the gut. It made him want to smile too, and more. He wanted to kiss her long slender neck, continue over her porcelain white skin, along her collarbone...

What the hell?

He swigged another mouthful of ale.

'I need to take these drinks out. I'm sorry if things aren't working out for you and Finlay but it's not my business anymore.'

She fiddled with her bracelet and didn't meet his eyes. 'It's such a pity....'

'What is?'

'How things ended for us.'

'Yup. But what's done is done.'

Something flickered across her face, but she remained calm and her lips quirked into a well-practiced smile. She worked for a travel company and dealt with people's holiday gripes and complaints every day. She'd learned to be the mistress of looking sympathetic but Aidan could tell this was fake and she was just covering her irritation.

'I suppose so.' Her gaze slipped towards the table where Lilah sat with Finlay and Hayley. Elise smoothed the end of her perfectly straight hair and seemed to be chewing something over. 'Who is that girl?'

'Lilah.'

'Hayley told me you'd taken in a lodger. Is that her?'

'Yes.'

'Isn't she the girl who smashed up your mum's stall at the fair?'

'That isn't what happened.'

'No?' Elise continued to watch Lilah, a slight crease forming on her immaculate brow. 'Ah, you're probably right. She doesn't look the type. Too young and naïve. She seems to have done well for herself since lodging with you. She looks beautiful.'

Aidan frowned at her. Where was this going?

'So, you and her,' Elise continued.

'There is no me and her. I'm merely helping someone in need.'

She blinked and nodded. 'Aidan, don't take this the wrong way, but are you sure she's not... You know?'

'No, I don't know. What are you talking about?'

'Well, isn't it more likely she's putting on an act of being a poor little thing, so she gets free lodgings? And maybe she's got her sights set even higher than that.'

'Set on what?'

'Oh really, Aidan. You're not that blind. When I saw her at the fair, she was scruffy and messy. But look at her now. She's all dressed up. Who do you think she's dressed up for? It's not exactly normal for a lodger who claims to be poor to be out in a place like this with her landlord.'

A few times he'd wondered if Lilah was going the extra mile to catch his eye, but he didn't want to dwell on the idea. She didn't need to do anything extra to get his attention. She had it anyway. Even when he tried to focus elsewhere, it was amazing how often it returned to her. 'She got a new job today. Hayley and I are helping her celebrate. That's all.' He lifted the tray of drinks.

'I'm glad.' Elise smiled at him. 'I'd hate for you to be hurt again. I really never meant to and well... Please take care.'

'Pardon? There's no need for your concern.' He took the tray and turned to walk to the table.

Elise took a step back and her lips quavered. 'I'm just looking out for you. Because once people get wind of that girl living with you, they'll form their own conclusions, whether you like it or not. Don't say I didn't warn you. Lodgers with benefits might be the next big thing. Who knows? Just don't be surprised if people start questioning your motives for taking her in.' She stalked off towards the bathroom.

Aidan's fists clenched at the sides of the tray. With a long, calming breath, he wove through the restaurant and outside to the table.

'Sorry I took so long.' He put the tray down. 'Finlay. Hi. Did you want a drink?'

'I'll get one myself.' Finlay got to his feet and left. Aidan didn't look at him. He placed drinks in front of Hayley and Lilah, then stashed the tray under the table.

'Are you ok?' Hayley asked, her expression filled with uncertainty.

'I'm good.' Aidan peered between her and Lilah. Lilah was on a padded bench seat in the corner of the deck, leaning against the railings. Normally Aidan would avoid that kind of seat – too much of a squeeze to get into, but Lilah smiled that face-splitting smile. The one that brightened everything it touched. She'd gone over and above to make his life easier since she'd crossed the threshold of Woodend Cottage and, so far, he'd heeded the warnings in his mind to keep her at arm's length. Even when he'd been gruff, she'd been there for him. And he needed that feeling right now. The sense that someone cared unconditionally for his welfare. He couldn't keep his distance. Not this time.

He muscled his way under until his thigh brushed against hers, causing a twitch in his groin. He ignored it. He had to. 'Congratulations, Lilah.' He lifted his glass and clinked it on the edge of hers, then Hayley's. 'Well done on your new job.'

'Thank you.' Lilah took a sip of her drink and beamed at him before her gaze drifted past him. 'They don't look very happy.'

Aidan followed her sightline. Elise had joined Finlay at the bar and they appeared to be exchanging heated words.

'Yup.' Aidan swigged some ale.

Hayley let out a sigh.

'Maybe we should just have these drinks and go somewhere else.' Aidan took a swig of ale. 'I don't think I can stay here.'

'You shouldn't have to leave,' Lilah said. 'You've done nothing wrong.'

'It was me who started this. I did loads wrong.'

'Maybe in the past, but not today.'

'It's just so awkward.'

'What does Finlay do?' Lilah asked.

'He's a high school teacher,' Hayley said. 'In P.E.'

Lilah winced and Aidan suspected she was recalling the hockey stick incident at a long-past P.E. session.

Before Aidan had lost his dad, he and Finlay had been close. They'd met up, gone on cycle rides together. Now everything was broken and disjointed.

He took another swig of his drink. *Please let Finlay and Elise get their own table inside and not come back out here.* But Aidan caught her looking over. Her eyes skimmed over Lilah then back onto him and she shook her head slightly. She took Finlay's hand and led him outside.

'Beautiful weather, isn't it?' she said, reclaiming her seat. 'It feels like such a waste being stuck at work all day.'

'I was off today,' Hayley said.

'Were you walking dogs?' Elise asked Aidan.

'Yes.'

'Sounds like the perfect job,' she said. 'For you anyway.'

He forced a little smile. 'We walked to the Old Schoolhouse for Lilah's interview.'

'What's the job?' Finlay asked.

'Supporting the residents with things like cooking and baking.'

'I see.'

'That reminds me,' Aidan said, addressing only Lilah. 'I saw something you'd like in a café window yesterday.'

'What was it?' Lilah sipped her drink as she turned to him.

'Little cakes that looked like bees.'

She smiled. 'Sounds like you quite liked them too.'

'I didn't try one, but I think I'd prefer them if you made them.'

Her cheeks coloured as they always did when someone gave her a compliment and maybe he'd said too much. That was verging on flirting, but it was hard to hold back, especially when she had her sophisticated make-up on. Her gaze held his and he didn't look away. His body burned with need, but it wasn't just lust keeping him fixated on her. That sense of knowing she was loyal to him flooded him with a desperate urge to seize her, covet her, and keep her close. Despite what everyone said about her, she was someone he could trust, even if it was just sitting beside him, making him feel less alone.

He breathed in and out very deliberately. His eyes dropped to her pink and glossy lips.

'I hate baking,' Elise said. 'It's so messy and the results aren't exactly great for the figure.'

'Lilah's a very talented chef,' Aidan said, lifting his glass. As he did, he caught Elise watching him.

'I wish I was,' Hayley said. 'I expect an invite to dinner soon.'

'You up for that?' Aidan asked Lilah.

'I'd give it a go.'

'I'll be your skivvy. I can peel potatoes and stuff,' he said.

Hayley laughed. 'Sounds perfect. I might cook better if I had someone doing the prep work.'

'I don't remember you being much of a cook, Aidan,' Elise said. 'But Finlay's a good cook, aren't you? Better than me. I find it such a bore. You should watch my friend, Genevieve Harrington, on YouTube,' she added to Lilah. 'She has her own channel and she does all sorts of vids. Quite a few cookery ones.'

'Sounds interesting.'

'I admit I hardly watch them anymore. I don't have the time. But tell me about this job,' Elise continued. 'Is this your first job since you left school?'

'Er...' Lilah frowned. 'Not exactly. But I left school like five years ago.'

'Really?' Elise said. 'You look so young.'

'I'm twenty-three.'

'Are you?' Elise raised her eyebrows. 'Wow.'

'I'm hopeless at working out people's age.' Finlay said. 'A third of my senior pupils look like they're in their twenties and another third look like they should still be in primary school.'

'And how is work?' Aidan asked.

'Fine.' Finlay pulled a noncommittal face and their eyes met for a moment. Painful memories surged in Aidan: a longing to go back to happier times, when they were friends and they both had fathers.

Aidan took a deep breath.

'So, Hayley tells me you've got some speaking gigs lined up,' Finlay said.

'Yeah. I've got a couple of motivational speeches coming up. Also hoping to make some money from honey eventually. So, lots going on. Not to mention my unofficial campaign to stop the council from building houses on the field at the back of the cottage.'

'Yeah. I heard about that. Some of the houses will be very close to the woodland.'

'Not something I want to be looking at every day.' Aidan gazed out over the river, before returning his focus to the group. Elise was talking to Hayley but her eyes roamed frequently to Lilah.

'Do you think we should head back and check Maya?' Lilah asked quietly, placing her empty glass on the table.

Aidan checked the time on his phone. It was early and they'd only had one drink. Why did she want to leave her own celebration?

Her eyes answered him with a slight shift to Elise. This was as uncomfortable for her as it was for him – possibly more so.

'Yeah, sure.'

'Already?' Elise pulled a face. 'Isn't this a celebration?'

'It is.' Aidan got to his feet. 'But it's an early start tomorrow, and you're here to check out some function rooms, aren't you?'

'Plenty of time for that,' Elise said.

Hayley looked at Aidan and gave a half shrug almost like she was asking if she should go too.

'I don't mind if you stay, Hayley. I don't want to cut your evening short.'

'Sorry you're going so early,' Elise said. 'But Hayley, you could look at the function room with us. You've got a good eye for that kind of thing.'

'Um, ok.'

'I'll message you,' Aidan said to Hayley.

Lilah followed him through the restaurant and out into the fresh air.

'Do you want to go somewhere else?' he asked. 'That wasn't much of a celebration.'

'It's fine. It doesn't seem right without Hayley.'

'Yeah. I hope she's ok.'

He pulled out his phone and pressed out a quick text.

AIDAN: sorry about that. Not the evening we planned. Let's do it again sometime but we'll check what E & F are doing first!

They'd only walked a hundred or so metres when a reply pinged in.

HAYLEY: Don't worry. I'm leaving as soon as I've had a look at the function rooms. Give Lilah a hug for me xx

He raised an eyebrow. No, he couldn't do that. It would cross the invisible line by a mile. 'Hayley sends you a hug,' he said.

'Oh.' Lilah wrapped her arms about herself, perhaps simulating said hug or perhaps she was cold. The temperature had dropped as the evening closed in.

'Let's go this way. It's steeper but shorter.' He led her up a side street that wound around the back of the shops at an abrupt angle. Further along, it passed a small green space and a little duck pond. Miracle really the council hadn't claimed this too for their house building.

'That's where I used to live.' Lilah pointed to a block of council houses on a street to the right of the pond. 'Rowan Way, the worst street in Glenbriar.'

Aidan knew its reputation well, though the worst street in Glenbriar was a lot nicer than some of the streets in big cities. But hidden poverty was everywhere. 'Do your family still live there?'

'No. My mum moved to Dundee with a boyfriend. Most of my family are either there or in Perth now.'

'Ah, right.' He remembered his mum ranting about the house that had needed gutting after Lilah's family left. Poor Lilah. She'd really had things rough.

The light was slowly fading as they skirted the edge of the duck pond. A reflected streetlight shimmered in it. 'When I was a teenager, I used to horrify my mum by joking about skinny dipping in this pond,' Aidan said, jumping on the low wall and balancing as he walked along it. 'She told me I'd be arrested.'

'Come down from there. You might fall in. And why did you say that to her?'

'Because I hated being stuck inside. When she wouldn't let me go out, I'd say stuff like that to annoy her. I wouldn't really have done it.'

Lilah giggled, then jumped as Aidan fake wobbled. He steadied himself and laughed, but Lilah seemed to think he was really going to fall. She reached out and swiped for his leg. The movement surprised him. He stumbled backwards and with a huge splash and a shock of cold, he landed in the water, fully clothed.

Lilah gasped, her hands flying to her mouth.

CHAPTER FOURTEEN

Lilah stood frozen, her hands clapped to her face as Aidan emerged from the pond, water cascading down his drenched clothes. This was a Mr Darcy moment if ever there was one.

'Oh my god. Are you ok?'

Aidan untucked his shirt, then shook his hands. 'That was a bit of a shock. Karma bit me on the backside, huh.'

'Or shoved you in. Karma, I mean. I didn't.'

Aidan looked at her, his eyebrow slowly rising. He took a step towards her and the left corner of his mouth twitched slightly. 'Oh yeah?'

'Seriously. I didn't. I tried to stop you from falling.'

'Did you?' The twinkle in his eye told her he was kidding.

'Sure. If I'd pushed you, I wouldn't still be standing here. I can run fast when I have to.'

'Not fast enough this time.' He moved quickly and scooped her off her feet. She let out a squeal, but for some reason she wasn't afraid. His hold on her wasn't rough or threatening.

'Fancy getting wet yourself?' A smile now filled his face.

'No. Put me down.' She faked an attempt to get free but really, she didn't want him to put her down. No way would he really throw her in. She knew he wouldn't. His low laugh rumbled close to her ear and she could hardly breathe, painfully aware of his arms around her, and water from his saturated shirt slowly seeping through her own top. But he didn't move. She opened her eyes and looked at him.

Their gazes locked, and her heart stopped. She dropped her focus to his lips for a second, briefly imagining leaning closer and touching hers against them. Every atom in her body was charged with the desire to have him.

'Not fancy it?' he said. And her eyes snapped back to his. Had he noticed her looking? Did he imagine she was going to kiss him? Jesus almighty, she fancied it all right, but no way did she dare. No freaking way.

'Fancy what?'

'Going for a swim?' He slowly spun her around, pretending to toss her into the water, but at the last moment, he gently placed her back down, their bodies mere inches apart.

Lilah stood rooted to the spot. 'I can't swim. Well, I've never tried, but I expect I'd have sunk straight to the bottom.'

'It's not that deep.' He raised his hand and gently tapped her cheek with his fingertip. 'I can tell you from experience.'

Giggles bubbled up from Lilah's chest and into her throat, then they burst out and Aidan laughed too. 'Oh god. Are you frozen now?' she said.

'Na, this is nothing. Let's get home and get dry.'

The cool evening air sent goosebumps racing over Lilah's bare arms. Her top was damp where it had been pressed against Aidan's wet shirt and was not helping her body temperature. She wasn't built from the same stuff as him. Something had changed, subtly maybe, but enough to expand a little balloon of hope in her chest. Maybe he liked her a teeny bit more than a lodger he felt sorry for.

He was walking again like he was on a mission, his legs going a lot faster than hers. She put on some speed and caught up with him. She didn't say anything but smiled and he looked at her, frowned slightly, then returned it with a little head shake.

Maya greeted them at the door of Woodend Cottage, sniffing all over Aidan.

'This is Eau de Pond,' he informed her. 'A new fragrance that's very in this year.'

'It certainly is,' Lilah agreed.

'You want a drink?' Aidan asked Lilah. 'I'll have a wash and change first.'

'Yeah, ok.' She went into her room and put on a dry, warm top. When Aidan emerged he was shower fresh and smelled masculine and hot. He had on dry jeans and a tight t-shirt, but his feet were bare. The desire fire burned in Lilah's stomach.

Aidan poured them drinks and handed her a glass. 'To a new job and a fresh start,' he said, clinking his drink on hers.

'Cheers,' she said, taking a sip of a red liquid she didn't recognise. 'What is this? It's really nice.'

'Chambord. My mum buys it for my Christmas every year.'

'I like it.' It tasted smooth and filled her senses with deep heat, kind of what she imagined kissing Aidan would be like.

'What a day,' he said, lounging back. 'I think you'll enjoy working at the Schoolhouse and even though the hours are short, it's a foot in the door and you never know what you might get.'

Passing the evening chatting with Aidan like this was better than being out. She liked Hayley but being alone with Aidan was so easy. Sometimes, he had an intimidating aura about him but Lilah trusted him and knew if anything happened he'd be for her, not against her.

It seemed like they'd been talking for just a few moments when Aidan checked his phone. 'Bloody hell. It's nearly ten o'clock. I'm going to take Maya out for a quick leg stretch, then get to bed.' His gaze lingered on her and he seemed to lean closer. His eyes dropped to her lips for a fraction of a second. Lilah's heart stopped. Was he going to kiss her? He frowned slightly and blinked, taking the moment with him. 'Well done on getting the job.' He reached out and gently patted her arm.

'Thank you.'

He increased the pressure on her arm a little then let go and got to his feet. 'You should get some sleep. I won't be long.'

She kind of wanted to go with him but she couldn't move. Her body was weak from the day and her pulse was fluttering after what had just happened. 'Ok.'

'See you in the morning.' He watched her for a moment from the doorway, then turned and left.

Lilah breathed slowly. What had just happened?

From her bedroom, she heard Aidan in the hallway talking to Maya, then the door closing. She grabbed a towel and took a quick shower before jumping into bed. Being alone in the house always made her feel a little edgy. When she'd been in the caravan at Malcolm and Brenda's, every noise had made her pulse race. Was it Malcolm sneaking around or an animal? Perhaps one of his son's dodgy mates. People who reminded her of her own family. How often had people knocked on the door looking for one of her brothers and threatened her with all sorts if she didn't know where they were? It had even happened once on Christmas Day.

Since she'd been with Aidan, she hadn't felt like that at all until now. This house felt safer. During the day, it was fine being alone. She was so busy she didn't notice, but this was the first time he'd been away so late. Normally, he walked Maya earlier. Lilah tried to read some more of *Jane Eyre*, imagining Rochester looking like Aidan. He fitted that image better than Mr Darcy. But she couldn't concentrate. Between the odd noises in the house and the recollection of what had just happened, her brain was all over the place. Maybe it was just her imagination on overdrive, but she could have sworn Aidan had been on the verge of kissing her.

Even earlier at the pond, it had seemed that way too. Did that mean... Well, what did it mean?

Maybe nothing. It could all just be inside her head.

This end of town was usually quiet but was that people talking outside? Perhaps a gang planning a break in. There was still a boarded-up window in the spare room. What if they were the people who'd broken it before? Should she arm herself? What could she hit them with? The bedside lamp?

The hall door closed quietly like someone was sneaking in and Lilah sat up, holding her breath. She tiptoed out of bed and lifted her hairbrush. Not much of a weapon but it was better than nothing, and it would be too noisy to unplug the lamp. Her pulse hammered so loudly in her ears she was sure it would give her away. She prised open the door just as she heard Aidan talking softly to Maya and the click of the lock on the front door.

'It's you,' she said, and Maya trotted up to her.

'Who did you think it was?' Aidan said.

'I just panicked that it was someone breaking in.'

'Ah. Sorry about that. I was trying to be quiet in case you were asleep.'

She let out a deep sigh. 'I'll sleep now I know you're back.'

His smile was evident in the dim light from his phone. 'Yes, I'm back. You go to bed and don't worry about anything.'

'I won't. Night-night.'

'Night, Lilah.' He reached over and gently pulled her into a side hug. 'Sleep tight.' Before she could return it or say anything, he pressed a soft kiss on her forehead, then let her go. 'See you in the morning.'

She stood frozen as he made his way into his room, then stumbled back into her own. She raised her fingers to her forehead. The spot where he'd kissed her was never getting washed again. She jumped under the covers and closed her eyes.

Oh my god.

The duvet was a substitute for Aidan's strong arms and she lay huddled under it, unable to stop smiling.

Safe again. Everything was fine. Better than!

Chapter Fifteen

Aidan

Aidan watched as a wooden panel from the boarded-up window hit the ground. Brann the builder moved straight to the next panel and started levering it off with his hammer.

'I'd like to find out who broke this in the first place,' Aidan said.

'You never will, mate,' Brann said. 'Probably kids thinking they were being clever.'

'Yeah.' Aidan ran his hands through his hair. Sickening to think kids had done this.

'I'm always telling my kids to behave themselves, but once they're out of my sight, there's bugger all I can do.' Brann cracked off another panel. 'I just have to hope the message has gone in, though it's not like I'm one to preach,' he added in an undertone. 'I wasn't exactly squeaky clean myself as a lad. Mark you, it's not easy when you come from a rough part of town, especially in a place like this where most people are well-to-do.' He ran his finger over the end of his nose.

Aidan's mind wandered to Lilah. She was the perfect example of someone who'd had that kind of rough ride. While she handled it well, she couldn't quite escape the constraints of her past. It made her both strong and vulnerable. Strong enough to stand up for herself against two thugs but vulnerable enough to be afraid of being alone in the house at night.

But she'd got herself a job despite her fears, and that showed some grit. Now she had to turn up and do the work. She'd left that morning full of excitement and the house felt empty without her.

He steered his thoughts away from the night before, but they wanted to dwell there. How often during the day and evening had he wanted to kiss her? This was getting bad. Maybe even that peck on the forehead was a step too far, but the urge was so strong. She'd needed comfort, and he'd provided it – that was all. Sure it was.

He checked the time on his phone. Patricia was due at any minute to start painting the barn.

'You fancy signing up for the tug-of-war at the Highland games?' Brann asked. 'You look like you'd be a good asset.'

'Yeah, I could do. I've never thought about it.'

'Give me a bell if you fancy it. We're looking for new people on the team. We had a few drop out.' He rolled his eyes. 'This year's committee hasn't been the best. Don't want to say too much but there's been a lot of falling out, which we've never had before.'

'That's a shame.'

'Yeah.'

A car pulled up on the road outside the cottage and Patricia got out. 'Ah, that's my mother. Better go and see her. I'll leave this to you.'

'Sure, no bother,' Brann said. He waved to Patricia as she opened the gate. She beamed as she waved back in a somewhat girlie way.

Aidan frowned as he met her on the path. 'What are you grinning like that for?'

'Me?' She appeared to have no idea what he was talking about. 'I was just waving to Brann.'

'So I see.' Aidan raised an eyebrow. 'Surely you don't fancy him. He can't be much older than me.'

'Of course I don't. Don't be ridiculous. He's just a very nice man.'

Aidan opened the door to the house, making a quick glance back at Brann. Not being an expert on what made men attractive, Aidan didn't like to comment one way or another, but there was undoubtedly some rugged appeal about the builder as he ripped another panel from the window. But the thought of his mum looking at him like that made Aidan cringe.

Patricia put her hands on her hips. Her motherly instincts clearly told her exactly what Aidan was thinking. 'Being fifty-seven doesn't mean I can't appreciate a nice man.'

'I didn't say that.'

Patricia pulled out her phone and scrolled through some pictures. 'This is the kind of thing I want to do with the barn.' The photos were Pinterest perfect sheds in shades of yellow with artistic wildflower and bee murals painted over them.

'And can you paint that kind of thing?'

'I haven't tried, but once I get the yellow on, I can see what happens after that.'

Patricia wasn't a fast painter and had done only one wall by two o'clock when Aidan returned from walking the dogs.

'Do you need a hand?' he asked.

'I might have to give up for the day. I think I've got an RSI from doing this.'

'I'll do some later if you want. Just got some admin to catch up with first.'

Back inside, he fired off some emails. After forty minutes, the front door clicked open and he heard Lilah chatting to Maya. He shut his laptop and went straight to the hallway.

'How did you get on then?' he asked.

'It was really fun and everyone was so friendly.'

'Great. That's good news.' He smiled at her and their gazes locked for a little too long but he couldn't break away. That simmering attraction was still there. After last night with the pond, the Chambord, and the forehead kiss, it had ramped up a notch and had got to a point it was almost impossible to ignore. The urge to kiss her again burned so strong inside him, he'd need a long, cold shower to cool down.

'I saw your mum out there. The barn is going to look really bright when she's finished.'

'Yeah. I'm going to give her a hand. It's hurting her wrist.'

'I'll help too if you want...' She blinked and turned away. 'Actually, she won't want me to.'

'I'd appreciate your help. She won't mind. I'll speak to her.'

'Ok. If you're sure. I'll go change, then come help.'

Aidan returned to Patricia.

'I'm done,' she said, shaking her wrists.

'I'll take over. Lilah's going to help too. She's very artistic, you know. I bet she could paint the flowers you wanted.'

'You think?'

'Yeah. Why not let her try? She could do a test one round the back. If you don't like it, you can always paint over it.'

'Ok, but don't do anything on the front or side until I've seen it.'

'We won't.'

'Hi,' Lilah said from behind.

Aidan and Patricia both turned. Patricia lifted one of her neatly shaped eyebrows and gave Lilah's outfit the once over. She was wearing one of her familiar outfits: denim shorts and a black vest top. 'Hello.'

'Maybe you should wear one of my old shirts,' Aidan said. 'To protect your clothes. I'll go get one. Mum wants some bees and flowers painted on the shed. Do you think you could do that? I suggested painting a test one on the back if you're up for it.'

'Um, yeah, I could try.' She cast a fleeting glance at Patricia.

'I'll send you some pictures of the kind of thing I'm interested in,' Patricia said.

'Ok,' Lilah pulled out her phone.

Patricia did the same and Aidan nipped off to grab an old shirt for Lilah. He chose a faded black and grey tartan one. An old fave but the seams had come away in several places, making it only fit for DIY.

When he returned, his mum was at her car. She waved to him and called, 'I'll be back tomorrow.'

'See you.' He took the shirt around the side and across the overgrown driveway to the barn. Maya was lying in the grass, close to Lilah, who was on her new phone, scrolling through pictures. He peered over her shoulder.

'Do you think you can paint that kind of thing?'

'Maybe.' She angled the phone so he could see better. 'If I draw the shapes, I just have to fill them in. It doesn't look too complicated.'

When she was close like this, her body heat radiated into him, along with a haze of sweet perfume. Again, he was struck by the vision of a flower fairy. She was a garden nymph, smelling of flowers and shining like sunlight. He wanted to capture her essence so he could absorb it when she wasn't beside him. That, or take her in his arms and kiss her until the sun set. The attraction was getting dangerous.

'I'm no good at drawing,' he said. 'But if you draw the shapes, I can help add the colours. Mum's got lots of little tester pots. We could try them.'

'Ok. Let's do it.' Lilah smiled at him and desire stung inside his chest.

Maya shifted forward and nuzzled his leg. He stroked her absently.

Lilah ran her fingertips over the soft fabric of his old shirt like she was testing the smoothest velvet, before she swung the shirt over her shoulders and pushed her arms into it. It was, of course, far too long and wide. She rolled back the sleeves, the main part falling below her shorts. Aidan's belly clenched at the sight and the urge to seize her and pull her close consumed him again. He balled his fists; this was ridiculous. What was happening to him? But seeing her dressed in his clothes gave him a furious desire to have her.

His phone buzzed in his pocket and he drew it out. The name *Finlay* on the screen made his insides recoil. A couple of years ago, seeing his cousin's name was a frequent thing. They would message back and forward about cycle rides or meeting up for a drink.

He opened it, half expecting to see something triggering like a photo of Finlay and Elise all loved up and happy, though he wasn't sure they were there yet. Would Finlay be that tactless?

FINLAY: Hey Aidan. After our meeting yesterday, I wanted to say a couple of things. I know the situation with Elise and me won't ever be easy for you. God knows I'd hate me if I was in your position. When Elise first asked me if I'd like to see her, I didn't know what to say. It was totally leftfield, and I have to admit I worried she was just doing it to get back at you. But as time went on, I realised it wasn't that. It's such a cruel thing that the person I ended up with is someone who you too had feelings for. Like everyone else, I thought your feelings for her had fizzled out when you went away. I now understand that wasn't the case, but you must see how it looked to us all, especially when you all but disappeared and no one could get in touch with you.

Aidan stopped reading and breathed slowly. Yes. He knew only too well, with hindsight, what a fool he'd been and people would be forever shoving it up his nose it seemed.

I miss your friendship. I have something I need to ask your opinion about. You know I have Granny's engagement ring and that I gave it to Elise? You might also know that she wasn't keen on it as it looked too old fashioned. Anyway, she's picked another one, and that's fine, but I'd still like her to have Granny's ring. I thought I could get it reset in a modern style and give it to her at the engagement party. Of course she wasn't just my grandmother though, so I'd like your opinion too. I already asked Hayley and she said she didn't mind what I did. Let me know what you think.

Aidan half closed his eyes. What could he say? He thought it was sacrilege messing with their grandmother's ring, but if he told Finlay that, it would look like him being stubborn and deliberately setting out to cause problems. Did it matter if Finlay changed the ring? He just wanted to do something nice for the woman he loved.

There was that thing called love again. All it seemed to do was make a mess of things.

'What's it to me now anyway?' Aidan muttered.

'What?' Lilah said.

'Ah nothing. Just stuff. First world problems.' He keyed out a quick reply.

AIDAN: You know how sentimental I am, so I'm the wrong person to ask. If you think Grandmother would be ok with it, you do it. Or if you think it's the right decision for the two of you, then go ahead.

Maybe it was a bit abrupt but he'd said his piece. Like most of the things in his life, it was out of his control anyway.

CHAPTER SIXTEEN

Lilah

'If we put a rubber band across the top of the paint can, we can wipe the brush on it and it avoids drips,' Aidan said.

'Should I paint a yellow patch on the back and wait until it dries before I try any of the designs?' Lilah asked, desperate to make sure she got this right the first time and not give Patricia any reason to criticise her.

'Just try a few. It takes too long for the paint to dry fully. Mum will soon let us know if she likes them or not.'

'She'll probably not like them if I do them. She and Scarlett aren't exactly my biggest fans.'

'Scarlett is really immature sometimes and Mum panders to her. It's easy for me to say this but Mum's not that bad normally. Neither is Scarlett. She just seems to have a thing about you. Probably jealous.'

Lilah scoffed. 'Why would she be jealous of me?'

'Because you're good at stuff – like this.' He pointed at the paintbrush in her hand. 'Or you're at least willing to give it a go. You're kind and thoughtful. That's threatening to Scarlett because she's brusque and used to getting her own way.'

'I'm not sure I buy it,' Lilah said. It might be part of the reason, but she was sure Scarlett hadn't been jealous of her at school. Who would have been?

She lifted a pencil and started sketching some shapes on the wood panelling – not the easiest surface to draw on but she got used to the uneven grain and the amount of pressure she had to put on to make an impression.

Lilah carried on sketching while Aidan painted around the front. His shirt gave her the same safe feeling she had when she was with him – like a protective shield infusing her with a sense of being invincible. Stupid? Sure. She knew that, but she liked it nonetheless.

After a while, he came around the back and peered at the faint lines she'd drawn. 'Why not paint some of that now? It looks good.'

'I kind of just copied the ideas your mum showed me.'

'It's amazing you can do it at all.'

They worked on into the evening, even as the spring sun was fading. The days were lengthening and Lilah liked watching the birds settle down for the night, filling the still air with their last soft tweets. Aidan remained at the front, slapping on the yellow paint and they didn't talk much but it was pleasant. When the light was almost gone, Aidan came around dusting his hands.

'Oh wow,' he said. 'I think that looks exactly how Mum wants it.'

Maybe it looked better in the dark because Lilah wasn't sure she'd achieved what she wanted and it was slow going. 'Well, if she likes it, I can try and do more but I've got work too.'

'I'll make sure she's well aware of that. I'd be happier if she paid you.'

'I don't mind helping out but it might take some time.'

'Don't worry. I'll see she understands.'

Aidan was busy with an upcoming speech and was also involved in some online podcasts about beekeeping, so by the time she left for work the following day, he was shut up in his study.

As one of her main roles at the Old Schoolhouse was to do cooking and baking with the residents, she decided to try out some recipes. The bee cakes Aidan had mentioned sounded fun and they'd be even better if they were made with honey. She'd taken a jar from the kitchen to play about with.

'This is a new recipe,' she told Toby and Lewis, the two boys she was working with. Both of them were in their late teens but seemed much younger. Toby was small and thin but had a sweet smile that melted her.

'We're going to use honey.' She pulled out the jar. 'Bees make it,' she said.

'Bees?' Lewis frowned at her. His language skills were better than Toby, who didn't say much.

'Yes. I live with a beekeeper. He looks after them and the bees make honey in the hives.'

'They sting?' Lewis asked.

'Sometimes, but not if you're careful and kind. Bees are gentle.' She smiled as she got the other ingredients. Before she'd met Aidan, she would never have talked about bees like this. They worried her as much as they worried Lewis.

The recipe didn't turn out exactly to plan but she hadn't expected it to, not when trial and error was involved and when her two 'helpers' were more interested in scoffing the raw ingredients than making things with them.

The finished result was tasty but didn't look neat enough to sell.

'These are delicious,' Marion said, catching Lilah before she left for the day. 'And the boys seem to have enjoyed themselves. I see you got them to wash up too. Very good.' She gave Lilah a pat. 'That'll be you finished, but I'll see you tomorrow.'

'See you,' Lilah said as she collected her bag. Aidan had leant her his bike and she jumped on it and whizzed down the hill. The bike was large but lightweight. Getting on and off it wasn't a pretty sight but it was quicker than walking.

Patricia's car was outside when Lilah returned home. She entered the house quietly and checked around. Neither Patricia nor Aidan were there, so she assumed Patricia was at the barn and that Aidan was out walking the dogs. She pulled out some veg, chopped it up, and threw it into a casserole dish. May as well prep something nice for dinner.

'Ah, you're back.' Aidan came into the kitchen behind her and she jumped.

'I didn't know you were here.'

'I was finishing off painting the barn.'

Would there ever be a day when she didn't find him hotter than boiling oil? Even when he was in his scruffy clothes, he looked edible. His tanned skin almost glowed on his neck and forearms. His deep musk aroma filled the room.

'Something smells good.'

It's you, she wanted to say, but didn't dare.

'Just roasting some veg.'

He smiled and it was that warm smile that went right to his eyes and lit up his whole face. Lilah didn't see it often, but when she did, it lit her whole world.

'You really are something,' he said.

'I hope that's a good thing.'

'Definitely.'

'Did your mum like the painting?'

'She did.' He leaned on the work surface. 'She was very impressed. You're really talented, you know? You can cook, bake, paint... What else can you do?'

'Nothing.' Just as well the kitchen was so hot. Her skin was burning.

'Don't underestimate yourself. Do you feel up to coming out and chatting to Mum about the painting?'

Lilah sucked on her lip. 'Ok. I guess.' She half hid behind Aidan as they made their way outside.

'Ah, the artist is back,' Patricia said, turning around and meeting Lilah's eyes. 'You've been hiding your light under a bushel.'

Did that mean Patricia liked what she'd done? 'I've always liked art. I just didn't get much chance to do it.' How could she? Art materials were expensive and opportunities were zero.

'Well, this is a chance, if you're interested.'

'Um, sure, as long as I can fit it around my work.'

'Yes, Aidan told me that and it's fine by me. I can pay you something for it too.'

'Well... Ok. If you're sure. I'm not sure how fast I'll be. The shed paint doesn't flow the way I remember acrylics working at school, but I kind of got a method where I was dabbing it. It wasn't quick.'

'No problem. I'm not in a great rush. I'm just happy you're willing to help.' Patricia pushed open the door. 'Oh, and Aidan, we really need plasterboard in here and possibly some insulation. Is that something you can do?'

'Maybe.' He went inside to look around.

Patricia smiled at Lilah. 'He's a good lad. Underneath that tough shell is a sensitive being. He always puts on a brave face, even as a boy. I can count on one hand the times he cried as a child. But that doesn't mean he's immune to hurt. He's been messed around enough by that silly Elise Reid. I really hate what she did to him.'

Lilah nodded.

'You've done well for yourself and you're a hard-working girl.'

'Thanks.'

Patricia crossed her arms. 'It's a pity about that unfortunate incident with Scarlett at school. You could have been a good friend to her.'

'I never meant to hurt her. It was an accident, I swear. I took a swing for the ball, she dived in trying to get it before me, and my stick smacked her in the face.'

'Hmm. It was a bad age to lose a tooth, but I always thought it was more likely to be an accident.'

'It all happened so fast I couldn't stop it; she was desperate to get the ball.' Which was Scarlett in a nutshell. She'd been so eager to stop Lilah from scoring.

Aidan came out of the barn and fiddled with one of the hinges on the door. 'I think I can do the plasterboard,' he said. 'Though I'm not sure how it would work around the windows and the door.'

'Well, there's the rather lush Brann the builder, who I'm sure could do it. I notice he made a great job of the window. He did my new kitchen last year and seems to be able to turn his hand to anything. I don't think he'd charge too much for putting up some plasterboard.' Patricia winked at Lilah.

'If you'd rather have him, feel free,' Aidan said.

'Let's see what you can do first. And, before I forget, I want to show you this, Lilah.' Patricia opened the door and pulled out a carrier bag. 'I bought some fabric in a warehouse sale at the weekend. It's beautiful but it has ugly markings all over it. I think it's just dirt. Do you think it'll come out?'

'I could try and do it,' Lilah said. She had the feeling Patricia was hoping she'd volunteer.

'Would you? That's very kind.'

After Patricia left, Lilah put on a load of washing and set to work scrubbing the pretty bee fabric. With Patricia off home and Aidan out walking dogs, Lilah was alone in the kitchen. Every time she thought about her interaction with Patricia, her stomach squirmed. Had she made a good impression? Was the air now clear between them? Each rub on the fabric made her wonder if this was a test. What if she pressed too hard and made a hole or scrubbed off some of the pattern instead of the dirt? She kept rinsing away the suds to check. So far, so good. Maybe Patricia was happy just to have some help. *Who knows?* Lilah was so unused to this kind of thing she wasn't sure how to judge.

Once she was sure all the marks were off, she emptied the washing machine and put the bee fabric on a short rinse cycle to remove the soap. The machine thundered around, sounding like it might take off, and she watched, cringing at the thought of opening the door and finding the fabric all chewed up.

While it spun, she took the washing basket outside. Aidan had told her she didn't need to do his washing, but it was as easy to do it all together rather than put on lots of little loads. Aidan did the same for her, so this was just fair. She lifted a pair of his black boxers and carefully pegged them on the line. *Just a pair of pants, idiot.* Nothing to get excited about. Though when she pegged her knickers alongside, it seemed to be an unspoken statement of something... Lust? Crap, she didn't need to advertise that. But how could she not lust over Aidan? He was gorgeous. Stop! She mustn't get any funny ideas about him. She unpegged her knickers and put them on the opposite side of the whirligig.

Lusting over Aidan maybe wasn't a 'funny' idea, but it was definitely a bad one.

Chapter Seventeen

Lilah pulled out the freshly spun bee fabric from the washing machine. Phew. No holes or any visible damage. The air was warm and heavy. Birds twittered and the bees hummed in the orchard. Nowhere on earth was as beautiful as this. If she could live here forever, it wouldn't be enough to fully appreciate it. A soft breeze rustled the grass in the field. Beyond it, way in the distance, were rolling hills. She tilted her head at a distant rumble.

Was that a truck on the main road that bypassed the town? That, and the distant sound of trains passing through, occasionally broke the silence surrounding Woodend, but the recent rumble was more like thunder. Hopefully not. She wasn't a fan.

Returning to the kitchen, she took a deep breath and checked the casserole in the oven.

Aidan eventually wanted to keep chickens. Once his veg garden was going, there would be supplies of food on hand. For now, they were getting boxes delivered from a nearby farm shop. It was fun and challenging working out how to use the surprise ingredients.

She stole a glance out the window. Dark clouds loomed in the distance, casting a shadow over the landscape. Was that a storm brewing? She wasn't sure how to read the weather. Now that she had her new phone, she often saw posts on social media from Rocky Rainman, who was connected to the Old Schoolhouse. Apparently, it wasn't a man at all. Brenda had talked a lot about the situation, claiming she knew the full story better than most, and told Lilah to watch *Destination Forecast* to see for herself. How Lilah was supposed to do that when Brenda never let her near the TV was one of life's mysteries. Lilah checked her phone and her heart sank at the little thunderbolts scattered across the map.

Where was Aidan? Hopefully he'd be back soon, especially if a storm was looming. Not that it was likely to bother him. He was so hardy she couldn't see him even noticing. But she'd feel happier if he was back. Maya probably wouldn't like thunder, so they could huddle up together.

As she wiped the work surface, her gaze remained fixed on the changing sky. The grey clouds slowly advanced and seemed to curl and swell into an ominous black shape.

A knock on the door made her jump. After taking a deep breath, she hastened to answer it.

'Hello.' She pulled it open to reveal Jim, the elderly neighbour. 'Are you ok?' she asked.

'Yes, yes, lovely girl. I'm quite ok and I'm terribly sorry to be a nuisance, but I'm wondering if you can help me with something.'

'Of course. What is it?'

'I'm thinking about buying an electric tin opener. These old joints can't work the manual contraptions. I've found some on my computer but if you could spare me five minutes, I wouldn't mind a second opinion. If my wife were still here, she'd tell you I never was any good at making decisions.'

Lilah smiled. 'Sure, no bother. I'll come right now.'

'Is Aidan about today?'

'He's out walking the dogs.'

'Ah yes. I caught him going by the other day with several of them. Lovely to see him back. Obviously, he misses Ben something terrible.'

'Is that his dad?'

'Yes. God rest his soul. He was taken too young. Don't think he was even sixty. Had that terrible motor neuron disease. Broke the poor man. He was so strong and to see him reduced the way he was... Well, it was heartbreaking. And poor Aidan. Ben was the most doting father alive. Loved Aidan since the moment he was born. I remember him carrying him up into the woods on his shoulders when Aidan was tiny. Always together, so they were. Both loved the outdoors and the bees. Such a tragedy. I'd love to see Aidan smile again but I don't know if he'll ever get over the loss.'

They'd reached Jim's door and he opened it with his gnarled old fingers. Lilah's heart was heavy, even though it was hard to fully comprehend what Aidan had been through, as she'd never been that close to anyone in her family. Getting through each day alive had been the style of her early life. No shoulder carries to the woods or anything like that. She didn't even know her dad. None of her siblings shared a father and none of those fathers hung around. A fleeting thought of Jaxon fluttered into her mind but she'd trained herself to let those thoughts carry on their journey. She wasn't going to start worrying about him or it would be a full-time job.

Jim's house was small and somewhat typical of a man of his age, but he kept it tidy and the fact he owned a laptop was fairly impressive. He had it all wired up at the little table in his kitchen.

'So, this is the one I'm thinking about just now.' He pointed at the screen. 'What do you think?' He sat down and indicated for her to sit next to him.

Lilah peered at the picture and read the reviews. 'Looks good to me. There are some rubbish reviews but most things have a bit of both.'

'That's what I thought. Shall I be brave and buy this one or should I look at some more?'

'Be brave, I think. Sometimes it's best. Go with what your heart tells you is right and don't muddy the water too much.'

'Yes, good plan. Here goes.' He manoeuvred the mouse into place and clicked *Buy Now*. With a smile, he winked at Lilah and she grinned back.

A loud rumble resonated outside, sending a shiver down her spine. The first droplets of rain splattered against the windowpane. 'That was thunder, wasn't it?' She squinted at the darkening skies beyond the window.

'It definitely sounded like it.'

'Oh no. I hate thunder and lightning.'

'Doesn't bother me too much, but I should unplug the television just in case.'

'Are you supposed to do that?'

'Yes. And probably this computer too. Best do it before the storm is directly overhead. Don't want to be touching electrics then.'

'I should get back and do that.'

'Take care. It's still far enough away not to worry too much and it might not even come this way.'

'I'll do it anyway.' She made a dash for it. The rain was getting heavier. As soon as she was inside, she pulled the plugs on the TV and the laptop in Aidan's study. Hopefully he wouldn't mind. Better than getting struck by lightning. A flash lit the sky and she jumped, cringing beside the old writing bureau against the wall. A long low rumble followed.

'Come on, Aidan,' she muttered. 'Where are you? Oh no!' She jumped to her feet. The washing was still out. And she didn't dare leave Patricia's bee fabric in the rain. She'd forgotten all about it.

She bolted into the kitchen and opened the door. Huge raindrops were battering the garden now and the washing was tangled and dripping on the line. Hands over her head, Lilah raced across the sodden ground. Another flash lit up the sky and she screamed. 'Oh my god. Help.' The rumble was like a firework this time, loud and ominous. Her fingers shook and her heart hammered as she unpegged the bee fabric.

'Lilah!' Aidan's booming voice called from the door. 'What are you doing? Leave the washing and get inside.'

'I need to get the bee fabric.'

He sprinted towards her. 'Are you mad? Get inside.'

She unpegged the last corner. He grabbed her hand and dragged her across the garden and inside the kitchen door.

'What are you playing at? Who cares about the washing? You shouldn't go outside during a lightning storm unless it's absolutely essential.'

Another flash lit the sky and the rumble came almost simultaneously.

'It was essential.' Lilah clung to the saturated bee fabric. 'This fabric... I volunteered to clean it and I didn't want it to get in a state or your mum might be mad.'

'Jesus Christ, Lilah. Hang my mother and her fabric. Look at the state of you.'

Her clothes were dripping and so was her hair. Not that he could talk. 'You're not exactly looking shiny yourself.'

'Yeah, but I was racing to get back, not throwing myself into it.'

'I'll have a shower and dry off.'

'You can't do that. You don't go near water or electrics during a lightning storm. I'll light the fire. That'll do to get us dry.'

'How can water have anything to do with lightning?'

'The pipes are conductors.'

'Really? Well, I unplugged the TV and your laptop... I hope that's ok.'

'Yes. Good thinking.'

'Jim told me to do it.'

A frown deepened on Aidan's brow.

'He came by asking me to help choose an electric can opener.'

The corner of Aidan's lip quirked. 'That was nice. Now, let me get this fire on. And I need to check Maya. She doesn't like storms.'

'I know how she feels.' Lilah made her way to the living room, where Maya was cowering under the coffee table. Lilah knelt down beside the trembling dog and wrapped her arms around her. 'I feel the same.'

Rain pounded against the windows, echoing through the room.

Aidan tossed wood onto the fire, and lit a knitted ball of sticks, prodding it deep beneath the logs.

'Come here, gorgeous.' Aidan crossed his legs and tapped his knee.

For a split second, Lilah thought he meant her. Her foolish heart leapt a mile until Maya dragged herself out from her hiding spot and moved to sit by Aidan, placing her head on his lap. 'You can come too.' He cocked his head at Lilah. 'If you want. I know you don't like lightning.'

She hesitated for a moment, glancing between the flickering fire and Aidan's dark eyes. Slowly, she moved closer and settled down next to him. The crackling flames warmed her immediately and heat returned to her veins.

'We can watch from here,' Aidan said, focusing on the French doors. Beyond, another flash lit the sky. Sheets of rain obscured the view as a rumble of thunder reverberated in the distance.

'This is my first thunderstorm since one I experienced in Canada last year. It was terrifying and it's made me more fearful of them than I ever was before.'

'What happened?'

'We were hiking up a narrow mountain path,' he began. Lilah's eyes slowly closed as she listened to his magnificent, deep voice. Nothing else was so soothing. 'The thunder was deafening, echoing through the valleys, and the rain was coming in torrents. The path was treacherous and slippery, and visibility was almost non-existent.'

Lilah opened her eyes to see why he'd stopped.

He ruffled Maya's head. 'I was terrified we'd be hit by lightning. Maya was shaking. We eventually found an overhang of rocks and hid under it. You were so brave.' He nuzzled Maya. 'But she still doesn't like them.'

'I don't blame her.'

'I've never felt so small in the face of nature's power. It's humbling and scary at the same time.'

Lilah let out a sigh. 'You've had such an incredible life.'

'Have I?'

'You've done so much.'

'And lost so much.'

'Yes.' She gave him a shy, hopefully sympathetic smile and pushed her hand into Maya's fur, close to where Aidan was gently stroking her. 'What was your job before you went to Canada?'

'I was an engineer for a big energy company. It paid well, but I'm not sure I want that life anymore. One day I might go back to it, but right now I'm happy making the best of what I've got.'

'You must have had guts to leave. If I had a well-paid job, I don't think I'd want to give up to return to this.'

His eyes met hers, and her heart stilled. 'Nothing mattered after Dad died. Money didn't seem important anymore. He spent all his life making good money but none of it made any difference in the end. It didn't keep him alive.' With a long sigh, he turned away and stared into the fire. 'He left me some money and valuable jewellery that belonged to his family. But that's just stuff. The most important thing he left me were words of wisdom. He said, "The closer you get to death, the more you realise nothing really matters in the end. Only love and happiness. Fill your days with them because you could spend your whole life searching and never stopping to enjoy what you already have".'

Lilah covered her mouth to stop her emotions from spilling out. 'That's beautiful.'

'Are you ok?'

'It's just such a...' She sniffed, holding her hand under her nose. 'Such a true thing to say, but such a hard thing to do. I've always lived from day to day, not knowing where my next meal will come from some days, and I've always thought there might be light at the end of the tunnel. Maybe I should stop thinking I'll reach it one day and just enjoy what I've got.'

'It doesn't mean you can't have dreams or aspirations. Just make the most of the journey, because you might never arrive at the destination you want. I've made some bad choices, thinking I was doing what would make me happy. I gave up my job and went off walking, hoping to make a difference to some other poor souls, but I should have stayed here, taken care of the house, done things properly with Elise.'

Lilah turned away. Of course, who else?

'Hey.' He curled his finger under her chin and gently turned her head to look at him. The intensity of their eye contact was almost as charged as the air outside. Time stopped as they held each other's gaze. A surge of need and desperation rocketed through Lilah. The urge to place her lips on his and taste them. *Master it.* For a moment, she could have sworn he was thinking about kissing her too.

Silence enveloped them, broken only by the distant rumble of thunder and the crackling fire. Their hearts beat in sync and they continued to stare at each other. She wouldn't want to wait out this storm with anyone else in the world. He was a person she wholly trusted. Maybe the first person she ever had. Everything had changed since moving in here. She was someone in his eyes. Someone she didn't need to be ashamed of. People liked her: Hayley, Jim, Marion at the schoolhouse, the residents... and Aidan. Yes. He maybe didn't feel as strongly as she did, but he liked her. He must. Why else would he let her stay? Why would he look at her like this?

'I'm not proud of where I come from or what I've done in my life so far,' she said.

'Well, you should be.' He ran his fingertip gently off the end of her chin. 'Because it's not your fault you were born into poor circumstances. You've done what you had to do to survive and now look at you.'

She shrugged. 'It's not like I've done anything much.'

'You're on the right track and that's what matters. You've got yourself a new job and you're giving it a shot. God knows, I wouldn't have coped here half as well without you in the last few months. You've helped my mum even though she's been off with you in the past. You're kind to Jim, gentle with Maya and the bees, and you're always willing to try. All of that is valid and important.'

'Thank you,' she said, her throat tightening. 'I wish I hadn't messed up and hit Scarlett with the hockey stick. Sometimes I don't know if it was an accident or not. I didn't set out to do it, but she was always so horrible to me. I'm not sure if I could have stopped myself. Maybe I just didn't try.' Unshed tears welled below her eyes. 'It seems so obvious to everyone else. But I actually don't know what's true anymore. Maybe I've lied to myself all these years and now I believe my own lie.'

'Lilah.' His deep voice called her gaze back to him. 'So what? If you inadvertently hit her because she'd spent years bullying you, I don't blame you. Sometimes we act rashly in the heat of the moment. If anyone understands that, it's me.'

'Should I tell her? Or apologise?'

'Hell no. It's water under the bridge. Let it die. No matter what happened back then, she behaved in an appalling way to you. I don't know if it'll make you feel better if I tell you that you're not the only one. One day, Scarlett's going to get a rude wake up call.'

'Not from me.' She swallowed, unable to deny the number of times she'd thought about giving Scarlett back some of what she dished out, but she wouldn't deliberately hurt her. Why lower herself to that level?

He glanced back at her again and his face seemed to move closer, then he stilled. His gaze locked with hers, and she willed him to say something else. The look he was giving her thrilled her and terrified her in equal measure. What if he did want to kiss her? How could she cope if her crush became real?

'Not from you.' He gently shook his head. 'Or me. But she'll meet her match at some point and she'll fall off her pedestal and realise she's breakable like everyone else.'

The storm was receding, the rain easing into a gentle drizzle. Aidan finally broke the magnetic connection, cleared his throat, and got to his feet.

'Storm's passed. I'll get us some warm drinks. You can have a shower if you want. It should be safe enough now.'

'Oh... Right.'

As he left the room, she sat a moment longer, her thoughts swirling in a tempest of their own. Her pulse was racing and she could hardly breathe. The way he'd looked at her was making her mind spiral further out of control. She reached out and stroked Maya, drawing comfort from her wonderfully soft fur.

The storm may be over, but the one in her heart was far more turbulent and unlikely to end anytime soon.

Chapter Eighteen

Aidan

'I want to tell you about a journey that has not only tested my physical limits but has also been a profound reminder of the power of resilience, determination, and the strength of the human spirit.' Aidan stopped talking and sighed, glancing around the buzzing hives in the tranquil orchard. Would that be too much of a mouthful to get out?

Since the thunderstorm at the weekend had cleared the air, everything felt fresher and greener. The bees flitted around, getting on with their work and being a very polite audience. He couldn't guarantee that tomorrow their human counterparts would be so receptive. Especially as he'd discovered the group he was to make the speech to contained several local councillors, who had decision-making power regarding the housing project threatening the field.

'This is a chance,' he told the bees. An opportunity to win over the councillors and persuade them to oppose the construction plans. If he could just convince them of the importance of preserving the natural beauty of the land and keeping it safe for future generations of humans and wildlife.

'Hi.'

He whirled around, spotting Lilah making her way towards him. She'd tied her hair back, exposing her long neck and somehow it always made her seem older. Just looking at her neck should be banned. Was he a vampire or something? Because he really wanted to put his lips on there and he frigging well had to stop thinking like that. She was getting to him in ways she shouldn't. The other night by the fire. Jesus. He'd had to work so hard not to do something completely inappropriate.

'Hi,' he said. 'Is something wrong?'

'No.' She smiled, a slight flush creeping across her cheeks. 'I've just been listening to you practising your speech all over the house, and now out here. I wondered if you'd like to practise it to a human.'

'You mean you?'

'I do.' She gave him a coy look.

'Yeah. Ok. But I'm struggling a bit.'

'With what?'

'I really need to make it better than good because I've discovered some of the councillors are going to be there. People who hold my destiny. Or the destiny of this field.'

'How do you mean?'

'The council want to build affordable housing all over it. The wildflowers and habitats will be lost.'

Lilah frowned and stared out over the green space beyond. 'I can see that would be a loss but you know that people from backgrounds like mine have always struggled with poor housing conditions. Isn't this a way to address that issue?'

Aidan rubbed his hand across his heavily stubbled cheek. He hadn't really thought about it like that. Housing people was of course as worthy a cause, but he also believed in the importance of preserving the green spaces.

'I hear you. And I confess I hadn't considered that. I understand the need for affordable housing, and I sympathise with the struggles people face. But this particular project threatens not only the field but also the delicate ecosystem it supports. There must be a way to provide affordable housing without sacrificing the natural beauty that surrounds us. I'm sure there are other solutions.'

'Maybe. I just know how hard it is on the other side. When you're told time and time again there are no houses.'

'Ok, good point. So, we need to find a solution – a way to address both the need for affordable housing and the preservation of our environment. But one thing at a time. This time, the fight is for the environment.'

Lilah put her hands on her hips. 'Seriously? Why does there have to be a choice? Why fight one battle and not the other? Wouldn't it be better to go to the council with an alternative for building houses? How can you fight against this project otherwise?'

He frowned and ran his hand through his thick hair. 'Because I'm not sure I can think of any other options.'

'But we need to find something. I agree with you that putting houses here would spoil a quiet and peaceful place, but what happens to the people who really need houses?'

Aidan let out a sigh. 'I wonder if we could think of a better location or some kind of compromise.'

'Won't the council already have looked at all the other locations?'

'Maybe. I'm not entirely sure how they go about scoping sites.'

'What about the place where the old amusement park was? I last went there when I was like twelve or something. It's sat empty since then.'

Lilah's gaze met his, and that electric connection opened again. Her eyes were full of passion and determination. Aidan suddenly felt too hot. He loosened his shirt and pulled in a breath, though it didn't seem to want to go in. She constantly had this effect on him.

He turned away and took a few steps, putting distance between them and blaming his crazy reactions on nerves.

'Ok. I'll put that to them as an idea if they're willing to talk to me.'

'I'd quite like to talk to them and tell them exactly what it's like to have nowhere to go.'

He quirked a little smile. 'If you do that, we can kiss goodbye to the field. You might succeed in getting them to build you something out there.'

She gave a little shrug. 'Yeah, sorry. I guess I should shut up.'

'Not at all. You're allowed an opinion and maybe...' He turned away and rubbed his forehead. 'Maybe you're right. Maybe I shouldn't fight this. I don't want to stand in the way of people getting what they need, but I'm also very fond of the planet.'

'Then make sure you mention some alternatives if you get to chat to the councillors. Why not try your speech again?'

'Ok. Here goes.' Once he started talking, he got into the flow and, after several attempts, he felt more confident. Lilah was a good listener.

'I appreciate you doing this,' he said. 'I know how busy you are with work and painting.'

'I'll never be too busy to help you,' she said. Her smile faltered.

'Thank you.' He glanced away. He had to; when he looked at her, his body burned in the most insane way. 'How was work today?'

'Good. We made macaroni cheese, and the boys ate it for lunch. They seem to enjoy the cooking. I'm only really with those two boys just now. They're the ones who need the most intensive care.'

Aidan smiled because she was smiling and it was infectious. 'You seem to be getting on well.'

'It's really good.' She pulled her phone from her back pocket and checked it. 'I said I'd help your mum paint the inside of the barn today. I didn't think you'd get that plasterboard in so soon.'

'You and her seem to be getting on a bit better.'

'She was pleased I managed to save the bee fabric from a thunderstorm but said I shouldn't have risked going out in it.'

'And she's right.'

'I just panicked that she was testing me, but she seems a bit more relaxed.'

'If you feel like that again, come and tell me. I'll talk to her.'

'No. I want to do this myself.'

He nodded. 'If you insist, but don't do anything risky just to please my mum. Ok?'

'Ok.' She pulled an almost Scarlett-worthy face.

'I should go get the dogs,' Aidan said.

Keeping busy was imperative. He had a jangle of nerves in his stomach like he'd never had before. So much hinged on his talk.

After dinner, he took Maya for another walk, but even that didn't dispel the tension. When he got back, Lilah was making use of the longer evenings and was still out in the barn painting.

He strolled into the orchard. Low sunbeams fell on it like lasers. A small swarm of bees had formed on the outside of one of the hives.

'Hmm,' he said, leaning in to examine them closely. 'Time to split you up, I think. You've outgrown your home.' He prepped a new hive and carefully removed some frames from the one where the swarm had gathered. Gently scooping the bees, he moved them to the new hive, before checking for queen cells. The job took time but it was perfect for focusing his mind. He spoke softly to them as he scooped more bees into their new home.

He flicked the last bees off his fingers and stood back, watching in the fading light as they buzzed around their new home.

A clattering and yelling made him jump. Maya barked and sprang to her feet.

'What the?' Aidan sprinted out of the orchard, round the back of the house towards the far side of the Crafty Bee Barn. Even in the gathering dusk, it shone bright yellow.

Some figures were legging it up the side of the garden, close to the fence between Woodend and Jim's garden.

'Get the hell away from here!' Lilah yelled, chasing after them with what appeared to be a hammer in her hand.

'What's going on?' Aidan shouted, his voice booming through the quiet air. Maya had caught up with Lilah and was running alongside her, barking.

'Keep going,' one of the figures called. But Aidan put on a burst of speed and vaulted the low wall beside the path, ready to intercept them. Maya raced around from the other side like she was rounding up sheep. Aidan grabbed one of them and rugby tackled him to the ground. Maya barked at the fence and the other two stopped, not wanting to pass her.

'Who are you and what the hell are you doing in here?'

'Trying to break into the barn,' Lilah said, catching up and pounding the hammer slowly and menacingly into her palm.

'Not to steal anything, man. Just wanted somewhere to hang out.'

'Hang out?' Aidan got to his feet and dragged the boy up by the back of his shirt. 'If you mean a place to drink, smoke or whatever else, then don't even go there. Take your stinking arses off my property and if you ever so much as breathe in this direction again, I'll put the dog on you.'

'We won't, man.' The kid put his hands up.

'We won't need the dog if I get you first,' Lilah said. 'I've got a long history of rearranging teeth and yours look like they need straightening.' She waggled the hammer.

'We're going, ok.'

'Hey, you're Brenda's son, aren't you?' Lilah asked the kid Aidan was holding onto.

'So what?' He narrowed his eyes at her. 'Oh, it's you. The caravan girl.'

'Yeah. That's right. So you better behave or I'll tell Mummy and I doubt she'll be happy.'

The other two laughed.

'And it won't be difficult for me to find out who your parents are either,' she said. 'So watch out.'

They both took a step back.

'Did you lot break the window here too? When Aidan was abroad.'

None of them answered.

'Did you?' Aidan said.

They shuffled around with their eyes down.

'Scram, the lot of you. And make sure you don't set even one toe on my property again, understand?'

'Yeah,' they muttered.

'Then get.' Aidan let the boy go and called Maya. The three of them scarpered.

'They gave me a fright,' Lilah said. 'I bet Brenda's son sneaks through the woods and across the field all the time without his parents knowing. It's not like I can blame him for wanting to escape but what a bunch of idiots. They remind me of my broth... Some people I know.'

'Little shits.' Aidan frowned at the hammer in her hand. 'Though maybe go easy with that.'

She smirked. 'First thing I could get my hands on.'

'You're a fearless one, aren't you?'

'Except in storms.' And sometimes the dark.

'Yeah. Well...' He caught her eye and for a moment, he gazed into the depths of her slate blue irises; the rising moon reflected in them, making them as deep as the sea, a portal to her soul. The urge to take hold of her, pull her close and kiss her seized him again. Hot blood roared through his body. This was unlike anything he'd felt before. Even when he'd first met Elise, it wasn't like this. The burning desire was raw, uncontrollable, and inexplicable. 'I – um.' He cleared his throat. 'I need to go to bed. Early. It's a big day tomorrow.'

'Of course. I won't be long out here. I just want to finish a couple of things.'

'Ok. Can you lock up when you come in?'

'Will do.'

With one more glance at her, he made his way into the house, knowing he wouldn't be able to rest until he knew she was safe inside with him.

Aidan stood before a room filled with expectant faces and mustered a smile. It was now or never. All the practising was about to get real. Lilah had made a good point about the affordable housing, so good he now wasn't entirely sure he was doing the right thing.

He took a deep breath. 'Thank you all for coming today. I'm here to discuss a journey that has not only tested my physical limits but has also been a profound reminder of the power of resilience, determination, and the strength of the human spirit.' This was the easy part; the bit people had paid to hear. What came later would be the test. As he spoke, he looked around the audience. He didn't know any of the councillors or who in the audience they were, but he saw a few likely candidates.

When he finished to loud applause, he took his seat and waited through the next speech before going into a secondary room where he was introduced to several people. Prominent among them were three councillors.

'Would you mind if I take this opportunity to mention the proposed housing on the field close to the west entrance to the Lower Briar Woods?'

'Oh?' One councillor frowned.

'I'd like to raise concerns regarding its environmental impact. Aren't there other more suitable sites? That particular site is an important ecosystem.'

The councillors shook their heads, their expressions remaining stoic. Aidan sensed their resistance, like he was pushing against an immovable wall, their minds already made up.

One councillor spoke up. 'You can raise your objections in the usual way, either on our website or by writing or emailing us. It's not a matter we can sort here.'

'I've raised my objections already, and I'd like to hope you're serious in your consideration. We can't simply disregard the value of preserving our green spaces. There has to be a way to find a compromise, to build affordable housing without sacrificing the natural environment that defines our community.'

'I assure you everything will be investigated thoroughly.'

Aidan sensed he'd get nothing more here. His resolve faded. 'Well, thank you for your time.'

He turned away, his steps heavy.

As he exited the building, he made his way quickly through the quiet streets of Perth towards the bus stop. He leaned against the shelter, staring at the passing traffic. What to do now? He wanted some reassurance. His speech felt like a pointless achievement now. He'd hoped it would gain him some favour with the councillors but apparently not.

A few drops of rain fell and more people gathered at the stop. It was only four o'clock, so the offices hadn't offloaded yet. It took forty-five minutes to get back to Glenbriar on a bus. Such a long time to be alone with his thoughts and it hadn't even arrived yet. Where was it? He drummed his fingers on his thigh and bounced his toes inside his trainers. Restless energy fizzed in his nervous system.

When the bus finally arrived, he sat tapping his knee and staring out of the window. His blood pressure rose to bursting point. What could he do to make people sit up and take note? He needed to find allies who believed in his vision.

The bus stopped on the main street of Glenbriar and the driver turned off the engine. What now? It seemed like they were swapping shifts. Aidan got up and jumped off into the rain. He'd be quicker walking the rest of the way and it would help dispel some energy. There was no rush to get back. Lilah was looking after Maya and he trusted her to do the job properly. What he needed was a drink.

Without conscious thought, he drifted towards the warm glow emanating from the doors of the Stagger Inn Bar. The muffled sounds of laughter and clinking glasses reached his ears, promising solace and respite. Plus, it was drier than outside.

He pushed open the door, scanning the dimly lit room. No way. There sat Elise and Finlay. He was about to hit reverse and go straight back out when Elise turned around and caught his eye. Since when did she frequent pubs like this? It wasn't bad but its rustic-verging-on-old-fashioned style wasn't her at all. She liked modern chic. Once upon another life, Aidan and Finlay had drank here together at least once a month. His cousin's influence on Elise was obviously more than Aidan had given him credit for – more perhaps than he wanted to believe. *She'd never have come in here with me.*

He gave her a brief nod of acknowledgement and went straight to the bar, keeping his back to their table. He'd just ordered a pale ale when a hand landed on his shoulder.

'You drinking alone?'

The sound of Finlay's voice made him start. He clenched his fists on the bar. 'Yeah. I've had a bad day.'

'Oh? Do you want to come and sit with us?'

'I'm not hanging around long.'

The bartender pushed his drink across to him and Aidan swigged it back

'Have you been at an interview or something?' Finlay asked.

'Been doing a motivational speech and trying to convince the local councillors to keep their hands off the field.'

'It's a tough one. And to be fair, there is a lack of affordable housing in the town.'

'Yeah, I know.' He slugged back more of his ale. Behind Finlay, Elise had got up from the table.

Finlay gave a little shrug. 'I guess it's the kind of thing nobody wants in their backyard.'

'It's not that.' Aidan clenched the bottle. 'If that was a disused warehouse or a scrubland, then I wouldn't have an issue, but it's not. It's a greenspace with a valuable ecosystem. There has to be a line somewhere.'

'Yeah, I hear you and you're right. It seems a strange place to choose, but options aren't exactly abundant.'

They never were. He wanted to do as his dad had said and enjoy every moment of his life but sometimes that seemed impossible – especially when hundreds of conflicting thoughts battered his brain. Finlay. Elise. The field. His dad. Councillors. Uphill struggles. Woodend Cottage. Lilah.

He took another large glug. 'I will make damn sure I win this battle.'

'I hope so,' Finlay said.

'I just need a moment to regroup before I go home.'

'Then I'll leave you to yourself.' Finlay left with a sigh and headed towards the bathroom.

Almost as soon as he disappeared from sight, Elise took a seat at the bar next to Aidan.

'What's up? You look stressed.' She reached out a hand and touched his arm.

He shook her off. 'Save it, Elise. I'm not interested. You made your choice, and I made mine.'

'No need for that attitude. I was just being polite. But does that mean you're seeing someone? Lilah?'

'Why do you keep saying things like that? Do you want it to be true?'

Elise shook her head, her eyes wide with concern. 'No, but I can read body language and she clearly likes you a lot. I wondered if maybe you—'

'And would it be so wrong if I did? What's it to you anyway?'

'Nothing. I just worry about you.'

'Why?'

'It's inbuilt, I suppose. I spent months worrying about you and not knowing if you were alive or dead. I had dreams you were eaten by bears and savaged by wolves. I don't want you to be alone and sad like I was. Lilah seems like a nice girl but I can't see her being the right person for you.'

'And what would you know about it?' He downed the remainder of his ale, smacked the bottle onto the bar and strode out. So, he shouldn't have got so mad, but after the day he'd had, he didn't want to talk. Hiding and drowning his sorrows seemed like a better plan.

Chapter Nineteen

Lilah

'Ca' the yowes tae the knowes. Ca' them whaur the heather growes. Ca' them whaur the burnie rows. My bonnie dearie.' Lilah sang as she dotted around the house, dusting the surfaces. Aidan wasn't back yet, but he'd said he might be late. Dinner was ready to heat up when he got back. The knack she had for suppressing worries about her family didn't seem to work with Aidan. Whenever he was later than she expected – or hoped – her tummy squirmed like it was full of wriggly worms, making her feel queasy. If she kept busy, it stopped her thinking about it quite so much, which was her only reason for dusting at this time in the evening.

Aidan's study wasn't off-limits, or he'd never said not to go in, but she always felt a bit naughty whenever she cleaned in here. As she dusted the front of the writing bureau, something made her want to open it. She slowly prised it down. Nothing inside looked particularly interesting. Not that she'd expected any intrigue.

It was mostly stationery but there were some nice wooden boxes. She flipped open the lid of one of them and gasped. Inside, jewels sparkled back at her. With trembling fingers, she lifted a necklace of intricately wrought crystals, possibly diamonds, though she hoped not. If Aidan had this many real diamonds in his possession, he should have them in a bank vault, not in an old writing desk. 'Wow.' She opened the other boxes and found more beautiful pieces. They appeared old and were very pretty and well made.

A knock at the door startled her. She hastily put the jewellery back into the boxes, closed them up and shut the bureau.

Hayley was on the doorstep. 'Hey,' she said. 'How are you doing?' She stepped inside and wrapped her arm around Lilah.

'I'm good, thanks.'

'Great. Is Aidan here?'

'No, he's in Perth doing his speech.'

'Oh. I thought he'd be back by now.'

Lilah's tummy gave a renewed squirm. Why wasn't he back?

Maya padded into the hallway, wagging her tail, and Hayley ruffled her hair. 'Ah, did you think I was Daddy coming home? Just auntie Hayley and I didn't even bring treats. Sorry, sweetie. But I did bring something for you, Lilah.'

'For me?'

'Yes. Look at this.' She held up a bag. 'More clothes.'

'Oh wow. Thank you.'

'I asked my friends if they were having a clear out to pass anything they didn't want to me, and I got some lovely things.

I think they'll fit you. I asked people I thought were about the same dress size as you.'

'That's so kind. Do you want a drink or anything?'

'No thanks. I can't stay long, but I want to show you something in the bag.'

They went into the living room and Hayley emptied the contents of the bag onto the sofa. Lilah spied a variety of tops and dresses.

'Look at this.' Hayley lifted a shimmering slate-blue dress and held it high. 'This was in one of the bags and I think it'll suit you perfectly. It's so like your eye colour. I think it'll be stunning on you.'

Lilah's eyes widened as she took the dress from Hayley. 'Wow, it's gorgeous.' She'd never had anything so beautiful.

Hayley grinned. 'I thought you might like it.'

Lilah held the dress against her body, envisioning herself in it. 'I've no clue when I would ever need to wear it.'

'You never know. Why not try it on?'

'Ok.' Lilah felt a pang of awareness. Should she change in here? What if Aidan came back and she was halfway through taking off her clothes? 'I should change in my room.'

'Sure. I'll wait here.'

Safely in her room, Lilah slipped out of her top and jeans and carefully stepped into the dress. The fabric felt luxurious against her skin, and how well it hugged her figure. She brushed her hands down the front. The only trouble was she couldn't quite reach the zip to fasten it.

'I can't do the zip,' she told Hayley, emerging into the living room.

'Oh, look at you. You look amazing. Turn around and I'll pull it up for you.' She tugged on it.

Lilah turned her back to Hayley, catching herself in the mirror above the fireplace. She could hardly believe it was her looking back. She coiled her hair over one shoulder as Hayley gently guided the zip up.

'It is an awkward zip, this. I had one like this before and it was a faf to get on. But it's not exactly something you'll need to worry about every day, so it shouldn't be a big problem.'

The reflection staring back at Lilah took her breath away. The dress accentuated her slim frame.

Hayley patted her shoulder, a wide smile on her face. 'You look stunning! It's like the dress was made for you.'

Lilah blushed, a shy smile playing on her lips. 'Thanks. I can't believe it.'

Hayley checked the time and sighed. 'I hate to rush off, but I can't hang about. Pity, because I'd love to style your hair to match. But another time. In fact, the next time you're going out, give me a call and I'll nip around and sort you.'

'Thank you. You really are such a kind person.' Lilah smiled at her, then threw her arms around Hayley's neck.

'Aw, not at all, my beauty. You're so welcome.' She rubbed Lilah's back. 'I'm so pleased you like the dress. You look like a princess.'

Once Hayley had left, Lilah stood alone in the living room again, her eyes drifting back to the mirror. Maya lay gazing up at her and seemed to be almost smiling.

'How do I look? I feel like Cinderella.' She pulled her hair up and secured it in a messy updo with a claw clip. Her neck stretched high and she rubbed her collarbone. What she need-ed to finish the look was a necklace. Of course she didn't have any jewellery. She stole into her bedroom and checked out the window towards the road. No sign of Aidan. If he was here, she would ask if she could borrow the necklace in his drawer. He wouldn't mind her trying it, would he?

She just wanted to see what it looked like. That was all.

Opening the top of the writing bureau, Lilah spotted the box tucked away in the corner as it had been before. Dusting it off, she carefully lifted the lid to reveal the assortment of necklaces, bracelets, and rings.

Her gaze landed on a delicate antique necklace adorned with shimmering gemstones. Carefully, she fastened it around her neck. She brushed her fingertips over it and her skin tingled under it. She'd never had anything precious before. Aidan didn't have a mirror in the study, so she returned to the living room and stood before it. Her eyes widened. Was this really Delilah Clarke? It looked like someone older, wiser, and more sophisticated.

She turned this way and that, checking herself out from all angles. Never in her life had she looked this good.

A click in the corridor made her heart thud. Maya jumped to her feet and raced out of the door, her tail wagging wildly.

'Hey, girl,' came Aidan's low voice.

'Shit,' Lilah muttered, her clumsy fingers unable to unfasten the necklace. If she couldn't get it off, what would she say? She could explain.

In the mirror, she saw the door open.

'Lilah.' Aidan froze in the doorway. 'You...'

She swallowed and turned around, her hand clutching the necklace. Was he angry or was there something else in his eyes?

'Wait a second.' His eyes narrowed. 'That necklace. Is that from my desk?'

Lilah's heart sank and a lump swelled in her throat. Could she just get away? His brows were grooved and he seemed to be trying to puzzle out something. 'Yes. I... I found it in a box in your study when I was cleaning. I didn't think you'd mind if I tried it on. I thought it would go with the dress...'

'And where did the dress come from?'

'I didn't *steal* it. I swear.'

'I didn't say you stole it. I just—'

'Hayley brought around a bag of clothes. I didn't take it from anyone and I'd never steal from you.' Holding her hand to her mouth, struggling to keep back her tears, she ran to the door, not looking at him. This was Aidan, the man who'd always made her feel like someone special. Someone she didn't need to be ashamed of, but now she was ashamed. She should never have taken the necklace without asking. How could he ever trust her again? Didn't this make her look like the little sneak thief everyone had warned him about?

'Hey, hey, stop.' He moved in front of her and his voice was softer. 'Christ, Lilah. I wasn't accusing you. I was just stunned to see you dressed like that. I've had a long and hideous day. My head is all over the place. If I reacted like I was angry, I didn't mean to.'

'I can't,' she said. Not sure what she meant or what to do. 'Please, just let me go.'

He didn't move. His solid form blocked the doorway. 'Lilah...'

'I'll put the necklace back.' Emotions overwhelmed her, and tears began to spill down her face. 'I wish I'd never touched it. I know I shouldn't have. I saw it there when I was dusting and I... Oh god, I've been so stupid. I'll leave. As soon as I get this stuff off, I'll go.'

'No, Lilah, you can't leave because of this.'

'I have to leave. I can't be here when—'

'Please don't go. I want you... to stay.' His burning palms gently clutched her on either side of her bare shoulders and he pulled her close. 'Please.'

'How can I? I'm as good as a thief.'

'No, you're not. Please, wear the necklace. Truly, I don't mind.' He leaned in and rested his forehead against hers. Then, without warning, he gently shifted his position and placed a warm kiss on her cheek. Lilah's heart stopped. Her mind jammed and she couldn't make sense of anything. *Aidan is kissing me.* And then he wasn't. It stopped so suddenly Lilah couldn't be sure it had really happened.

'I'm sorry. So sorry. I shouldn't have done that,' he said.

'It's ok.' She placed her hand on her cheek where his lips had been.

'No, it isn't. It will never be ok for a person to kiss someone without asking. Never. I'm bloody ashamed of myself.'

'You and me both.' She pushed past him and ran towards her room. He might be ashamed of kissing her but it couldn't be anything like how she was feeling. Why had she taken the necklace?

Everything was suddenly a horrible, ugly mess. Just like the usual state of her life. The happiness and joyful moments of the last few weeks were nothing but a quick blip. Survival mode kicked in. She needed to get packed up and go.

Footsteps approached her door. 'Lilah, please don't go,' he said from the corridor. 'Please, give me a chance to make things right.'

'Go away.' She could never face him again. She'd taken the jewellery from his desk when she had no right and she'd been caught. The fact he'd kissed her made no sense, but it wasn't as upsetting as the necklace. Maybe it was wrong of him to have done it, but her foolish heart had craved it for so long, she couldn't see it like that. Why had he done it? To try and appease her? Did he know about her crush? If he did, that made everything so much worse.

'Lilah, please. I know you very rarely get the chance to dress up and wear nice things. I really don't mind. In fact, you looked so beautiful...' He trailed off his words so quiet she wasn't sure she'd heard right.

'What?'

'Please, let's make things right between us.'

'I don't know how.' How could she get over the fact she'd betrayed him? 'Just leave me alone.'

'Ok, but I'm begging you not to leave. Not yet. Not like this. Let's at least talk.'

Lilah held her breath as his footsteps receded. She walked over to the mirror, gazing at her reflection, her tear-streaked face shown off by the offending necklace.

She wiped away her tears and fiddled with the clasp until the necklace fell into her hand. After placing it on the bedside cabinet, she bent her arm around her back to unzip the dress. But no matter which way she stretched, she couldn't get the zip pull and tug it. No wonder someone had thrown the dress out. It may look beautiful, but it was completely impractical. Her breathing became rapid and she felt too hot. How could she get this off? Cut it?

That seemed rash. The dress was so pretty. Aidan could help her, though she really didn't want to see him. How could she look him in the eye? How could *he* look at *her* and not see a thief? She couldn't stay here. That being the case, she could ask him to help her before she left – forever.

She hadn't had the chance to find out how things had gone at the meeting or anything. He'd said he had a shitty day, and she hated the idea of him being alone, but her shame was like a club bashing her over the head every time she remembered the necklace.

Swallowing all her emotions, she made her way back to the living room. He wasn't there. She peeked outside. Maya was lying in the garden, but Aidan wasn't visible. Perhaps he was with the bees.

Something clicked in another room and she heard movement. He was somewhere about. Maybe in his study? As she moved into the corridor, she realised the noise was coming from his room.

'Aidan.' She knocked on the door, her voice shaking slightly.

He opened the door, his brow furrowed. Lilah froze. Jesus Christ. Where was his shirt? A slab of hot, tanned chest stood before her. Across it was a light smattering of dark hair. His life in the outdoors had honed him into a rugged shape. He was glorious. She clamped her mouth shut and forced her focus to his face.

'Are you ok?' he asked, his voice soft and low. 'You're not leaving, are you?'

'I can't get the zip down on this dress. I can't reach it. Can you do it?'

Aidan stared at her. 'Lilah.'

'What?'

'I'm not sure I should do this.'

Lilah turned around. 'If you don't, I'll be stuck in this dress forever.'

'Fine.'

She closed her eyes, turning her back to him again, and barely breathing, as his hands touched her back. He moved closer, his warmth closing in on her. His breath sounded laboured and it grazed her neck as he spoke.

'If you want to keep the necklace, please do. It's yours.' He edged down the top of the zip.

'I can't. I don't want people to think I stole it.'

'I'm giving it to you. I would have given it to you if I'd been here.' The zip moved another inch. 'Tell everyone it was a gift.'

Was this really happening? Why would he give her something that valuable? 'I don't get why. You know I shouldn't even have touched it.'

'Curiosity isn't a crime. Neither is wanting to look good, and you do look good. You suit the necklace better than anyone I can imagine.'

'Do I?'

'Yes.'

She tilted her head to one side, drugged by the heat of his breath and the depth of his voice. Her eyes were heavy. 'What will people think if you give it to me?'

'If you think it's an inappropriate gift, then that's fine. Don't take it. But you're welcome to wear it whenever you want. Assuming you're staying here and I hope you are. I really don't want you to leave.'

'I don't want to leave, Aidan. But I feel so shit about this.'

'Then don't. Put your mind at rest,' he whispered. The soft hairs on the back of her neck lifted like they'd been caught in a gentle breeze and their movement tickled her. The zip moved gently down her back and Aidan's warm fingertips made contact with her skin, sending pulses of desire rustling through her. 'I know you weren't stealing anything. You looked so stunning when I came home; it took my breath away. I'm sorry I kissed you. I don't want you to think I'd take advantage of you. It was comfort I was looking for, but I should have asked.'

'Stop beating yourself up about it. I get it and I'm fine. It was a kiss on the cheek, that's all.'

'Yes. That was all.' He pulled the zip right down and stepped back, taking all the warmth with him.

Lilah breathed very deliberately. 'What if that wasn't all?'

'I don't follow.'

'What if I want more?'

'I can't do anything else. It wouldn't be right.'

'Why not?' Lilah turned to face him. 'Because I'm too—'

'Don't finish that sentence. You're not too poor or ugly or anything like that. I just don't want to put you in an awkward position.'

'And what if I don't care?' She ran her fingers around the neckline of her dress.

'But what will that make us? Make me? It'll look like I'm using you. Christ, I *will* be using you.'

'No, you won't.' She stepped forward, her heart thudding. The skin beneath her dress tingled. Her breasts, still held tight in her bra, strained as if trying to pull closer to Aidan's chest. 'Not if I want to.'

'You know it's risky. If we do this, there's no going back.'

'I want to be with you. I've had the world's biggest crush on you for the longest time.'

'Sometimes I wondered.' He raised his hand to her cheek and ran a fingertip across her skin. His eyes were dark and intense, but his slightly crinkled brow looked like he was trying to solve some kind of puzzle.

She let go of the dress and it pooled at her feet. 'I want you so badly it hurts.' Body trembling, she drew closer. He looked her over and there was no disguising the hunger in his eyes. He clutched her face in his hands and his grip was firm but gentle. Bringing his lips close, he held her gaze. Lilah let her eyelids fall. Electricity zipped between them as their mouths met. It was a kiss like no other. One she'd wanted for so long. It made her heart soar and she edged closer, sighing as his warm hands wrapped around her and pulled her in tight. Nothing could ever be as beautiful as this.

His need pressed against her, sparking fire inside her. He whispered something close to her ear, and the heat of his words tingled on her skin. She moved her mouth back to his and her heartbeat accelerated. She couldn't get much closer but she wanted to. His fingertips tangled in her hair, the kiss deepening every second. As their tongues met, fire erupted inside her.

His deep voice vibrated on her lips. 'Lilah.'

The last vestiges of control were slipping from her. She glided one of her hands around the back of his neck, while the other clasped the side of his face. Her fingers traced his jaw before moving into his hair. He tightened his grip around her and she was lost.

Jesus. She wanted him so badly. Normally, sex creeped her out. The guys were often sleazy or only interested in a quickie. But already she felt worshipped by his kisses.

He pulled back and stared at her. The desire in his eyes was matched by something else. Something questioning. What was he thinking? 'You really want this?'

'Yes,' she whispered, her breathing heavy. Her gaze locked on him but it was dreamy and unfocused.

'Then tell me what you want, what you like.'

She blinked and sucked her lip, running a palm across his beautiful hard chest. 'Just you. I don't know what else.'

'Have you done this before?' He gently pushed some loose hairs behind her ear and frowned slightly.

'Yes.' She gave a little shrug. 'But I haven't found out what I like.'

'Ok. Let's try this.' He gently lifted her and carried her to his bed. It had to be the biggest bed she'd ever been in. Laid on the soft sheets, she allowed her head to roll back as he kissed her neck, then moved slowly downwards. He slipped off her bra and his warm palms cupped her breasts, making her arch into him and moan.

As his breath skimmed her nipples, and he kissed his way to her belly button, Lilah let out a soft cry. The heat from his body warmed every part of her. Then he got up and she watched him remove his jeans. When she saw just how hot for her he was, her breathing grew rapid again. She closed her eyes as he prised off her knickers, kissing the inside of her thigh while he was there. She trembled beneath him, but not out of fear. His touches were soft and adoring. He didn't seem in any rush. Most of her previous times would be over by now. Foreplay was non-existent. The guy would have got what he wanted and be dressing to leave while she was lying naked, usually in some discomfort, wondering what she was supposed to do next.

'Aidan,' she gasped. 'I'm not on the pill or anything.'

'That's ok. I have protection, but we won't need it for a while.'

'Why?'

'You'll see.' He brought his mouth to hers and kissed her again, warming her to the core. His fingers moved low, touching her until she squealed and panted. No one had ever worked magic on her like this before.

Between his lips and fingers, he had her reduced to a quivering ball of delight and she lay back in a state of deep contentment. Not only was she already deeply satisfied but he seemed to draw pleasure from her enjoyment too.

He nudged in beside her on the bed, resuming a kiss that hadn't really stopped all evening, and moved on top of her. This was the moment. She would become one with Aidan and nothing would be the same again. With a brief second of anxiety, she waited. This had been painful in the past. Guys had rammed their way home without any concern for her feelings. But Aidan was gentle, kissing her softly and holding her. She relaxed for him, wrapping her arms around his neck and linking her legs around his waist.

His strong, deep thrusts pushed her to a new level of delirious pleasure and she lost conscious thought as she spiralled over the edge, feeling completely loved. Not used. Here was bliss at last.

Chapter Twenty

Aidan

Hot blood pumped through Aidan until he woke sweaty and overheated. He lowered the covers to allow the air to cool his chest. But hang on... Waking to an empty bed was nothing new, except this morning it shouldn't be empty. Where was Lilah?

He sat up, his body still heavy with sleep, and his head like a lead brick. 'Oh god.' He groaned and clutched his face. What a mess he'd made of things. The useless exchange with the councillors yesterday afternoon had wound him up. He hated how helpless it made him feel. It had driven him to be short with Elise. And then, worst of all, he'd upset Lilah. *Lilah*. A little voice chirped away inside his head, reminding him how much he liked Lilah. She'd confessed to having a crush on him. And he'd definitely had something building inside him as he got to know her. But last night had transcended everything.

She was fun, exciting, and a pleasure to be with, though he wished he hadn't kissed her when he was begging her not to leave. The actions of a desperate man. He groaned and massaged his forehead. No denying life was good when Lilah was in it. But what now? Where did they go from here? Would people find out? Maybe Lilah would want to tell people or expect to do this again. Should they? Or was this a one off? If they had a repeat performance, that would look like he was using her for sure, and he didn't want that. She was too nice for that. People had used her all her life one way or another, and she didn't need him coming along and doing the same.

Getting out of bed was a struggle. He'd drunk more than he meant to last night before he came home. Another thing to add to the ever-growing pile of reasons why he should not have done what he did. 'Christ. I'm an idiot.'

Maya was waiting in the kitchen to go out and he opened the door for her.

'Lilah?' he called. No response. Where was she? He knocked on her bedroom door and waited.

Nothing.

'Lilah,' he said again, gently opening the door and peering around. The bed was made and the room was empty. 'Oh, come on. Where are you?'

With his heart thudding, he pulled out his phone and sent her a message.

AIDAN: Where are you? I'd like to talk.

Minutes turned into an agonising wait as he kept checking the screen. He showered, dressed, fixed himself some breakfast and still the message remained unanswered.

A knock on the front door made him jump. But Lilah wouldn't knock. Probably just a delivery. He dragged himself to his feet and along the corridor, opening the door to find the moody face of Scarlett glowering back at him.

'Morning,' he said. 'Why are you here?'

'I'm dropping Mum off at the barn. Her car's at the garage. Just in case you hear someone in there, it's her.'

'Right. Thanks. Why couldn't she come and tell me herself?'

'Because I want to talk to you.'

'What about?'

'Where's Delilah?'

'Lilah,' he muttered. 'And why do you want to know?'

'Is she about? Because I don't want her to hear me.'

'She's...' He glanced at the clock. 'She's at work.' He knew it was too early for that but Scarlett didn't need to.

'Good. Because we need to talk. I had a message from Elise last night, which is pretty unusual. She's not like a close friend or anything. But she's really worried about you.'

'I can take care of myself. I don't need people worrying about me.'

Scarlett shook her head. 'Yeah, but you made a big mistake with Elise and I can see you doing the same kind of thing with Lilah. She's a really clever actress and she's spun you a right little sob story. She's even more cunning than I thought, because she's taking her time about it. I thought she'd waltz in and bold as you like steal your money or whatever. But no, she's milking it.

Now, she's living here thinking she owns the place. Next thing we know, she'll be jumping into bed with you—'

'That's enough.'

'Oh jeez. Don't tell me she already has. Well, that's it. Next up, you'll be dating and she'll be bleeding you for every penny. Or she'll be pregnant with your kid and you'll never get rid of her.'

'I said that's enough. You mind your own business and stop being so childish. Lilah is a good person. That hockey stick thing was a long time ago and you've had more than enough revenge for it. Time to let it go.'

Scarlett raised an eyebrow. 'Whatever.' She spun around and stalked off down the path, her bright red pixie cut like a raging fire atop her head.

Unable to sit still, Aidan strolled out to the bees. 'Good morning,' he said. 'Or at least I want it to be good. But I need to find Lilah. I hope she hasn't left us.'

The bees buzzed around, getting on with their business, their presence as soothing as ever, even if the relief was only temporary. Nothing could take away the tension in his shoulders. If Lilah would just come back or reply to his messages. They needed to talk. A wave of sickening realisation washed over him. Was this how Elise had felt when he went to Canada? This was what he'd done to her – gone off and not replied to messages. Admittedly, some of that had been because he didn't have signal or battery life, but not always. Sometimes he'd wanted to be alone. Was that what Lilah wanted? Needed?

Come ten o'clock, she wasn't back and he hoped she'd gone to work. He resisted the urge to ring up the Schoolhouse and see if she was there.

'Morning, Mum.' He opened the barn door and looked around. Of course, Lilah wouldn't be there, but he had to talk to someone. Being alone was killing him.

'Morning.' Patricia turned and smiled, placing some hand-sewn fabric sachets on a shelf. 'Are you alright?'

He took a deep breath. 'Yeah, just pissed off about the field. I had a really unproductive talk with the councillors yesterday and I get the feeling they're not going to listen to anything I have to say.'

Patricia frowned. 'Very frustrating.'

'It is.' He rubbed at his forehead. 'I'm not even sure I'm fighting for the right cause anymore.'

She raised an eyebrow. 'How do you mean?'

'I don't think I should be blocking affordable houses. People need them.'

His mother sighed. 'Hmm. That may be true but it doesn't stop the field being an important ecological site, does it?'

'No. That's why I need to come up with alternatives and find a way to make them listen.'

'How?'

'I'm not sure. I have to go and collect the dogs but I'll think about it on the way.' He closed the door on her and pulled out his phone, sending another message to Lilah. His chest squirmed as he saw the first one still unread.

AIDAN: Did you get to work ok? Please reply. I want to know you're safe.

He called Maya and they walked down the hill to pick up the other dogs for their walk. Once they were altogether, he, Maya, Max, Bella and Coco returned by the same road and headed towards the gate to the woods. An unmarked white van was parked at the fence beside the field and two people in hi-viz jackets were walking across it carrying handheld devices. Aidan let out a growl and the dogs turned to look at him.

'Sorry,' he said. But it looked like people making official measurements. Even their heavy footfalls were sacrilegious.

Birds sang in the trees, oblivious of the threat to their homes.

The weight of what he'd done last night pressed heavily on his shoulders. Maybe the worst part was how much he'd enjoyed it. It wouldn't be easy calling it a one off and walking away while Lilah was still in the house. This had always been the risk. Was that why she'd disappeared? Had it dawned on her too?

As he followed the familiar path, his mind wouldn't shift from her. He walked through the woods all the way to Clachnabronnachan. She wouldn't be finished work for some hours – assuming she'd gone in. He couldn't march up to the door with all the dogs, so he turned and went back to the town. After dropping off the dogs and getting some lunch, he took Maya back to the woods and returned to the path he'd taken earlier, searching for a place he could sit and mull things over. It was after two now and Lilah should be finished. Would she come back this way? Had she ever gone in?

As thoughts peppered his brain like missiles, he looked up and, there on the path ahead, he saw her.

She darted behind a tree, as if to hide. Aidan quickened his pace and Maya bolted towards her. 'Lilah!'

Maya was jumping around wagging her tail and Aidan sped up.

Lilah took a deep breath, tucked her hair behind her ears, and peered at him with wide, pleading eyes.

'There you are. Why did you run off? I've been worried about you.'

Her gaze dropped to the ground, her voice barely a whisper as she spoke. 'How can I stay?'

'Why not?'

She gave a little shrug. 'After what happened last night, I can't live under your roof anymore. I can't bear the thought of being there and not... Well, you know, and what will everyone think?'

'But...' He stared into her glossy, fearful eyes. 'Those risks were always there.'

'I know.' She looked away. 'But it's different in the light of day, isn't it? I mean... What's to stop it happening again? Instead of me cleaning the house to go towards rent, what if I start jumping in your bed? Would that cover the payment?'

'Don't say things like that. You know I don't want that. I told you plain as day I don't want you to think I'm using you.' This was exactly why they should never have acted on impulse... And yet, he couldn't swear that given the chance again, he wouldn't want to do exactly the same thing. Because the raw level attraction hadn't gone away. If anything, it had intensified.

'I'm just confused.'

'I understand. We crossed a line and I'm sorry.'

'Which is another thing. If I stay, I'll feel... dirty. Like you gave in for a night because of my stupid crush, but you'll always regret it.'

'I said I'm sorry because I'm upset that you're feeling this way. I didn't say I regretted it. Do you?'

'Of course I don't, but I regret putting myself in this position.'

He nodded and glanced around, letting out a low sigh. Beside him, Maya panted as she waited for them to restart the walk. 'I think I know the solution.'

'You're going to kick me out?'

He let out a half laugh and took a step closer. 'No. I'm trying to avoid you leaving.'

'There is no solution other than me leaving. We have to accept that, Aidan. It'll be too awkward otherwise.'

'I think there's another way.'

'Really?'

'Yes. Let's make it official.'

'What?' She gaped at him. 'Make what official?'

'Let's date and be a couple. You can be my girlfriend and I'll be your boyfriend, your partner or whatever it's called at the moment.'

She shook her head and drew closer to the tree. 'That won't work. No way.'

'Why not? Am I that bad?'

'No... But.' She held out her hands like she was trying to grasp invisible words. 'Will it be real not just pretending so people think we're together, when actually it's an excuse for us to...?'

'It'll be as real as we want it to be.' He closed the distance between him and Lilah and resting his palm on her cheek.

Maya nuzzled up Lilah's thigh and she patted her somewhat manically.

'I don't see how it can work. You won't want to be seen out with me, will you?'

'Why not?' he rubbed the pad of his thumb across her cheek, enjoying the deep pleasure of skin on skin contact. 'I've been seen out with you before.'

Lilah opened and closed her mouth but no sound came out.

'What do you say?' He trailed his hand down her neck and over her shoulder, bringing it to rest on her upper arm.

'Well, ok. If you're really sure.'

'I am. How about we start by telling my mother?' He closed his grip gently around her and she visibly swelled at the touch, her chest rising in a way that reminded him how she'd come undone for him last night. She'd been so responsive, so happy, and so full of affection. Quite a different experience from what he was used to.

'Your mum has enough reasons to dislike me already.'

'Well, she's not allowed to hate my girlfriend.' He bent in and placed a long kiss on her cheek. She let out a breathy moan. 'Let's go home,' he whispered. 'Together.'

CHAPTER TWENTY-ONE

Lilah

Lilah's head was a dizzy mess of wild imaginings. What had just happened? Aidan wanted to date her... For real? How was that possible? Things that dreamy didn't happen to Lilah Clarke. Yet here she was, walking hand in hand with him towards the bright and sunny crafty bee barn. Did that mean he really liked her? She'd grown so used to his company he was like a friend, but this felt like so much more.

The decorating was complete. Even with the bright colours, the barn fit perfectly into the surrounding garden.

Only one problem. Patricia was in there. She'd been a lot nicer recently but she was unlikely to appreciate this.

Aidan let Maya into the front garden and started to walk towards the barn again, but Lilah tugged his hand and stopped him.

'This really isn't a good idea.'

'It's not up to my mum to decide who I date. That's my business. I'll tell her straight she's not to give you any grief about it. If we're doing this for real, she has to find out at some point.'

Lilah let out a sigh as they started walking again. She appreciated what he was doing, but she wasn't sure it would work, especially when Scarlett was on the scene.

Aidan pushed open the door to the barn and before Lilah could see inside, Patricia spoke, 'Ah, you're back. A man came around asking who owned the house. I think he was measuring the field or something.'

'Did you get his name?' Aidan opened the door wider and held out his arm for Lilah to walk in before him.

'Oh, hello, Lilah,' Patricia said. 'His name was Jacob McCash. He left a number. I wrote it down.'

'Thank you.' Aidan took a slip of paper from his mum. 'Um... We've got something to tell you.'

Lilah smoothed the front of her top, not making eye contact with Patricia.

'Oh, what is it?'

'Lilah and I are dating.'

'You're dating?' She shifted a decorative wooden chair from the craft table and blinked. 'My goodness.'

'Yes.'

'Well... That's... lovely. I can understand why. Lilah, you've grown into such a kind person. The painting you've done around here is perfect.'

'Thanks.' She smiled weakly, trying to detect any hints Patricia wasn't being truthful.

'I wonder if you have a moment to help me with something else.'

'Um, ok.'

'Is that ok with you?' Aidan said.

'Yeah.' She gave him a weak smile.

'Fine then. But don't keep her too long,' he added to Patricia. 'And don't expect her to do any unpaid labour.' He studied Lilah for a moment, then leaned in and placed a soft kiss on her cheek. 'See you in a bit.'

He closed the barn door on the way out, leaving Lilah and Patricia.

'Well, I must say I'm not actually surprised. I could see you liked each other.' Patricia sat back at her table. 'I had this idea for bookmarks, but I need a second opinion. Normally I'd ask Scarlett, but she's off with her boyfriend and you have an artistic eye.'

Was it too good to be true that Patricia was ok with this? Hardly daring to believe it, Lilah moved to the worktable and took a seat.

Although Aidan had said there was no need to keep their relationship a secret, Lilah felt weird just randomly telling people. At work, she wanted to say something, but what? 'Hey, guess what? I've got a boyfriend – the guy I've been living with and I had a crush on for weeks.' Nope. That sounded dodgy. A whole week passed, and she said nothing to anyone.

'Lilah, we've got visitors coming,' Marion said. 'You might know them already.'

'Who?'

'Well, Marcus Bowman is Toby's brother. It's Marcus who pays for him to be here. He's the weatherman who presents *Destination Forecast*.'

That was the program Brenda told her to watch, but she still hadn't seen it.

'Marcus's girlfriend is Willow Roxburgh, and she used to work here.'

'Oh, she's Hayley's cousin, isn't she? The one who's behind the Rocky Rainman thing.'

'That's right. They're coming to see Toby today and Toby tends to get very excited when he has visitors, so maybe you could do something calming with him this morning.'

'Ok. We could wash something. I know it sounds a bit weird but he likes washing up and I always find that relaxing too. I think having my hands in warm water helps.'

'Sounds like a great idea.'

Lilah filled a basin with warm, soapy water and went to find Toby. 'We've got some things to wash today,' she told him, taking him by the hand. 'Come and see. You have to be careful. It's some ornaments and we're going to clean them and take care of them.'

'Ok.' Toby nodded.

He was still elbow deep in soap suds when Willow arrived alongside Marcus Bowman. Lilah recognised him as soon as she saw him. He'd been a weather presenter for some time. A distant memory of living in the old house at Rowan Way surfaced. She and her mum were waiting for a TV programme to come on and her mum was saying, 'At least the weather guy is eye-candy but can they just get a move on with it?'

'Hi,' Willow said, taking the seat next to Lilah. Lilah smiled at her, checking out her very long blonde hair. She had rosy cheeks and a youthful smile. She looked younger than Marcus who was very tall and resembled an Italian model. Not that Lilah could comment on age gaps. Aidan was ten years older than her. 'I hear you know my cousin, Hayley.'

'Yeah, she's really nice.'

Marcus had taken the seat next to Toby, and he put his arm around his younger brother. 'This looks fun.'

'Fun,' Toby repeated, then flicked bubbles at Marcus.

Marcus laughed.

'And you live with Aidan,' Willow said. 'I think that's what Hayley told me.'

'Yeah.'

'He has a nice house.'

'I love it. And Aidan and I are... Well, we're dating.' Finally, she'd said it aloud.

'Really? That's great.'

'Hayley said he was involved in an eco-campaign,' Marcus said. 'She wanted us to get behind it. I haven't had a chance to find out about it yet.'

'He wants to stop the council building houses on the field behind Woodend. The thing is, people need affordable housing. I agree it would be a shame to build on the field, but I really believe we need houses too.'

'Tricky one,' Marcus said.

'I thought the site of the old amusement park was a better place but I don't think the councillors will listen to me if they wouldn't listen to Aidan.'

'We can try and help,' Willow said. 'But there are no guarantees.'

'Any help would be good.'

When Lilah got home, she looked around for Aidan but he wasn't there. The sun was out and she sat down in the orchard, under a tree. She scrolled through her phone, searching the council website until she found the name Jacob McCash. Maybe Aidan had called him already, but there was no harm in adding her voice to the campaign. Lilah keyed in the number and waited. Her stomach turned over as she did. She'd never done anything like this before and wasn't exactly sure what to say.

'Jacob McCash, planning department.'

Lilah sat up and took a breath. 'Hi... I... Um, believe you were here about building houses on the field.'

'Pardon? I was where?'

'Woodend Cottage.'

'Yes, I was. I've spoken to someone about this already.'

'Good, but I also live here and want to say some things.'

'What kind of things?'

'Have you considered any other sites for these houses?'

'As I told the other person, you can request that information in writing. I can't discuss it right now.'

'Then make time. When can we discuss it? Get your diary and find a date. This is important.'

'What's your name?'

'Lilah Clarke.'

'Well, I don't have any space until next Wednesday. I suppose I could see you at ten o'clock.'

Lilah would be working and she wasn't sure if she could get the time off, but Aidan could go. She certainly wasn't going to turn down the chance of a meeting. 'Ok. Put it in as Lilah Clarke and Aidan McBride.'

'All right. It's in my calendar.'

'Thank you. We'll see you then.' Lilah ended the call and gazed out over the field, seeing its full beauty in the sunlight. Of course, she didn't want that spoiled, but she was acutely aware of the lack of affordable housing, having grown up in such dire conditions.

'Hey,' Aidan said from behind.

'Oh, you're there.'

He slumped onto the grass beside her. 'Just been out with the dogs. Maya's lying in the shade.'

Lilah tossed back her head and let her long hair tumble down her back. It grazed her skin softly. Aidan's hands landed gently on her shoulders from behind and she leaned into him. The rows of blooming apple trees, their branches laden with fragrant blossoms, smelled sweet in the warm air. The gentle hum of bees going about their busy work provided a pleasant soundtrack. All of it was too perfect to be true.

'How was work?' Aidan murmured in her ear, running his palms down her upper arms and leaving a trail of goosebumps.

'Good.' She told him about Willow and Marcus and how they'd offered to help. 'And I hope you don't mind, but I called Jacob McCash, the guy from the council. He's agreed to meet us next Wednesday. I'll probably have work but you could go.'

'Oh, Lilah.' He pressed a kiss into the crook of her neck. 'You are amazing. How did you get him to agree to a meeting?'

'I just insisted.'

He chuckled onto her skin, and it tickled her. 'Then I'll definitely go. You could ask for the time off, though it's quite short notice, or I could see if Gabe would come with me.'

'That would be fine.' She smiled and closed her eyes as Aidan kissed her neck again. Was this a dream? Their daily life hadn't changed much... Except now they shared a bed and when things went bump in the night Lilah had someone to hold her. And not just hold her. Previously, she'd never got the thrill of sex or why anyone would want to do it. Now she understood. With a partner like Aidan, it was beautiful, breathtaking, and made her feel more wanted than she'd ever been.

She fiddled with the edge of her denim shorts. Maybe this wouldn't last. 'Oh god.' She threw back her head. Who was she kidding? How could it last? When she thought about this flimsy new life collapsing, it made her want to scream, cry or run away and never see anyone ever again. Doubt and uncertainty gnawed at her, whispering that she didn't belong in Aidan's world. *Control. Must stay calm.*

'What's wrong?' Aidan asked, kissing her again.

'Oh, er, nothing. I just remembered I said I'd help your mum with something, but I'd rather stay with you.'

'Then stay. Mum can manage on her own.'

'You know I can't do that.'

He groaned.

'I better go. I think she's a bit lonely now that Scarlett's always off with her new man.'

Aidan huffed out a laugh. 'I never thought I'd see the day. But I should check in with the bees, so off you go and I'll see you later.'

She gave him a long kiss, then headed for the Crafty Bee Barn. Crafting was fun and she enjoyed helping Patricia now that she was a lot more chilled.

Voices beyond the door caught her attention. Patricia appeared with Scarlett.

'Oh, you're here,' Patricia said. 'I thought you must be busy.'

'I was, but I'm free now.'

Scarlett rolled her eyes with a disdainful noise.

'Let's hope Aidan's not about,' Scarlett muttered. 'We don't want to witness you slobbering all over him.'

'Scarlett! Don't be rude,' Patricia said. 'Come in, Lilah. I'll show you what I made yesterday.'

'Sure.'

Scarlett sat down by Lilah and muttered, 'I'm not fooled. I knew you were trying to wheedle your way into his life. So what now? You get to live rent free? Or is it to get some revenge on me?'

'Neither of those reasons.' Lilah glared at her. 'We happen to like each other.'

Scarlett scoffed a laugh. 'Yeah. I'm sure Aidan loves you. He's a man, after all. Of course he wouldn't say no. But he'll regret it. I'm the only one who can see it, it seems.'

'Scarlett,' Patricia said, sitting down opposite. 'That's enough.'

Scarlett rolled her eyes again.

Lilah's throat tightened, her breath catching in her chest. Scarlett's words cut deep. 'Think what you want,' Lilah said to Scarlett. 'But I know the truth.' The words rolled off her tongue even though as soon as she said them, she wasn't sure. Did Aidan only like her 'because he was a man' and she'd offered herself to him? It didn't seem like that but he hadn't ever said how he felt.

'How do you like these?' Patricia pushed some fabric in front of Lilah. 'Wax wraps.'

'They're nice,' Lilah said. 'I thought I could attempt making some honey fudge. If it was any good, you could wrap it in this.'

'I like that idea,' Patricia said.

Lilah didn't look at Scarlett but sensed yet another eye roll.

Patricia checked her watch. 'Scarlett, if you're going into town, can you nip into the hardware store and get me some varnish?'

'I can't,' Scarlett said. 'I've got another job to do for Zeb.'

'I could go,' Lilah said. A walk would clear her head.

'Oh, thank you,' Patricia said. 'But no need to make a special trip.'

'I don't mind. It's not exactly far.'

'Well, if you're sure, let me write down exactly what kind I need and I'll give you some money.'

Scarlett crossed her arms and pulled a face. Lilah ignored her, waiting as Patricia scribbled something on the paper.

The streets of Glenbriar weren't too busy. As she headed towards the hardware store, Lilah saw two women outside a shop talking. Almost simultaneously, she realised the shop was the hair salon and one of the women was Hayley. Lilah stopped when she saw the other person. Elise. Could she perhaps cross the road? Had they seen her? Too late. Hayley waved.

Lilah lifted her hand in return and slowly made her way towards them. Maybe the wave would be enough and she could walk on by. Did they know about her and Aidan? Should she tell them? Would they believe it?

'Well, hello you,' Elise said in a manner that seemed friendly but somehow didn't extend into her eyes. They remained cool and guarded.

'Hi,' Lilah replied.

'Hey.' Hayley stepped forward and hugged her. 'And how exciting is this news about you and Aidan?'

'Oh, you know.' The heat in Lilah's cheeks was burning.

'Indeed, I do. Aidan messaged me. I was going to text you about it, but this is even better.'

'He messaged you?'

'Yes. Why do you look so shocked?' Hayley chuckled.

'No reason.' But her eyes drifted to Elise.

'Don't worry about me.' Elise's hand fanned across her chest. 'Aidan and I are done. I'm thrilled he's moved on and found... you.'

Lilah blinked and smiled, then glanced at Hayley. 'Thank you.'

Elise took a step closer. 'I need to get to work but I really hope the two of you find happiness together. Catch you later, Hayley.'

Lilah echoed Hayley's wave, watching Elise march up the street.

'So, how did it come about?' Hayley said with a grin. 'Did you seduce my cousin? Or did he capture you with his brooding looks and charm?'

'I'm not sure I know.' Lilah giggled.

Hayley looked at her for a long moment. 'I think he's made the perfect choice.'

'Do you really?'

'Yes. Why wouldn't I?'

'It's just... It's hard for me to believe. I mean, I've never had any kind of relationship. I'm scared that I've read him all wrong. What if deep down it's her he still wants...' She motioned her head in the direction Elise had walked.

Hayley reached out, gently squeezing Lilah's arm.

'Oh my god, I shouldn't have said any of that. Please, pretend I didn't.'

'Hey, it's ok,' Hayley said.

A shiver passed up Lilah's spine. Why had she spoken like that and to someone who was so friendly with Elise? Hayley always seemed so nice but would she keep this to herself?

'I won't repeat it to anyone,' Hayley insisted. 'But I can't forget you said it and I can't deny it worries me. Why would you think he still wants Elise?'

'Well, I mean, we have fun together, you know.'

'Hot sex, you mean?' Hayley said with a grin.

Flames lashed Lilah's cheeks, making her feel sunburnt. 'Well, yeah.'

Hayley chuckled. 'Nothing wrong with that.'

'I know. And that's all good, but he doesn't really say much. Not about anything important.'

'Hmm.' Hayley let out a sigh. 'That's pretty standard Aidan, to be honest. He can be reckless and gruff, short-tempered and totally uncommunicative. But ever since you arrived in his life, he's been a different man. I've never seen him smile as much. The fact he's moved on is great and he's loyal to people he cares about. If he's dating you, of course he cares about you.'

Lilah rubbed a circle on her forehead, massaging away the niggles that kept coming back whenever she thought about her future with him. 'It's just... Well, I've fallen for him so hard it scares me. Maybe he'll never like me as much as I like him.' *Love him.* Because she loved Aidan more than she'd ever loved anyone. But he'd loved Elise like that. How could she expect him to transfer that love to her? Just like she couldn't transfer her love for him to anyone else. She knew it wasn't possible. He could pretend to be over Elise, but could she ever really be gone from his heart?

'Give him time,' Hayley said. 'You've only been seeing each other for a short while. He maybe doesn't even know what he's feeling right now.'

'But how can I ever be good enough for him?'

'What? Don't look at it like that. Make sure he's good enough for you.'

'What do you mean?'

'You said before you haven't had much experience. Maybe Aidan is just one guy and nothing will come of it. Don't beat yourself up about it. Enjoy it, but don't set all your hopes on it unless that's what you want. Put yourself first.' Hayley pulled Lilah into an embrace and patted her back. This sisterly show of affection and kindness was like nothing Lilah had ever known before and it warmed her deeply. 'Now, I need to do some work. My first client cancelled but there's always stuff to do. Remember, trust in Aidan, trust in yourself, and take things one step at a time.'

Hayley's words played over and over again as Lilah entered the hardware shop and located the varnish. Was this just a step on the relationship ladder? She couldn't imagine feeling this strongly about anyone else.

As she passed Jim's house on the way back, she poked her head in to say hello. He was grinning and called her in to show off his new tin opener in operation. 'I love it, Jim. It's excellent.'

'Thank you, lass. Now you run off and see Aidan. The lad'll be missing you.'

'You think?'

'Yes. I see how he looks when you're not with him. I know the feeling well. Every day I feel like that without my Jenny.'

'Oh Jim, that's sad.'

'Not to worry. Now, you run along and live your young life to the full. Don't waste a second when you could be together.'

'Thank you, Jim.' She gave him a brief hug. 'You're such a lovely neighbour.'

'Away with you.' He chuckled to himself as she headed out the door. She entered the garden through the gate and went around the side of the house, following the sound of the strimmer. Shirtless and covered in beads of sweat, stood Aidan, moving from side to side as he progressed through the long grass. Lilah stood still, taking him all in. How was it possible such a man was hers? Hayley and Jim had faith. Could she?

Chapter Twenty-Two

Aidan

The soft touch of Lilah's lips on his sent surges of agonising delight through Aidan's stomach. With his back to the door, he had nowhere to go, and that was fine by him. No other woman had ever made him feel this raw with desire. Even Elise. It had to be said… Though not out loud or at this moment. Lilah tasted good. She kissed him harder, clamping her hands to the back of his head and moving him closer to her. What a way to start the weekend.

He slammed the Crafty Bee Barn door shut behind him as Lilah wrapped a leg around his thigh. He lifted her, turning her around and holding her against the door, so they were face to face. She squealed and clung to him before placing a beautifully soft kiss on his cheek. His need for her was off the charts. He couldn't get enough of her.

Her breathing was rapid and close to his ear. 'I just want you, Aidan,' she whispered.

Aidan met her mouth and kissed her again. Then he heard a voice on the path. Someone talking to Maya.

'Shit,' he muttered and Lilah climbed down from him. 'She's here on Saturday.' He took a deep breath and kissed her brow, then stepped back as Patricia opened the door.

'Oh, what are you two doing here?' She frowned at them.

'Just taking a gander. The place is looking good,' Aidan said, adjusting the neckline of his t-shirt. 'Do you think it's time to open to the public?'

'Yes,' Patricia said. 'I need to bite the bullet and do it.'

'I think I'll make a new gate,' he added. 'And fence off the entrance, so we don't have customers wandering into the garden.'

'Yes, that would be sensible.'

'I'll go and pace it out, then you can look into the kind of panels you fancy.'

'Thank you.' She beamed at him, then turned to Lilah. 'Would you come with me a second? Let me show you what I made earlier.'

'Um... Yeah.'

Aidan gave Lilah a quick wink before he left. So much for thinking it would be a good idea to set her up as his girlfriend to show people he'd moved on. He hadn't expected to enjoy it quite this much. Or to want her quite this much, though it shouldn't surprise him. She'd always had a way of setting his insides on fire.

As he made his way back to the cottage, he paced a line where he could make a new gate in the fence that ran along the street. It would be the easiest and shortest access point to the Crafty Bee Barn. At the gate, a small red car was parked. Scarlett. She'd obviously dropped off Mum again but why was she hanging about? Aidan would happily avoid her, except for a slight pang of worry. Was she ok? As he got closer, he peered in and saw her deep in a text message. Her fingers raced as she typed.

About to walk the other direction, he'd just stepped onto the path when Scarlett looked up. Her expression had the usual angry frown but something else lingered in her eyes. Sadness? Worry?

Aidan leaned over the fence and spoke into her open window. 'Everything ok?'

'Obviously.'

'Good. Just checking.'

She let out a huff.

'What's your problem?' Aidan said. 'Why the constant scowl? You should take anger management classes.'

'Hark who's talking. Says the man who looks like he's chewed a wasp.'

Maybe she had a point. Often he felt angry and didn't know what to do about it, but since Lilah, nothing had felt so bad.

'Well, I'm happy now. I must be doing something right.'

'Oh, please. Just you wait until it all goes tits up. You'll see I was right all along.' Scarlett leaned her elbow on the edge of the open window, her expression unyielding. 'It's blatantly obvious by the way she's not really your girlfriend. You're only doing this to annoy Elise. If you're still so obsessed with Elise, go back to her and tell her to break off her engagement with Finlay. You could get back together before it's too late.'

Aidan shook his head then glanced behind him. Lilah stood on the path, her eyes narrowed and her arms folded. *Crap.*

'Well, I gotta go, lovebirds,' Scarlett said. 'Have fun.' She started the engine and drove away.

Aidan's heart sank as he took a step towards Lilah. 'Is everything ok?'

She stared back at him, then glanced sideways. 'Sure. Your mum wants to know if she can order a white picket fence. She says that'll look nice.'

'Right. Yes, she can order whatever she likes. I'm sure I'll work out how to put it up. Listen, what Scarlett said there...'

'Yes?'

'It's not true.'

'Ok.' Lilah seemed to be x-raying him to the point where he started to wonder if he'd said something wrong.

'I'm never going back to Elise. You know that, don't you?'

'Sure.' Lilah nodded. 'I should go tell your mum about the fence.'

Aidan watched her go and his chest tightened. She was only going to the barn but even that seemed too far away. He didn't want to be without her.

On Wednesday morning, Aidan paced outside the council building near the riverside in Perth, his mind racing.

'Hey.' Lilah took hold of his arm. 'Are you ok?'

'Sure. I just want this to get started.' He hated hanging about. Lilah's employers had been generous enough to give her the day off to come to the meeting and for someone who'd never done anything like this before, she seemed remarkably calm. Maybe that was *why* she was so calm; she didn't know what to expect.

'Your friend is definitely coming?' Lilah asked. 'I know you said he's a busy man,'

'Yeah, he is. He has so many commitments it's almost impossible to tie him down to a time and place, but he said he would come along.'

'Could that be him?' Lilah pointed with her eyes and Aidan spun around.

'Aidan!' Gabriel Wilder marched up to him and bear hugged him.

'You made it.'

'I did. And hello. You must be Lilah.'

'Hi.' She shook his hand.

'Nice to meet you: the woman who managed to get an elusive meeting.'

'I just said I wanted one.'

'Well, you got a better result than either of us. He wouldn't even talk to us on the phone.'

'Third time lucky,' Lilah said.

'Let's make it count.' Aidan gave her a gentle pat on the back.

'I've got all the results from the polls on my blog and people are definitely against houses on that field,' Gabriel said.

'That's great,' Aidan said. 'Because I've had another idea. How about we consider a community buyout? I've been researching it and there have been quite a few examples in other places. That way we could preserve it but there's also scope for environmentally friendly developments like a Climate Café.'

'I'm loving the sound of that.'

'And let's not forget the site of the old amusement park for the affordable houses,' Lilah said. 'I want to suggest it to him. How do we know if it's been thought of before?'

'We'll definitely get that in,' Aidan said.

'Right, we have a plan.' Gabe gave him a clap on the upper arm. 'Let's see if we can get him listening.'

As they entered the meeting room, Aidan took a deep breath. Jacob McCash wasn't alone. Two of the councillors Aidan had spoken to previously were there too.

'Is it ok if they sit in?' Jacob asked. 'They're interested in what you have to say.'

'The more the merrier,' Lilah said before Aidan had even opened his mouth.

Their expressions didn't exactly exude 'interest'. If anything, they were a mix of irritation and disdain. Aidan's resolve hardened. *Nothing will deter me.*

He, Lilah and Gabriel took their place together at one side of the table, ready to present their case.

Jacob asked for some introductions and Aidan said who they were.

'You already know my thoughts on the ecological importance of the field, its role in preserving biodiversity, plus the negative impact a housing development would have on the local ecosystem as I've detailed these in my formal objection. But today we come with further ideas for moving forward.'

'So Miss Clarke indicated during our phone call,' Jacob said. 'But it's somewhat irregular, I might add.'

'Maybe,' Lilah said. 'But three of you turned up and that must count for something.'

Aidan smirked. This tenacious Lilah was a force to be reckoned with.

'I've canvassed the proposal on my blog and my podcasts,' Gabriel said. 'And local opinion is strongly opposed to the development. I have the results of all the polls and questionnaires. The preferred use for the field is to leave it as it is or use it in an eco-friendly way that would benefit the community.'

'I have some ideas that are both environmentally friendly and less invasive than a housing development,' Aidan said. 'Starting with a community buy-out and moving on to the installation of a wildlife hide and possibly a climate café. I'd also like to draw attention to the site of the old amusement park as a more sensible site for new houses.'

Aidan watched the reactions of the council members from the corner of his eye. One scribbled notes, the other leaned forward with renewed interest, but Jacob McCash remained impassive. 'That site is in an awkward location.'

'What does that mean?' Lilah asked.

'Its proximity to the railway line makes it less than ideal.'

'But a site that would crush an ecosystem is ideal, is it?'

Jacob looked like he was biting his tongue. 'It's still under investigation.'

'Then I hope you're investigating other options too. Otherwise, it makes the council look like a bulldozer,' Lilah said. 'What happened to all these green initiatives? Even when I was at school, we were being told how the council wanted to preserve the environment and we had lessons about reduce, reuse and recycle. How does this proposal go with that?' Lilah's red hair made her look fiery and not someone to cross. She was more threatening than she had been armed with the log.

Aidan exchanged a look with Gabriel and they both grinned. Neither Jacob nor the councillors seemed to have an answer.

'Well, thank you for your take on the position,' one councillor said. 'Obviously there's still much discussion to be had, but it's given us an interesting insight.'

'When can we expect to find out your decision?' Aidan asked.

'It's impossible to put a time on it, but we'll give everything you've said due consideration.'

Aidan, Lilah and Gabriel left silently and walked down the stairs well away from the room before Aidan spoke. 'I think you terrified them.'

'Me?' Lilah stared at him.

'You terrified me,' Gabriel said.

'Oh god. Did I say something stupid?'

'No, you just said it like it is.' Aidan patted her on the back.

Gabriel chuckled. 'You sure did, and it's exactly what they needed to hear. That council needs a good shake up. Some of them are like giant planks blocking the way of sustainable progress. They're so backward thinking.'

'There's not much else we can do now except wait,' Aidan said.

After a brief lunch with Gabriel, they went their separate ways and Aidan and Lilah caught the bus back to Glenbriar. 'You were great,' he said, smiling at her, his chest swelling. 'The first time I saw you, you were ready to tackle two big guys with a log. But today you took on three high heidyins in a war of words and you've given us a fighting chance.'

'I hope so.'

They returned to Woodend and Aidan checked in on his mum in the barn. She was dog-sitting Maya, who jumped up from her position at the door to greet Aidan.

'How did it go?' Patricia asked.

'Lilah was amazing. She told them straight.'

Patricia smiled. 'That's good. She's not at all like what I thought when we first met.'

'I wish you'd tell Scarlett that.'

'I have, but you know Scarlett. So stubborn.'

'Yup. Thanks for looking after Maya.'

'No problem. She's so well-behaved, I hardly have to do anything.'

Aidan went back to the house and into the kitchen. Lilah had a small envelope in her hands. Maya ran to her and Lilah cuddled her.

'What's that?' Aidan asked.

'An invitation.' She handed it to him. 'For you and me to Finlay and Elise's engagement party.'

Aidan's heart sank. 'Oh, great.'

'Don't you want to go?'

'Do you?' His fingers tightened around the invitation. Part of him wanted to accept and show the world that he had moved on. But another part of him balked at the thought of it.

'I don't know. I've never been to anything like that. Do you think I'd look out of place? Everyone will be so glamorous.'

'You're just as good as any of them.' That settled it. He was doing it. Lilah deserved to be seen and he wanted to be seen with her. 'You can wear my favourite dress.'

'Why is it your favourite?'

'Because you look so good in it... And because it's fun to take off.'

Lilah grinned.

'We'll show them,' he said.

CHAPTER TWENTY-THREE

Lilah

At the door of the Crafty Bee Barn, Lilah stopped. What was that noise? Had Maya got in? It sounded like her sniffing around but it couldn't be her; she'd gone out with Aidan for her walk. Lilah pushed open the door and was met by the warm scent of the flowers Patricia had put on the side table.

Her eyes landed on Scarlett, sitting alone at one of the crafting tables, tears streaming down her face. What on earth? Lilah froze. She never expected hard-as-nails Scarlett to cry. *Should I approach?* Did she dare? She didn't want this thrown back at her.

'Scarlett?' Lilah murmured. 'Are you ok?'

Scarlett's head snapped up, her eyes red and puffy. She quickly wiped away her tears. 'What do you want?'

'I don't want anything. I just wondered if you were ok.' Lilah took a seat at the other table. 'It's not like you to be upset. Do you want me to get someone? Or I'll go away if you want to be alone.'

Scarlett pushed away her tears and didn't make eye contact. 'Have you seen my mum?'

'No,' Lilah said. 'I've just got back from work, so I don't know if she was here or not. Have you called her?'

'She's not replied to my message yet.'

'Do you want me to call Aidan? Or your boyfriend, though I don't know his number.'

'No. Don't call Zeb.'

'Ok.' Lilah fiddled with a stack of bookmarks on the table. Should she say more or just leave? 'Are things not going well with Zeb? Have you split up?'

'Do I look like I need a pity party?' Scarlett muttered. 'Just because you've wormed your way into my brother's bed doesn't mean—'

'It's not pity, Scarlett. It's called concern.' Lilah got to her feet. 'We may not be friends, but that doesn't mean I want to see you hurting. I was only offering help. If you don't want it, then fine. I'll leave you to it.'

'If you really must know, things between Zeb and me... they're not good,' she muttered.

'I don't need to know, but I'll listen if you want to tell me.'

'What? So you can go and tell everyone?'

'Who would I tell? You're so fond of reminding me that I don't have any friends. I'm not begging you to tell me. I was offering to listen because I thought you might need someone but you've got such a crazy, warped opinion of me, it's probably better if I just leave.'

'I don't get men,' Scarlett mumbled. 'Why do they change as soon as you start dating?'

Lilah wasn't sure she understood. Aidan hadn't changed since they'd started dating, except he was more affectionate, but that wasn't a bad thing. 'Um... I don't know.'

'It's like, well, he's controlling. He keeps asking me to do weird stuff he says is for his job but I'm not sure it's legit. I've seen strange guys hanging around outside his flat and they kinda give me the creeps.'

Lilah took the seat opposite Scarlett. 'What do you think he's up to?'

'I don't know. Maybe drugs or something.'

'Could be,' Lilah said with a sigh. 'That's what it was like with my mum, only she'd be the one hanging about outside, trying to get what she couldn't afford.'

'Fucking hell,' Scarlett said. 'What can I do?'

'Split up with him. You don't want to have a serious relationship with someone like that, do you?'

'But what if he gets mad and comes after me?'

Lilah gave a little shrug. She'd seen that happen to her mum more than once. It was part and parcel of her normal. 'Get Aidan to go with you when you tell him. That might do the trick.'

'Do you think it will?'

Lilah nodded. 'Yeah. That kind of people are usually class-A cowards hidden behind a tough-guy front. He sounds like my little brother.'

'Jaxon?' Scarlett said.

'Yep, the very one.'

'Zeb knows him.'

'Does he?' Lilah frowned.

'Yup. He mentioned him yesterday. Apparently, Jaxon has been hanging around Glenbriar for a week or so now.'

Lilah had changed her number when she got her new phone and hadn't given him her new one. She'd also avoided checking her old one for messages. Keeping away from Jaxon's troubles was better for her sanity.

'Well, I've no idea why. I don't really talk to him much anymore,' she said sadly, though it was partly self-preservation. 'In fact, I don't really see my family at all.'

'That's like me and my dad,' Scarlett said. 'He walked out a few years ago and since then, we've hardly spoken.'

'Families can be so complicated.'

'Sure can.' Scarlett gave Lilah a long hard stare. 'Thanks.'

'For what?'

'Listening to me, when, well, I've been—'

'A bitch?'

'Yeah. I guess I deserved that.'

'You did. And hey, I won't tell anyone about what you just said, but you should tell Aidan. No way will he let a guy push you around.'

'Yeah, ok.'

'I'll go and see if he's back,' Lilah said. 'You should talk to him ASAP and get this thing sorted.'

Scarlett sucked on her lip, apparently in two minds about it. 'Maybe.'

'The sooner you do something about it, the better you'll feel.' Lilah left Scarlett in the barn and returned to the house. Aidan wasn't back and she sent him a message asking if he was far away. He replied within minutes.

AIDAN: Just been to the shop. Back in fifteen minutes. Is everything ok?

LILAH: Scarlett is upset and needs to talk to you.

AIDAN: Has she been nasty to you again? I'll kick her out if she has.

Lilah smirked at his words.

LILAH: No, she's having issues with her boyfriend. She's told me not to tell, so best you hear it from her.

AIDAN: Ok. On my way. See you shortly x

Lilah touched the little 'x' with her fingertip like somehow it connected her to Aidan and she felt his kiss for real on her cheek. She returned to the barn and opened the door. 'Aidan's on his way back. Why not come in and wait for him?'

Scarlett followed Lilah into the cottage through the French doors.

'I'll put the kettle on.' Lilah left Scarlett in the living room and headed to the kitchen. This situation was surreal. She appreciated the thaw in Scarlett, but she wasn't sure she trusted her. As she made the drinks, she heard Aidan's voice in the garden and she opened the side door. Maya greeted her with slobbery kisses and a waggy tail before padding onto the grass and lying down under a shady bush.

'Where's Scarlett? he asked.

'In the living room.'

'And you're making her tea?'

'Just being polite. She isn't her usual self. She's really upset.'

Aidan frowned and closed the side door. 'Really? That doesn't sound like her, not unless she's having a tantrum about something.'

'It's definitely not a tantrum. Come and see.' She took Aidan by the arm and led him into the living room.

'Hey,' he said to Scarlett. She stood by the open French door, fidgeting with her rings. 'I hear there's something you want to talk to me about.'

'I... I can't.'

'You really should,' Lilah said quickly. 'Or let me if you don't want to say it.'

'Ok. Fine. You tell him.'

'Her boyfriend has been asking her to do stuff she doesn't like.'

'Like what?' Aidan frowned.

'Deliver stuff to people. Take messages. He won't take no for an answer,' Scarlett said, without looking at either of them.

'She wants to break up with him,' Lilah continued. 'But... Well, will you go with her?'

'Sure,' Aidan said. 'If that's what you want.' He glanced at Scarlett. 'Is it?'

'Yeah. Cause he's freaking me out.'

'Then we'll go,' Aidan said. 'Right now, if you want.'

'Yeah, ok,' Scarlett said. 'I need to grab my bag. Give me a minute.' She darted out the door and Lilah half-wondered if that was her doing a runner, but before she could act on that thought, Aidan sat on the arm of a chair and beckoned her forward. He took her hands and pulled her onto his lap. 'When did you and her become friends?' He kissed her cheek and she melted into him.

'We didn't. But I don't like the idea of her getting hurt.'

'You're a sweetheart.' He stroked her hair.

'Am I?'

'Yes. You always put others before yourself, even when you don't really like them.'

She wasn't sure that was true. She definitely didn't feel that way about her own family. Had she done enough to help them? Mostly she buried her head in the sand and pretended they didn't exist.

She leaned her head on Aidan's shoulder. 'I'm so nervous about this party. What if no one talks to me?'

'We don't have to go if you don't want to.' He pulled her close and she loved being here so much. The strength of his arms around her made this the safest and happiest place in the universe.

'If you're there, it'll be fine.'

Scarlett returned with her bag and Lilah jumped off Aidan's knee. It wasn't like she was doing anything wrong, but she wanted to keep Scarlett in this nicer mood and she doubted Scarlett seeing her 'slobbering all over' Aidan – as she'd put it – would please her.

'Let's go then,' Aidan said. He whistled Maya and they headed down the hill. Aidan was tall, upright, and commanding. Lilah could almost touch the power radiating from him. If someone like him had turned up at her mum's flat, all the unsavoury guests would have run a mile. Hopefully Zeb would do that. Scarlett wasn't her best friend and never would be, but Lilah knew only too well the horrible crawling dread of having nasty people creeping about in your life.

None of them spoke; the tension built in Lilah's chest to the point of hurting. She half expected Scarlett to chicken out before they got there. Scarlett was chewing her cuticles and glancing around every few seconds. They passed the little pond Aidan had fallen into and turned onto Rowan Way. Lilah glanced at the box-shaped maisonette she used to call home but didn't feel much. The unfamiliar curtains had shut out her old life. Other streets led off this one and further along was The Back Wynd that eventually led down to the main road. Most of the buildings on that street were older Victorian-style buildings but nothing as large as the tenement blocks like the ones in Dundee where Lilah's mum now lived. The houses on the Back Wynd were bleak and very square. At one time, they'd probably housed families who worked in the distilleries or the old mill.

Scarlett turned into a close halfway down the road and headed up the old stone steps. Lilah followed behind Aidan. Maya panted as she bounded up. Scarlett stopped outside a door with bashed paintwork, then knocked on it, her hand trembling slightly. Aidan stood beside her, a pillar of strength, while Lilah stood a few steps back, holding Maya. She'd been in places like this so often but it didn't make her feel any better. Definitely not. It made her aware of exactly the kind of thing they were likely to encounter.

After a few seconds, the door swung open, revealing Zeb. He might have been handsome if he was better nourished but his skin was grey and his eyes sunken. Longish, somewhat unkempt hair hung around his face.

'What's all this?' Zeb sneered, his eyes darting between Scarlett and Aidan. 'Scarlett, babe, where you been? Are these your mates?'

'This is my brother.'

'Ah, you're the brother, are you? And who are you?' He glowered at Lilah.

'Never you mind,' Aidan said. 'Scarlett's got something to tell you. Then you can consider yourself out of our lives forever.'

'Oh yeah?' He glared at Scarlett.

'We're finished, Zeb. I don't want anything more to do with you.'

Zeb's smile faded. 'You think you can just leave me?'

Aidan stepped forward. 'Yes, Zeb, she does think that because she can. You don't own her. So say goodbye and stay away from her if you know what's good for you.'

Zeb's eyes narrowed at Aidan. 'Seriously, you're threatening me?'

'Well spotted,' Lilah muttered.

Aidan stepped even closer, his voice low and dangerous. 'Watch your step, mate. I've got a lot of friends in this town. A lot. And the kind of friends you have are no match for them, so back down.'

'Like I care anyway. She wasn't exactly a world-class shag. Fuck the lot of you.' Zeb slammed the door shut.

Maya's head turned swiftly from the door to look up the steps towards the next landing. Lilah held her tight, but she understood why Maya was curious. A shadow wavered around the bend in the stairs like someone was standing there, just out of sight. Lilah hadn't heard any doors closing or footsteps coming down, but then, she hadn't been listening. If someone had come down, she didn't blame them for not wanting to get involved in this.

Scarlett let out a shaky breath, tears welling up in her eyes. Lilah moved closer and wrapped an arm around her. 'It's ok.'

'Let's get you back to Mum's.' Aidan guided her back to the stairs.

'Hopefully you won't be seeing him again,' Lilah said.

'She won't be.' Aidan rubbed his fist across the palm of his hand. 'I don't believe in violence but I won't let anyone hurt my family.'

'I think he got the message loud and clear,' Lilah said. 'His type are quick to hide in their shells and he doesn't seem like a big enough fish to have any influence.'

Scarlett nodded. 'He's not a big fish. He wants to be but he's too scared. That's why he was always wanting me to do his dirty work.'

As they walked away from Zeb's flat, Lilah turned around. She had a feeling someone was at the door of the close where they'd just exited.

'Right, we'll walk you to Mum's and you take it easy for a bit, ok?' he said.

'Ok,' Scarlett rubbed her eyes with the heels of her hands. The houses in Patricia's street were a lot pleasanter than the ones they'd just left. They were Victorian in style too but had bay windows and well-kept gardens. Patricia wasn't home, but Scarlett had a key and Lilah and Aidan left her in the house. She gave them both a watery smile.

'She always chose to hang about with idiots,' Aidan muttered as he and Lilah headed up the hill towards Woodend Cottage.

'Really? At school, her gang used to think I was the idiot.'

'Exactly, and look how wrong she was about that.' He tipped her a wink.

'Thanks.'

'Just saying it like it is.'

As they got back to Woodend Cottage, it started to drizzle.

'Let's grab a jacket,' Aidan said. 'Then we can take Maya for a walk before the rain gets heavy.'

They'd barely got to the gate at the woods when it started to pour. At a jog, they went around the shortest circuit, letting Maya do her business before hightailing it back to the house.

'I'm getting soaked,' Lilah laughed, holding her hands above her head.

'Me too.' Aidan was ahead on the path and he turned as he ran, a smile on his face. Stopping, he waited and as Lilah caught up with him, he took her face in his hands and gazed at her.

'Kissing in the rain is supposed to be very romantic,' Lilah said, unable to focus anywhere but at his deep, dark eyes.

'Shall we find out?'

She nodded and Aidan dipped in and placed a soft kiss on her lips. Raindrops dripped from Aidan's forehead to hers and ran down her nose. Their lips meshed and she moaned as Aidan's tongue touched hers. Her clothes were sticking to her. Aidan drew her close and the wet friction between them was hot.

'Let's take this home,' he murmured.

'Ok.'

He took her hand and they ran down the path, Maya bounding ahead. She loved the sense of belonging she had when their hands were linked like this. As they approached the cottage, Lilah squinted through the rain. Sitting on the cottage doorstep was a hunched figure. 'Who's that?'

'No idea,' Aidan said.

The person looked up at the voices and Lilah froze, clinging to Aidan's arm.

'What's wrong?' he asked.

'That's Jaxon. My brother. What's he doing here?'

Aidan opened the gate and Maya bounded up to Jaxon. He drew back, shaking slightly and giving Lilah and Aidan a pleading glance.

'Maya, come here,' Aidan said, and she moved away from Jaxon directly.

Lilah stiffened. Why did it look like he was laying on the *I'm-in-trouble* act a bit too thickly?

'What are you doing here?' Lilah asked, wiping wet hair away from her eyes.

His soaked clothes were worn and stained and he peered at her, his eyes slightly glassy. 'I... I have nowhere else to go. I've been sleeping rough for days, and I thought maybe you could help me.'

Lilah crossed her arms. 'How did you know where I was?'

'I was at Zeb's. I heard you and I followed.'

'At Zeb's?' Aidan said.

'Well, I was going to see him when you guys came in, so I hid up on the next landing.'

'What were you doing at Zeb's?' Lilah asked.

'Looking for somewhere to stay, you know? But I figured he wouldn't be best pleased after busting with his girlfriend, so I thought I could ask you guys.'

'We can't take you in just whenever you feel like it. You need to sort yourself out and take responsibility for your own life.'

'I am,' he said, huddling his arms around himself and shivering. 'I just need a couple of days. I utterly swear. Two days and I'll go. Please.'

'Let's get inside,' Aidan said. 'We're all getting soaked.'

'And what about me?' Jaxon asked.

'We'll talk inside.' Aidan unlocked the door and let him in. 'Go in there and sit for a moment.' He opened the door to the living room and let Jaxon in.

'Thanks, man. I really appreciate this.'

Aidan closed the door behind him and Lilah shook her head. 'This is not good. He's up to something, I'm sure.'

'I can't in all conscience leave him out on the streets. Let's give him the benefit of the doubt, shall we? Like I did for you when everyone said I shouldn't.'

Lilah's eyes met his. He gave her a little smile and ran his thumb over her cheek, wiping away some excess water. Yes, he was right. Scarlett had lectured him about her the same way she now wanted to let rip about Jaxon. Aidan had been right to trust her and she'd be forever grateful he'd given her that chance. She should let her brother have the same. But it threatened the sanctuary she'd found with Aidan.

'I know you're right. I just don't know if I can trust him. He's caused so much trouble in the past, and I don't want him to spoil what we have here.'

Aidan placed his hand on her arm. 'I understand. Let's give him the two days that he wants. I know some safe places he can go to after that. He's just a kid. He shouldn't have to sleep on the streets.'

'Fine. Just two days.' That might work. Sure, she wanted him to be safe but she didn't like the idea of him hanging around. He always brought trouble.

CHAPTER TWENTY-FOUR

Aidan

Aidan stood in front of the mirror, straightening his tie with a sigh. He glanced over his reflection, adjusting his jacket, and ran a hand through his thick, dark hair. Finlay and Elise's engagement party was upon them. The prospect of facing Elise and her judgy friends was not appealing. He'd half-hoped Lilah would decide she didn't want to go but she seemed quite determined. And really, he quite liked the idea of being seen out with her. It would send a very clear message to everyone – he'd moved on.

Lilah entered the room, wearing the slate blue dress that encased her slender figure perfectly. Aidan watched her in the mirror. She bit her lip nervously, her eyes flickering between him and the door.

'So beautiful.' He turned to her and smiled before placing his hands on her pale shoulders and kissing her neck. 'Shall I zip you up?'

'Please.'

He tugged the zip gently up her back. 'I'll get the necklace for you too. It goes perfectly with this dress.'

'Are you sure?'

'Of course. I gave it to you and I can't imagine it on anyone but you.'

Lilah stroked her fingertips around her neck.

'Give me two minutes and I'll get it.' He left the room and went into his study, locating the box of jewels in the writing desk. In his mind, Lilah now owned the necklace, though she wanted him to keep it with the other jewellery. He'd never offered any of the pieces to Elise. She liked modern jewellery, as Finlay had recently discovered with the engagement ring, and would have scoffed at these. But Lilah had such a classical natural beauty that they suited her perfectly.

Had Finlay already had their grandmother's ring reset? Did it even matter? It wasn't his concern anymore.

He took out the necklace and put the lid back on the box. He probably should have them valued. His dad always said they were worth something but who knew if that was true? As he left the study, Jaxon came out of the bathroom. This was day two of his stay. Tomorrow was D-day. Aidan had spoken to him about taking him to a safe house and Jaxon seemed ok with it.

'You want me to do anything while you're out?' Jaxon asked. 'Cut the grass or anything?'

'That's kind, thanks. But just rest. Use the time to chill.'

'Thanks, mate. You're one of the good uns.'

Aidan closed the door to his bedroom. Lilah stood at the mirror, gazing at her reflection. He moved in behind her and lifted the necklace over her head. 'Stunning,' he whispered, just below her ear, turning the word into a kiss. He kept his lips on her skin longer than was necessary but the taste of her was addictive. Pulling back, he focused his attention on the clasp. Otherwise, all he'd want to do was remove her clothes and take her to bed. 'There, you look like a princess. You'll outshine everyone.'

Lilah blushed and fidgeted with a dangling jewel on the necklace. 'You think? I'm just... nervous, you know? It's my first party with you, and...'

Aidan ran his hands around her waist and pulled her closer. 'It'll be fine. Together we can do this.' He pressed another kiss on her neck, then another, until she turned around in his arms and met his lips full on.

'I would rather...' he said, barely breaking the kiss. She hadn't stopped. 'Spend the evening here doing this with you.' He drew back. 'But your brother being here is a bit of a passion killer. So let's get this party done and dusted. Tomorrow we'll get him somewhere safe and we can get on with our lives.'

Lilah sighed, her gaze shifting to the door. 'Yeah, about that. Well, about Jaxon. I'm not sure it's a good idea to leave him alone at the cottage. What if something happens?'

'Such as?'

'I don't know. It just makes me nervous.'

'Well, unless he burns it down, I think we're ok. But I'll drop Maya into my mum's just in case. She's the most precious thing I have here.'

Patricia was giving them a lift to the party, so it was a natural thing to do. Scarlett wasn't going as she was still feeling rough after the breakup and Maya would be good company for her.

'Ok.' Lilah sighed.

Aidan leaned in and kissed her forehead. 'Come on, let's go.'

They said bye to Jaxon, collected Maya and walked towards Patricia's house.

'Thank goodness we're not walking the whole way,' Lilah said. 'These heels are killing me already.'

Aidan scanned her up and down. No one would believe this was the same person he'd mistaken for a boy at the fair all those weeks ago. Almost as soon as he'd realised she was a woman and they'd got talking, he'd seen something in her, but he'd never been able to pinpoint what. Even now, when she looked utterly stunning, he couldn't place what it was about her that made his heart stir.

Scarlett seemed relieved at having Maya to look after and Aidan felt a little sorry for her. Hidden deep behind the angry exterior was a sensitive soul. He knew the feeling. Perhaps if he'd been a bit more sensitive towards Elise, none of this would be happening. Whether that was good or bad, he wasn't sure.

Patricia ran them to the Cross Keys Inn. Not so long ago, this was where he'd run into Finlay and Elise, and they'd interrupted his drink with Lilah and Hayley.

It was all decked out with bunting around the outdoor seating area, fluttering in the wind. The river rushed by, swooshing over pebbles and rocks. Glasses clinked and people chattered while soft music played. The outdoor deck was like the prow of a ship and Aidan leaned on the railing, looking out, sipping his champagne.

Hayley had found Lilah and pulled her over to introduce her to some of her other friends. Aidan didn't feel like socialising. Mostly he wanted to limit time spent with Finlay and Elise. Difficult at a party meant to be celebrating them. He focused on the water, following its progress across a cluster of stones. Some kids sat near the bank, close to the wobbly bridge, laughing and chucking pebbles. Aidan and Finlay had done stuff like that together as kids. How had it all gone so wrong?

'Hey, you.'

He glanced around at a woman's voice and came face to face with Elise. She interlocked her fingers and leaned her wrists on the railing beside him.

'Hi.' He took a large swig of the champagne he'd been handed on arrival. It was a drink he didn't particularly like and the bubbles tickled his nose. 'Nice party,' he said. 'This place is... Nice.'

'Nice?' Elise laughed. 'You have such a way with words.'

He didn't miss the sarcasm. 'What's that supposed to mean?'

'Let's face it, Aidan, you never say how you feel. It's ironic you've gone into public speaking because you're useless at personal speaking. If you'd said something, I might have waited for you. If I'd known that's what you wanted. And if I knew it was worth my while or you cared enough. Because it wasn't like you ever actually told me.'

'What? That's not true.'

'Isn't it? Did you ever once tell me you loved me? Did you ask me to wait? Did you explain why you thought it was a good idea to put our relationship on hold for a year and what I could expect when you came back?'

'Well... No.'

'No. Exactly.'

'Why are you saying this now?'

'Because this is all... all wrong,' she said through gritted teeth.

'What is?'

'This engagement. I'm not sure I can do it.'

Aidan shook his head at his glass. 'No way, Elise. No way. You can't say that now.'

'Why not? We could still—'

'No. I'm with Lilah now.'

'Oh, come on.' She glanced around. 'Lilah is sweet and you've had your fun with her. It's not like she's going to stick with you forever. Let her go.'

'But—'

Elise held up her hands. 'Listen, this is not my call but if she's all that to you, then I hope you've told her how you feel because if you don't, she won't stick around. No one will.'

Aidan turned away, and his eyes found Lilah in the bar just inside. She was laughing and appeared happier than ever. Hayley laughed too and so did some others. And there were men in the group. Men who were checking out Lilah with undisguised admiration. Aidan's blood heated. He couldn't blame them for finding her attractive but he couldn't bear the idea of her going off with someone else. What he once felt for Elise was a poor second to this. He downed his champagne and plonked the glass on top of the wooden rail. 'See you,' he said to Elise.

He made his way across the deck and inside, then in beside Lilah.

'Hey.' He threw his arm around her shoulder. 'What's all the hilarity?'

Lilah glanced up, her eyes sparkling. She leaned into him. The sound of laughter and chatter faded into the background as they focused on each other.

Aidan couldn't tear his gaze away from her. He would never look at anyone else, ever. She was radiant and her good cheer was infectious. She'd brought joy and hope to his life where it had been empty before.

'Are you having fun?' he asked.

Lilah's cheeks tinged with a rosy hue. 'Yeah, it's a good party. What about you? This isn't really your thing, is it?'

Aidan's grip on her shoulder tightened ever so slightly. 'Don't worry about me. I'm happy if you're happy. You deserve happiness. You're so good at making other people feel good about themselves. Jim, Scarlett, people at your work, me.'

'I haven't done very much.'

'You always do your best. Now, will you dance with me?'

'I'll try but I'm not sure I'm any good at dancing.'

'Then we can be terrible together. Come on.' He led her inside to the dance floor, not caring if people were watching or gossiping.

As they swayed gently to the music, his gaze remained solely on Lilah. The outside world faded away, and all that mattered was the connection they shared. This was where he belonged and he wasn't going to let her get away or leave it to chance this time.

CHAPTER TWENTY-FIVE

Lilah

Soft music filled the room, and Lilah closed her eyes. That way her senses were heightened and being pressed close to Aidan with his arm around her was like being in a cocoon – a safe place she never wanted to leave. Somewhere nearby people still laughed and chatted, glasses clinked, and chairs scraped on the polished floor. But in that moment, there was only her and Aidan.

They swayed to the gentle rhythm, and Lilah let out a sigh. When she opened her eyes, her heart flickered. He was looking intently at her. His dark irises were almost as black as his pupils, and they were boring into her. Should she say something? She wasn't sure what. Her mind had jammed and she was little more than mush in his arms.

The heat of his palm on her back sent tremors through her; her heart was racing. Did this feel as good for him as it did for her? She rested her head on his shoulder, inhaling his familiar scent.

Aidan's hand tightened slightly and Lilah smiled. If time could stand still, this music play forever, and she could stay wrapped in Aidan's arms, then everything would be perfect. But other niggles played in her mind. She caught Elise's eyes on her and the pangs intensified. And then there was Jaxon. What might he be doing?

The final notes of the song echoed through the room, and Aidan released her. Reality rushed back in.

'I think we should go,' she said.

'Why? I thought you were enjoying this.'

'I am. I'm just worried about Jaxon.' Her focus strayed to Elise and although she wasn't making direct eye contact, Lilah was convinced she'd been looking just seconds before.

'Ok, let's go,' he said. 'Maya will be pleased to have us back.'

Lilah rubbed her arms; they were suddenly a little cold.

'I'll see if Mum's ready.'

'Can we walk? I need some air.'

'All the way? In those shoes.'

'I'll give it a go... Or you can piggy-back me.'

He raised an eyebrow. 'I'm not sure that'll work.'

She gave him a playful nudge. They said a few goodbyes and discovered Finlay's friend Oliver was also leaving. Lilah gave in to accepting a lift part of the way. Oliver had a very fancy car and Lilah sat in the back feeling like a celebrity. He didn't say much and Aidan spoke mainly of generic subjects like the weather and how the night was lovely and clear. Lilah was quite glad to get out close to Scarlett's house.

They collected Maya and she wagged her tail furiously. Scarlett yawned as she waved them off, already in her pyjamas.

Lilah clutched Aidan's hand as they trudged up the hill towards Woodend Cottage. Maya trotted alongside them.

'She seems none the worse for an evening with Scarlett,' Aidan said.

'Scarlett was probably glad of her company. She'll be worried Zeb might come searching for her.'

'If he does, he'll have me to answer to.'

'Yeah. But she'll still be anxious.' The feelings were all too sharp for Lilah. She'd known them all her life... Until recently. Only since Aidan came on the scene had she felt truly safe. 'She seems to have lost some of her spark.'

'Yeah. It's not like her to be so quiet. Maybe this is karma catching up with her.'

They passed the pond and Lilah smirked.

'You remember when you fell in there?' she grinned.

He laughed, a warm sound that filled the night air. 'Fell? Was pushed I reckon. I was soaked to the bone.'

She squeezed his hand. 'It was quite something to look at.'

'Glad you appreciated it.'

The sky was darkening but even though it was past ten, they could see well enough. The joyous long days of a Scottish summer. This had been an amazing night. No one had questioned her about being with Aidan or treated her like she belonged anywhere else. She hadn't made a fool of herself and people had been friendly and kind. Only Elise's sharp glances had given her anything to worry about.

'Aidan. I don't want to hurt you, but... I need to know something.' It was hard to say it but she couldn't go on without knowing. Since she'd been with him her confidence had grown. She was a different person, a stronger one. But if he chose to go back to Elise... Well, she hoped she didn't have to test her new strength, which was why she had to find the words.

'What?' He frowned and clutched her hand.

Lilah's smile faltered. 'I saw you talking with Elise. What was it about?'

He ran his fingers through his hair. 'She's having second thoughts about the engagement.'

Lilah's heart flickered. If Elise ended her relationship with Finlay, would Aidan reconsider their own future? 'Oh.'

Aidan's grip on her hand tightened as they approached Woodend Cottage. 'Why is the door open?'

'What?' Lilah swung her focus to it. 'I bet my idiot brother went for a walk and didn't shut it. Honestly, he's such a dick.' She marched on ahead, almost running up the path.

'Hang on a minute,' Aidan's voice boomed. He caught up with her and took hold of her arm. 'Let me go in first. Just in case.' He flicked the light on in the hallway. 'Hello,' he called.

Silence greeted them. He checked around every room and Maya sniffed about.

'Anything?' Lilah asked, rubbing her arms and frowning. Where had he gone? Or had someone broken in and taken him by force? Such thoughts were part and parcel of life with Jaxon.

'No. I'm going to lock up. Maybe you could text him. If he comes back, he'll have to knock. I'm not having him sneaking back in.'

Lilah tapped out a quick message, but she didn't expect a response. She sighed as she entered the bedroom and put her phone on the bedside cabinet. Jaxon had always been unpredictable, disappearing without notice, and generally causing trouble. Her usual avoidance tactic wasn't working. Something felt wrong. An uneasy knot formed in her stomach.

Aidan stuck his head around the door. 'I'm just going to check the barn in case he's hiding in there.'

'Can I come too?'

'If you really want to but I'll only be minutes.'

Lilah got to her feet and followed him to the door. 'I'll wait here.' She watched him cross the side garden where the painted barn stood next to Jim's fence. Maya sat by Lilah, her ears pricked, eyes following Aidan's every move. He unlocked the barn and disappeared out of sight. Lilah's heart raced but moments later, he reappeared and locked the door. He jogged back to the house, shaking his head.

'Empty,' he said. 'Let's get in.'

'I'm sorry,' Lilah said. 'This is why I don't make more of an effort to keep in touch with him. He just brings worry after worry.'

'I know.' Aidan took her face in his hands. 'But let's not assume the worst. He might just have gone for a walk.'

She sighed, wanting to believe that was true but pretty certain it wasn't.

'Can you get me out of this dress?' she asked.

'With pleasure.' Aidan pulled down the zip and placed a gentle kiss on her neck.

Smiling weakly, she dressed in her pyjamas as Aidan went to the bathroom. She stood by the window, gazing out towards the road. Why would Jaxon go for a walk at this time of night? The sky was velvety purple and the three-quarter moon cast a soft glow over the countryside. But Jaxon wasn't someone likely to enjoy a moonlit stroll – unless he wanted to get something he shouldn't.

Aidan came in and unbuttoned his cuffs.

'I can't undo the clasp on the necklace,' Lilah said. 'My fingers keep slipping.'

'Here.' Aidan took hold of it and gently slipped it off.

'Should I put it back in the box?'

'Do it tomorrow. Let's go to bed.'

'I'm so nervous about Jaxon. Why did he have to come here?'

'Because he needed help.' Aidan tugged off his shirt.

'I'm not so sure. I wish I could trust him but... Something isn't right... about any of this.'

'Come to bed,' Aidan said. 'We'll try to get some sleep. If he isn't back in the morning, we can go to the police. Ok?'

'Ok.' Lilah pulled back the covers and got in beside him. She wanted to forget about Jaxon, wished she could press rewind and come home to a normal house or at least a note or a message saying he was fine and had simply moved on again. Which may still be the case, only the not knowing was horrible. All through her life she'd managed to detach herself from worrying about her family, but that wasn't happening tonight, even with the distraction of a hot and naked Aidan.

He moved in close behind her and wrapped his arms around her. 'Close your eyes. Whatever happens, I'm here.'

She rolled over to face him. He kissed her and she returned it. Maybe she could be distracted after all. When their clothes were off and Aidan moved on top of her, Lilah's mind let go of her troubles. These moments were precious and she wanted to savour them, because who knew how long she'd have this in her life.

Aidan had unlocked her doors, broken her barriers and discovered exactly what made her squeal, moan and beg for more. Tonight was no different. Aidan took his time kissing her, touching her, and thrusting intensely, until she was little more than putty in his hands.

She loved the feel of him on top of her, surrounding her, in her. She kept her legs wrapped tightly around his back, holding him deep inside, until her world splintered into a kaleidoscope of light and she climaxed so intensely she couldn't breathe.

A tear rolled from the corner of her eye as he let out his final groan of satisfaction. She clung to him, digging her short nails into his hard shoulders, not wanting him to move off her, but trying to keep her face to the side, so he wouldn't know she was crying.

Why am I crying?

'Are you ok?' he whispered. His naked body seemed sapped of its usual strength as he raised his hand to her cheek.

'Uh-huh,' she said, trying to turn her head into the pillow and wipe off the tear.

'Are you crying?'

'Kind of… But I think it's happy tears.' It was something big anyway.

He raised himself up slightly and gently pressed a kiss at the side of her eye, as if kissing away the tears.

'Please, don't go,' she said.

'I'm not.' He shuffled about in the bed for a moment, then moved close again, pulling her into his arms. 'It'll all be ok.'

Right now, she believed him. It was easy. His voice was so commanding, his hold so assured, and she was warm and safe. But would it still be true in the morning?

Sleep wouldn't come.

When Aidan's breathing grew heavy and she knew he'd dozed, she still lay awake in his embrace. Her mind raced back to the party and his talk with Elise. He hadn't really answered her properly. Would he go back to her? He'd never made any formal promise and, other than asking her to date him, he'd never really spoken about their relationship or where he hoped it to go... If anywhere.

Why can't I shut off? She needed to close down her thoughts and not only that, her feelings. She'd been so good at that before. But Aidan had pulled emotions out of her she didn't know she had. Could she shut off her feelings for him too? Maybe that was the answer. Then, if he chose to go back to Elise, she could detach and not care. Another tear leaked from her heavy eyes. How could she ever not care for Aidan?

Lilah opened her eyes and blinked. Aidan stood at the dressing table with a towel wrapped around his waist.

'Is Jaxon back?' Lilah sat up quickly.

'No.' Aidan let out a sigh. 'Are you sure this is normal for him?'

'Unfortunately, yes, but I have a really bad feeling about it this time.' She stretched, pulled off the covers, and got to her feet.

'Well, we can go to the police station this morning and see what they can do.'

She picked up her phone and checked it. Unsurprisingly, nothing. As she replaced it on the bedside cabinet, she knocked the necklace to the floor. 'I need to put this back. I'm scared I lose it or it gets damaged.'

'Can you check if Maya wants to come back in too?'

'Sure.'

She called her from the French doors and Maya padded back inside, greeting Lilah with her waggy tail and slobbery kisses. 'You're such a lovely dog. Thank goodness we didn't leave you here last night with Jaxon.'

Lilah went into the study and opened the writing bureau. She shuffled things around but couldn't see the box for the necklace. In fact, none of the boxes were there. Had Aidan moved them into a safer place? 'Aidan.' She returned to the bedroom. 'Yesterday, when you got the necklace out, where did you put the jewellery box?'

'I left it in the bureau,' he said. 'Where it always is.'

Lilah's heart slumped to her feet. 'It's not there. None of the boxes are. I think Jaxon has taken them.'

'Seriously?' Aidan shook his head and headed for the study. 'He robbed me. What a prick. After I let him have a place to stay too.'

'Yup.' Exactly that. Lilah handed him the necklace. How could Jaxon betray their trust like this? And though she agreed with Aidan, she felt a sting in his words. None of this would have happened if he hadn't taken her in to start with.

What a mess.

'I definitely need to talk to the police now. Not that they can do anything much. The jewels probably aren't even worth much but they belong to my dad's family. My family. He kept them and passed them to me.'

'I'm so sorry,' Lilah said. If only she could remove herself from her family connections. But somehow, they always found a way back. Perhaps she should remove herself from Aidan. Would he be better off in the long run without her? She brought trouble with her without meaning to.

She kept out of his way as he checked on the bees.

Jaxon had dragged her down deep enough. She shouldn't make things any worse. Aidan was likely to come to his senses any day now. See her for the bad news she was and possibly go crawling back to Elise. Maybe Jaxon had simply paved the way for her retreat. Now all she had to do was walk the path. Would that make her look guilty? Perhaps people would think she was his accomplice and now he'd got the goods, they would split it halfway. That's what people she'd grown up with would think, but Aidan wouldn't. He trusted her, but that didn't change the facts. Wherever she went, trouble followed.

Chapter Twenty-Six

Aidan

The afternoon sun cast a warm golden glow over the orchard. Aidan made his way to the hives. The hum of the bees echoed the thoughts in his head, buzzing around, though, unlike the bees who had clear purpose and direction, his thoughts didn't know where to go next.

With a gentle puff from the smoker, Aidan calmed the bees. The air carried the sweet scent of flowers and beeswax. So cleansing and refreshing, but not enough today to work its magic on him. Nothing could clear up the mess surrounding Lilah and Jaxon. Should he let Jaxon have the jewellery and be done with? What was its value anyway? But he felt betrayed. After offering Jaxon a safe haven this was how he'd repaid him. Lilah had been right not to trust him.

And there he was, back to Lilah. He let out a sigh as he took out his hive tool and delicately prised open the lid, revealing the bustling colony beneath.

As he lifted one frame at a time, he marvelled at the weight and richness of the honey-laden combs. The honeybees zoomed around and Aidan spoke calmly. 'Hello, friends. I wish I knew what to do for the best.'

He'd hardly seen Lilah that morning. But then, he'd left early to report Jaxon. Or had he made a mistake and she'd been keeping out of his way? After the way things had gone with Elise, could he really trust himself?

He carefully brushed away the remaining bees with a soft-bristled bee brush, ensuring that the honeycombs were clear, then placed the combs in a sealed container.

After securing the hive, Aidan moved on to the next one.

Once all the honey-filled frames were safely collected, he carried them to the shed. He uncapped each honeycomb with a knife, revealing the sticky, amber-hued honey within, then placed them in the extractor.

He turned the crank, spinning the extractor. Droplets of honey splattered against the sides. Gradually, the golden liquid pooled at the bottom, ready to be collected and poured into jars. He'd half hoped Lilah would come and watch this, but she hadn't returned from work yet. He tried not to let the idea worry him. Sometimes she worked overtime and that was fine, but his insides chilled with the fear she might not come back to him.

The police had taken descriptions of the missing jewellery, which wasn't easy as Aidan couldn't remember what it looked like, not in great detail anyway.

After collecting the honey in the jars, he made his way to the barn. As he approached the bright yellow structure, he shook his head, giving way to a brief smile. The once ramshackle space was now vibrant and welcoming. Lilah had worked magic here. Just like she had on him… The travel weary, grief-ridden wanderer had learned how to smile again.

A cheerful sign had appeared featuring the hand-painted whimsical bee motifs she'd got so good at while decorating the barn. She'd placed it facing the street to invite passersby to explore the treasures within. Colourful bunting, fluttering in the breeze, adorned the eaves.

He peered inside to where Patricia sat at her craft table in front of the shelves, made from reclaimed wood, displaying her handmade designs. Some of Lilah's work was there too. Pieces of jewellery and bookmarks.

'Hello, son. Is everything ok?'

'Yeah. Just checking in.'

'How's Lilah? I haven't seen her since the party.'

Aidan sat on the craft table with a sigh. 'Some stuff's happened with her brother and it's not very pleasant.'

'Poor girl.' Patricia shook her head almost in time to the soft music coming from her iPod. She got to her feet and adjusted a pretty little hand-painted canvas with a scene of the hives in the orchard with the field behind. She was a good artist. Hopefully that scene wasn't one that would become confined to rustic paintings and memories. A housing estate wouldn't make for such a charming picture. 'Her family were always dodgy but she's done well for herself. What's happened to her brother?'

'He took some stuff from the house,' he said.'

'Valuable stuff?'

'Sentimental more than valuable. Lilah's really cut up about it. I know what she's thinking. She's scared she'll be tarred with the same brush, but I know she'd never steal from me. She's only ever been kind to me.'

'Yes. She's a delight really. I completely misjudged her when I first met her. Go and talk to her, make sure she's ok.'

'I'm not sure she's back yet.' He stepped outside onto the path that led through the garden. Everything was tidier now and in full bloom. Sunlight filtered through the leaves, casting a dappled pattern on the ground. Maya trotted towards him, tail wagging, and he crouched to pat her. 'Hey, girl. I'll take you out soon. I've got a couple more things to do first.' She nuzzled him, then licked his face, and he chuckled.

He reached the cottage and pushed open the kitchen door. Lilah stood inside, her fingers tapping at her phone screen.

'Oh, you're back,' he said.

'Yeah. I got back ten minutes ago. I can't get in touch with Jaxon. I left my old phone on charge and I've just tried calling some people I thought might know him but no one knows where he is. What are we going to do? I want to get your stuff back. This is all my fault.'

'No, it isn't. You tried to warn me and I didn't listen. So if it's anyone's fault, it's mine. I don't even care about the jewellery. It's the principle. I don't think he should be allowed to get away with it.'

'He shouldn't. I just don't know how to find him.'

'Let's hope he's not in trouble with worse people than us.'

She buried her head in her hands but as Aidan approached, she took a step back and flicked her hair over her shoulder. 'I'm fine,' she said.

'How about you come and look in my shed? See the honey I collected. That'll distract you.'

'Sounds good.'

'Two secs. I need a drink; I'm parched.' He crossed the kitchen and opened the cupboard. How could he make this better for her? Finding Jaxon might be the only way. Perhaps that idiot Zeb might know. Aidan had no desire whatsoever to see him again, but it might be worth it if he could help restore Lilah to a happier mood.

He could walk Maya that way later. She was good company – and backup. A knock on the door startled him. Was it Jaxon returning the jewels? That didn't seem likely but an odd sensation gripped his stomach, making him hesitate.

'Should I get that?' Lilah asked. 'It might be—'

'Jaxon, yeah. I think you should wait in here. Let me talk to him.' He could imagine Lilah losing her cool and whacking him with the first heavy object she could find.

'Ok.'

He closed the kitchen door and made his way into the hall. When he pulled open the door, he was completely unprepared for the sight of a puffy-eyed, ashen-faced Elise.

'What's happened?' he said, his mind spinning through zillions of thoughts in a split second but dwelling heavily on the most morbid ones. Was Finlay dead?

'Can I come in?'

'Ok.' He stepped back and let her in. Was she going to collapse into his arms? 'Has something happened to Finlay?'

She nodded and Aidan's heart shot into overdrive.

'What? Is he ok?'

'We split up.' She put her hand over her mouth. 'It's so...' She stamped her foot and gave an irritated grunt. 'Ugh. It's just awful.'

'Why are you telling me this?'

'Because I need to talk to someone but I don't want anyone else to know yet. I hate it. It's humiliating.'

'I'm not sure I can do anything to help.'

'You know why we split up?'

He shook his head. 'No.'

'Because of you. We had a big row. Finlay thinks I never really got over you.'

'After what you said at the party—'

'I know, Aidan. That's the point. He's right. I should have waited. It annoyed me that you thought it was ok to go off and leave me like that but I miss you. I miss us.'

Aidan stared at her and no words came. What could he say? How often had he dreamed of this moment? But why now? It was too late.

CHAPTER TWENTY-SEVEN

Lilah

Lilah's heart raced as she stood in the cottage kitchen, her ear pressed against the weathered wooden door. This was it. The moment she'd dreaded, a culmination of the fears that had lingered since she first allowed herself to believe she had a genuine chance with Aidan.

Deep down, she'd always suspected that Aidan would choose Elise. Who wouldn't?

The old light, with its irritating hum, cast gentle shadows on the worn table. Its surface, marked with countless scratches and stains.

The kitchen seemed to hold its breath alongside her. The old-fashioned clock ticking on the wall echoed in her ears, counting down the precious moments in which she'd foolishly hoped things would be different.

She should just be happy she'd stolen this time with him, because this outcome seemed inevitable.

As she waited for Aidan to speak, a sharp pain pierced her heart. Elise had said she missed them. Did he miss her? *Have I been nothing but a distraction?*

She let out a sigh and pressed her forehead to the door. Just why? She didn't need constant reminders of her own inadequacy. Jaxon's behaviour was more than enough to do that. And still Aidan wasn't speaking. Neither of them was. Her heartrate trebled. *Oh, no.* Could it mean…? Was he drawing closer to Elise, his lips making a bittersweet reunion with hers? A sharp pain stabbed Lilah deep in the chest. She couldn't bear it.

What now? Retreat quietly and let the tears flow? Sit in her room all day and wallow? No. She'd come a long way in a few weeks. Maybe Aidan didn't want her anymore but officially they were still boyfriend and girlfriend. If he was kissing Elise, he was nothing but a cheat.

Unable to contain herself any longer, she flung the kitchen door open. The hinges creaked and it burst open faster than she'd meant it to. As she stepped into the dimly lit hallway, her eyes darted around. Both Aidan and Elise turned to look at her. But he wasn't even beside her. Lilah opened her mouth, not sure what she wanted to say. She'd been so sure she was going to catch them kissing. What were they doing? Just standing staring at each other?

'I… um…'

She glanced at her feet and the old worn carpet runner that stretched along the hallway. The air held a faint scent of the lavender she'd cut a few days ago. Back when she was kidding herself this could work.

Her gaze shifted between the two of them. She wanted answers, but her voice caught in her throat and she didn't want to make herself look stupid. Anymore stupid than she already did.

'Hello,' she said after a beat.

'Hi,' Elise said with a brief, almost curt, smile. 'I was just leaving.' She cast Aidan a look equal parts harsh and sad. 'We can talk another time when it's more convenient.'

An uncomfortable silence filled the hallway as Lilah and Aidan locked eyes. 'Are you ok?' Aidan said, shifting his weight from one foot to another, his gaze flickering towards the door.

'I heard everything she said.'

'She didn't say anything I mind you hearing.'

'She wants to get back together with you. It's so obvious.' The exhaustion of the last few days caught up and hit her like a brick. She was so tired of watching her back. Even when she suppressed her worries, they were never really gone. If it wasn't Jaxon bringing her down, it would be someone or something else. Aidan would be better off back with safe and sensible Elise. 'You're never going to be over each other, so why don't you get back together?' She wanted to trust him the way she always had but could he ever trust her... Or what she brought with her? 'I'll leave you to it. You'll be happier that way.'

'No, Lilah. You mustn't leave. I'm not going back to Elise. I'm with you.'

She swallowed back a lump of what should have been joy but it was bitter tasting. 'What does that really mean, Aidan?'

'I don't follow? What do you think it means?'

'I don't know. That's the point.' What she really wanted was love. Just love. Real love. Not him 'doing the right thing' or whatever he thought he was doing.

'It's ok, Aidan. You don't have to be with me anymore. I'll not force my company on you. You'll be better off without me. I always bring trouble.'

'What are you talking about? Have I ever said that?'

She didn't reply.

'If that's what I've made you think, I apologise.'

'You only started dating me because you felt sorry for me, but you don't need to do that anymore.'

'That wasn't the reason.'

'You might think it's not, but deep down, it is. You're always blind to what's right in front of you. Why did you let Elise go when you cared for her so much? Now you're kidding yourself you're doing some noble deed by dating me because it looked like you were moving on and it was appeasing me and my silly crush at the same time.'

'Lilah.' He rubbed his forehead. 'That's not what I'm doing.'

'I can't talk right now.' She opened the main door and marched off down the path, just holding back the tears.

'Where are you going?' Aidan shouted.

'I need space,' she said. Her feet carried her down the hill, the pavement beneath her echoing her slamming footsteps. The route to the main shopping area was so familiar now, the narrow pavement by the side of the country road winding its way downhill. As she walked, she passed the big houses with their meticulous gardens. The earthy fragrance of freshly cut grass filled the air. But none of it soothed her mind or calmed the tears pushing their way ever closer. It just served as a reminder of things that didn't really belong in her world.

She needed more than physical distance. If she could recall the knack for shutting down she'd fostered all her life. She'd closed off memories of her family and forced herself not to think about them. That had stopped the worries and fears but only on the surface. Deep insecurities ran into her bones and her very being. Now the barriers had cracked open, doubt and panic seeped through the gaps.

The pavement stretched ahead, seemingly endless. A dark path towards an uncertain future.

Where was Jaxon? She wanted to murder him for thieving.

What was she going to do about her relationship with Aidan? What could she do? She couldn't change who she was or where she came from.

Lilah raked about in the pocket of her jeans. She had some loose change in one and her phone in the other. Those coins might be enough to get away from here. She could get on the bus to Dundee and go to her mum's. Not that she particularly wanted to see her. But eventually Jaxon would turn up there. He always did. And Lilah would be ready.

CHAPTER TWENTY-EIGHT

Aidan paced back and forward across the floorboards in the living room, his footsteps echoing in the empty space. Lilah's absence weighed heavily on his heart. She'd gone off before and he'd chased her. Would she come home this time? If she didn't, what would he do? He couldn't go after her, as he didn't know where she'd gone. But he couldn't live without her.

'She'll be back,' he told himself. She'd said she needed space but that was an hour ago. He'd checked the barn and his mum hadn't seen her. She'd been locking up, ready to leave. It was a warm afternoon, and she wanted to spend some time at home in the garden.

He couldn't settle to anything.

With a heavy sigh, he headed out the French doors and called Maya. He needed to clear his head, and perhaps a walk in the woods would help. It would stop him wearing a hole in the rug anyway. Maya wagged her tail as she bounded towards him.

Sunlight filtered through the leaves in the woods, bringing back memories of the time he'd brought Lilah back home on his bike. Even then he'd wanted her with him, though he hadn't quite understood why. He understood better now. It still didn't make complete sense. He just knew whenever they were apart, it was harder to function.

Perhaps Lilah had gone to see Zeb herself. A prickle of panic stabbed his chest. He didn't want her doing that. She was a tough cookie but that would be playing with fire.

Jaxon knew Zeb, so he was definitely a connection Aidan needed to check out. He walked Maya back to the cottage and stopped momentarily. When he was sure Lilah still wasn't back, he headed down the hill, making his way towards Zeb's street.

He took the steps in the close two at a time, Maya on his heels as they approached Zeb's door. He knew better than to trust anything Zeb said, but if he could get anything at all out of him, it might help. With a firm fist, he knocked on the worn wooden door.

The door swung open, revealing Zeb's hard face and greasy hair. The second Zeb made eye contact, he pushed the door to shut it again. Aidan's hand shot out, preventing it from closing. He needed answers.

'Get off,' Zeb muttered.

'Tell me about Jaxon,' Aidan said.

'Who?'

'Don't play games. You know who I mean.'

Zeb hesitated, his gaze shifting nervously. 'Yeah, so what? I dinny ken a 'hing about him.'

'When did you last see him?'

'I dunno.'

'Then think, because I'm going nowhere until you talk.'

Zeb pulled a face but Aidan kept his shoulder on the door.

'What the fuck-ever,' Zeb muttered. 'He came by last night. Idiot that he is. Wanted to trade me some ugly necklaces for, well, stuff. But I'm not that stupid. It looked like he'd raided his granny's cupboard and found a pile of worthless shit.'

'So you threw him out, did you?'

'He wasnae for going, but then he started getting hunners of messages. His phone was red hot. I thought it was some bint wanting him but he said it was his sister and he better get the hell out or she'd be after his guts. I just shut the door on the idiot. No idea where he went after that.'

'And no one else has been here looking for him?'

'Naw. Why? What's he done? He better no have dropped me into anything. Or he'll be in a shit heap of trouble.'

Aidan's frustration mingled with his growing panic for Lilah's well-being. Where had she got to? The pieces of the puzzle were falling into place, but her section was agonisingly missing.

'He's not done anything that affects you, but it does affect me. So if he comes round here again, you let me know straight away. Ok?'

'Yeah, whatever.'

'I'll give you my number and I mean it. You call me if you hear anything.'

After he'd given him his number, he released his grip on the door, allowing it to swing shut. He stood for a moment, then sighed. Jaxon would be an idiot to come back here. And Lilah hadn't been here... yet. Would she?

Maya bounded down the stairs before him and Aidan checked his phone once again, hoping for a message from Lilah, but there was still nothing. His unease grew as he made his way back to Woodend Cottage. Empty silence greeted him, and Lilah was still nowhere to be found.

With the weight of worry bearing down on him, he needed someone to talk to. A year or two ago, he'd have gone for a drink with Finlay. Finlay was calm and laid-back enough to be horizontal, the kind of person he needed right now. Someone just to be present, listen if need be and not overreact. But given recent events, Finlay was more than somewhat out of the question as a listening ear. There was Gabe, but they didn't really talk about stuff like this. In fact, Aidan didn't really talk to anyone about this kind of thing. Did anybody?

What about Hayley? She was bubbly and easily excited, but she was always kind.

Even though she never took sides, she was still in contact with Elise. But she'd also stayed friends with him throughout and he needed her now.

He messaged her, then decided he couldn't wait for a reply, so hit call.

'Hey. How you doing?' she said.

'Not so good. Listen. Where are you? Can I come round and talk to you or can you meet me somewhere?'

'Sure. What's up?'

'I'd rather not say anything on the phone.'

'Ok. I'll drive up to yours,' she said. 'I'll be there in about twenty minutes.'

He boiled the kettle and waited.

Hayley didn't bother to knock. She bounded in all smiles and threw her arms around Aidan's neck.

'Hey.' She pulled back and frowned at him. 'I guess this has something to do with Elise and Finlay splitting up.'

'Let's get a drink and sit down.' Aidan fixed them both a coffee and they sank into chairs in the living room.

'Where's Lilah?' Hayley asked, glancing around. 'Is she at work?'

Aidan shook his head. 'She's... out. She said she needed space.'

'What?' Hayley clutched her mug. 'Why? Please not because of Elise.'

'I think so.'

Hayley shook her head and let out a sigh. 'Elise is my friend but she's hurt so many people I love. Finlay is absolutely crushed by this. I know you felt the same when you came back and found out she'd given up on you. Please tell me you're not getting back together with her.'

'I'm not. No way. She's out of my life, but I don't think Lilah really believes I'm over her.'

'Well, you need to tell her.'

'I did, but she thinks she always brings trouble.'

'Oh no. That's sad because you're right... Because you were right to choose Lilah. She's the one who's always been loyal to you. She's loved you right from the start.'

'She what?' Aidan furrowed his brow. 'She... loves me?'

'Aidan!' She gaped at him like she'd never seen him before. 'Are you a total idiot?'

'I don't think so.'

'Then you must know how much she feels for you.'

'Well... I...' He half closed his eyes. Love? He'd never thought anyone could love him. Actually love him just as he was. 'She just said it was a crush.'

Hayley shook her head. 'And how do you feel about her?'

'I... Well, I don't know.' He'd closed his mind to the possibility of love after Elise. It brought too much pain... Pain like he was feeling now.

'You don't know?' Hayley glared at him. 'Then sorry, but you're a total twat.'

'Am I?'

'Well, duh. You're dating her. You're living with her. You're sleeping with her. Doesn't that kind of imply you feel something for her? Or are you just using her?'

'Of course I'm not.' His stomach squirmed. Was that what Lilah thought? Was that why she'd said left? She didn't believe he could ever love her. But he could. He'd already been loving her for a long time. He just hadn't wanted to see it for what it was.

Love was what was all this had been building up to... Yes, love. It was different from how he'd felt about Elise. That love was less raw and all-consuming. Perhaps he'd loved the idea of her more than the real thing. The necessity of his love for Lilah fought against the agony of knowing what it was like to lose it.

He'd been brought up on love. Loved as son by a wonderful father. This kind of love was different, though in other ways similar, as it had left an aching chasm in his heart when it was taken away. This was why it was easier to be in denial and shun love.

But he loved Lilah and he wanted her in his life.

'I should have told her.'

'Yes, you should have. When she comes back, you have to tell her and if you don't, then you don't deserve her.'

'I never told my dad.'

'What?' Hayley blinked, her brow furrowing. 'Told your dad what?'

'That I loved him. He often told me but I didn't say the words back. When he was ill, I was angry. Not with him but with life. I shouldn't have wasted those days nursing my own rage. I should just have sat by Dad and told him I loved him over and over.' His voice cracked and Hayley moved in beside him.

'Hey,' she said, taking him in her arms.

'I'm ok.' He patted her back. 'Just disappointed in myself. I was still angry after he died. And I wasted another chance. Instead of telling Elise how I felt, I ran away to wallow some more. And that lost me her. Now I've done it again. Why can't I spit it out?'

'Because it's not easy to make yourself vulnerable. But try, Aidan, please.' She stared at him. 'You have to.'

'I know. I know. I know.' He groaned at the ceiling. 'But it's too frigging late.'

'Of course it isn't.'

'I don't think she's coming back.'

'What? I thought you said she'd gone out.'

'That was hours ago and she's not replying to my messages. There was an incident last night with her brother.' Aidan explained as Hayley sipped her coffee.

'I'll message her and see if she replies to me,' she said. 'I'm sure she won't have gone too far. She doesn't have anywhere else to go, does she?'

'Not really.'

'If she replies to me, I'll let you know straight away.'

Come evening, there was still no word. Aidan lay atop his covers, unable to close his eyes. He'd made such a mess of everything. Giving into feelings hadn't crossed his mind – not consciously. Whenever he was with Lilah, his mood changed and his heart lifted. Now he understood why. This was love. True and pure. But she was gone.

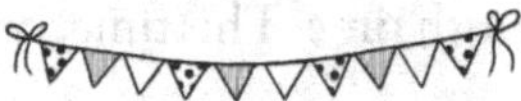

He dozed fitfully, making him crotchety in the morning. With it being Tuesday, he had the dogs to collect. No messages had come in from Lilah or Hayley. He took the path through the woods but instead of doing the usual circuit, he carried onto Clachnabronnachan. First he called in at the Old Schoolhouse and asked if Lilah had shown up for work. The woman frowned at him.

'She called in sick. Why do you want to know?'

'I, um, no reason.' Aidan left quickly. Calling in sick wasn't a good sign. His next visit was a longshot but worth a try. The old caravan where Lilah had stayed before she came to Woodend was almost hidden by junk in the McManus's garden. Aidan took the dogs to the door and knocked.

Brenda appeared with a menacing expression and her arms folded over her giant bosom.

'Hi,' Aidan said. 'You haven't had a visit from Lilah recently, have you?'

Brenda raised an eyebrow. 'Why are you asking me that? Isn't she your live-in lover?'

'Just answer me, will you?'

'Never clapped eyes on her since she left here.'

Aidan sighed and returned to the woods. He checked his phone for the umpteenth time. This time, he noticed a new email from Jacob McCash.

Dear Mr McBride,

Following our meeting with you, Miss Clarke and Mr Wilder, we have noted your objections and those of the wider community. Further investigations have been undertaken with these objections in mind and you'll be pleased to know the plans for the housing development on the field at Woodend have now been dropped.

A committee has been set up to look into the of the former amusement park as a future development site.

The council were also interested in your ideas for a community buy-out of the field at Woodend and would welcome a meeting with you to discuss this further. If you could forward me contact details for Miss Clarke and Mr Wilder, I would like to invite them to the meeting also.

Aidan could hardly believe it. He wanted to run home, pick up Lilah, and twirl her around while she squealed for joy. Except she wasn't there and he still didn't know where she was.

CHAPTER TWENTY-NINE

Lilah

Lilah stood in front of the old tenement building on the dirty pavement. Litter swirled around, blown out of overfilled bins. The weathered exterior had graffiti painted on it and the tiny garden had the remains of an old kitchen piled up outside. This was where her mum was living now. Rowan Way wasn't the best street but surely it beat this sorry place in the centre of Dundee? But Mum had her reasons for moving, the proximity of the off license being one of the more unfortunate ones.

Taking a deep breath, Lilah pushed open the creaking door and stepped into the dimly lit close. She covered her mouth and edged her way past a suspicious looking wet patch on the ugly concrete floor. When she got to her mum's door, she knocked. It took a few moments for her mum to get to the door.

The familiar scent of stale smoke and neglect hit her as the door opened. Her mum peered at her through the gap and took a puff from a cigarette. 'Delilah? What are you doing here?'

'Come to visit.'

'Have you now? You better come in then.' She undid the chain with unsteady fingers. Lilah was confronted by a somewhat gruesome, if not unexpected, scene. Dirty dishes piled high in the sink, clothing strewn across the floor, and empty pill bottles scattered like fallen soldiers.

Her mother, Claire, sank into the worn-out couch, a distant look in her eyes. Her frail frame trembled as she tapped ash into a tray. 'This is a bit strange.'

'Can I stay here for a bit?' The idea made Lilah a little sick but it was slightly better than sleeping rough. She sat on the edge of an armchair.

'Eh?' Claire pushed a strand of her lank, heavily bleached hair behind her ear, as if that might help her hear better.

'You heard. I need somewhere to stay. Just for a couple of nights.' She was horribly aware of how like Jaxon she sounded. That was exactly what he'd said to Aidan. Was she really any better than her brother? She'd already lied to Marion at the Schoolhouse and said she was ill, but how long could she keep that up? It wasn't like she was ever going back, but quitting felt like giving up something almost as precious as Aidan. The first real job she'd had... Something she really liked.

Claire looked away; her gaze fixed on a distant corner of the room. 'Aye, sure. Just whenever you fancy. You're all the same. You only ever come to see me when you want something.'

Lilah clenched her fists, fighting back tears. Mum had never come to see her. She wouldn't even message if Lilah didn't message her first. *I've never asked for help before!* Yet she still felt like she was imposing. 'Ok, never mind.'

'I didn't say no,' Claire said. 'I just don't know where to god I'm going to put you.'

'There's a spare room here.'

'Yeah, but Jaxon's already in it.'

'He's here?'

'Yes.'

Lilah jumped to her feet.

'Where are you going?'

She stormed out of the living room and straight towards the spare room. With a swift motion, she shoved open the door, startling Jaxon, who was lying on the bed lost in his own world, his headphones on. Startled, he leapt up, flinging his phone away and standing frozen before Lilah.

'What the hell?' he said, his eyes wide. 'You scared the shit out of me!'

She shut the door behind her, obstructing his escape route. 'You deserve it. I'd like to scare you a bit more, you sneaky little thief. How dare you steal from Aidan? What have you done with the jewellery?'

Jaxon's eyes darted around the room. He opened his mouth and shrugged. 'What you talking about?'

'Don't you try that. I know you took it. And you weren't even smart enough to shut the door behind you.'

'What?'

'You left the front door of Woodend hanging open, which made you look guilty before we even knew what you'd done.'

'Oh, fuck's sake,' he muttered, sitting on the bed. 'Ok, fine. I took the stuff. But it was old shit I'm sure he doesn't need. I was desperate.'

'Desperate? For a quick fix? You're a sad excuse for a human being. Give the jewellery back. You better still have it or I'm taking you back to Aidan and he can sort you out himself.'

Aidan would never hurt Jaxon but he was a lot bigger than him and Lilah was relying on Jaxon's cowardly nature to do the trick. She put her hands on her hips and glowered at him.

Jaxon's shoulders slumped. 'Fine. I've got it.' With an over-the-top sigh, he dragged himself up and picked up an old rucksack from beside the bed. 'There.' He pulled out the jewellery all clumped together and handed it to her.

Lilah held the weighty jewellery in her palm. 'You were really stupid to take this. Aidan would have helped you, you know? He's a generous man. And whatever he did for you, it would be better than giving you money for your next fix.'

'What's going on in here?' Claire pushed her way into the bedroom and frowned between Lilah and Jaxon. Lilah saw herself in the pale, freckly skin and the delicate build, but she hoped she never let herself go the way her mum had.

'Jaxon stole this from Aidan. I need to give it back to him.'

'Who's Aidan?' Claire frowned. 'Is he in the gang from the Hilltown?'

'He's her boyfriend,' Jaxon said.

'Ah nice,' Claire said. 'You've got a boyfriend. Can I meet him?'

'We've split up,' Lilah said.

'No kidding,' Jaxon said, and he let out what was really a very annoying and rude laugh 'Ha! I'm not surprised.'

'What do you mean?' Lilah frowned at him.

'Come on, Li. Not being funny, but he was a bit, you know...'

'No, I don't know. A bit what?'

'Well, a bit much for you.'

'What?' Lilah stared at him. 'A bit much? In what way? Are you being disgusting?'

'Na. But he's got a house and dosh. He wasn't likely to stick with you, was he? Not after...' He looked her up and down. 'He'd got what he wanted.'

'That's not very nice,' Claire said. 'Why would you say that to your sister?'

'Don't get at me,' Jaxon said. 'But really, if an older guy with his own house takes in a twenty-year-old, what are people going to think, huh? Pretty obvious what he was after.'

'Shut up,' Lilah said, but her heart cringed. 'And I'm not twenty, I'm twenty-three.'

Jaxon shrugged like it made no difference, which was so infuriating coming from a teenager like him. *Imagine not even knowing how old your sister is!*

'How old was he?' Claire said. 'Creepy git.'

'Not *that* old, mum.' Lilah shook her head. 'He's thirty-three.'

'Is that all?' Claire frowned at Jaxon. 'I thought you were talking about some dirty old man. Was he nice?'

'Yes,' Lilah said.

'So, why d'you split with him? I don't think there's anything wrong with finding a nice stable guy with his own house. Sounds sensible if you ask me. Unless he *was* using you. If he was, then ditch the prick.'

'We split because of you.' She eyeballed Jaxon. 'Sure, he seems "too much" for me because I'm related to thieves and junkies. Why the hell would he want to date someone whose brother turns up and steals from his house?' That was the short version and the one that made her feel better, as she could get it off her chest without sounding bitter. The other version included Elise, and Lilah hated thinking that she couldn't ever take Elise's place in Aidan's eyes.

'Whatever,' Jaxon said.

'Stupid boy.' Claire shook her head and folded her arms, keeping her lit cigarette raised so the smoke wafted unpleasantly under Lilah's nose. 'Ruining your sister's chances like that.' She turned to Lilah. 'What if you give him the stuff back? He might want to get back together.'

'No. He won't. But I do need to give him that jewellery back.' Maybe she could post it. Was it safe to send this kind of stuff in the post? Or she could go to Glenbriar and leave it on his doorstep. Or with Hayley, though she didn't want to see her either. Hayley was kind and her messages were always lovely, but Lilah should kiss goodbye to the Glenbriar connections permanently. Who needed someone like her darkening their lives?

Still, that aside, she had to find a solution to a more immediate problem. Where was she going to live and what should she do next? Would it be possible to live at the Old Schoolhouse? At least then she could keep her job, but could she bear being that close to Aidan?

The worn-out sofa sufficed as a place to stay that night. But the hours of darkness passed fitfully. The absence of Aidan's comforting presence brought a fresh swell of tears. She yearned for the safety and warmth of his arms.

Morning came, casting a greyish light through the tattered curtains. She rubbed her tired eyes and sighed at the reality of her situation. She couldn't live like this for long.

Heavy footsteps reverberated through the small flat, and her heart sank.

Claire stumbled into the living room, slurring her words as she addressed Lilah, 'Morning, love. Sorry 'bout the mess. Steve's here. You remember Steve, right?'

Lilah's lips pressed into a tight line, her gaze drifting towards the man who stood beside her mum, reeking of alcohol. She'd spent countless hours like this witnessing the toxic life her mum led with men who entered and exited their lives like people through shop doors.

Steve leered at Lilah, his gaze lingering a moment too long before he broke into a gruff chuckle. 'I'm not sure we've had the pleasure.'

'Oh.' Claire gave a little shrug. 'I thought you'd met before.'

Lilah couldn't with all honesty remember if she had or not. All her mum's boyfriends kind of rolled into one big unpleasant type of man, who looked a lot like Steve.

'Hi,' was all she could manage. Getting away from this flat was a priority. She had to do it soon, and the Schoolhouse might be her best bet.

Claire shuffled towards the sofa and plopped down heavily, an unsteady smile on her lips. 'What are you up to today?'

'I'm going out for a bit.'

Anything to escape from this suffocating atmosphere. Aidan's absence was a constant ache, a reminder of the stability and love she'd briefly tasted. *Put it behind and move on.* Just as she always did.

She showered in the bathroom that was like something out of a scary TV show, then walked to the park. Schools were still in, so there were no kids. She sat on a swing and checked her messages. Aidan and Hayley. Both of them asking where she was and when she was coming back.

She would be going back but when she did, everything would be different.

CHAPTER THIRTY

Aidan

'Feels a bit weird opening to the public without Lilah,' Patricia said. 'She's been a godsend to me.'

'Yeah. She turned out ok in the end,' Scarlett said. 'Actually, she was good to me. Kind of wish I'd had her as a friend. She helped me with Zeb when no one else did.'

'Took you long enough,' Aidan muttered, throwing the door wide open. It was agony not knowing where she was or if she was even ok. He'd had one message from her saying she was fine and that was all. It told him nothing except that she didn't want him pestering her. How had he blown his chance so thoroughly?

Scarlett and Patricia exchanged glances across the Crafty Bee Barn, a gesture not lost on him. Scarlett leaned against a shelf. 'What's going on with you and her? Talk to us.'

He glared at her. 'It's none of your business.'

Patricia stepped forward. 'Aidan, we care about you. Don't shut us out. Why did Lilah leave?'

He crossed his arms. 'Seriously?'

'I want to know what's happened to her,' Patricia continued. 'Have you actually split up or is this a break, or what?'

'And it's obvious you like her more than Elise,' Scarlett added. 'Otherwise you'd be running back to her now she's ditched Finlay.'

'Of course I'm not going back to Elise.'

'Because you love Lilah,' Patricia said. 'It's blatantly obvious.'

Aidan looked at the floor. 'Yup.'

Patricia sighed. 'Love is complicated. It's messy and unpredictable, as I know well, otherwise I wouldn't be divorced twice. But it's also worth fighting for. Don't let stubbornness keep you from finding happiness.'

Aidan furrowed his brows. Maybe she had a point but he wasn't sure what he could do about it. Not unless he found out where Lilah was.

Scarlett adjusted a bee pin on the same log Lilah had yanked from the stall the previous month. 'You're lucky, Aidan. You found someone so devoted. I don't get why she'd leave you.'

'Because I was stupid,' he said. 'I didn't say everything I should have.'

'You're so like your dad,' Patricia said. 'He never told me how he felt. It broke me in the end and our marriage fell apart.'

'But he learned his lesson,' Aidan said. 'Because he told me how much he loved me every day.'

'Then you need to take a leaf out of his book. We may have been divorced, but he was a good man and a good father. You're a good man too. Just remember, people aren't mind readers.'

Aidan nodded and pulled out his phone. His heart stilled. A message from Lilah. Finally.

LILAH: Will you be at the craft fair in Glenbriar tomorrow? I have your jewellery and I don't want to post it. But that's all I want. Just to pass over the jewellery and be done with it. No big song and dance. Ok?

His mind raced. *What?* Part of him was relieved she was willing to see him, but all she wanted was to hand back his jewellery. He didn't even care about the jewellery. Only her. Old insecurities resurfaced, whispering in his ear: *everyone you love leaves. You're better on your own.*

Taking a deep breath, he pushed the doubts away. He could do this. He just needed a plan.

He replied to her message.

AIDAN: I'll be there with Mum at the Crafty Bee stall and yes, of course I want to meet. Just tell me when. X

He hit the send button and headed into the garden.

'Maya,' he called. She bounded up to him, wagging her tail. 'Hey, girl. I think she might be coming back.'

He couldn't settle to anything for thinking about how things might play out, but something else was bothering him.

Finlay.

Since his split with Elise, Aidan had stayed away on purpose, but he needed to clear the air. With his mum calling him out on his uncommunicativeness, here was a chance to put things right.

Finlay had a pleasant, modern apartment close to the river. Aidan hadn't visited for some time. He pressed the entry button and waited.

'Hello.' Finlay's voice crackled over the intercom.

'It's Aidan, can I come up?'

Silence for a moment, then the main door clicked open. Aidan entered and leapt up the very clean stairs two at a time until he reached Finlay's door. Finlay was waiting, leaning on the frame, his arms folded. They were the same height, similar build and both with dark hair, though Finlay was usually better turned out, while Aidan did rough around the edges without even trying.

'Why are you here?' Finlay asked. 'To gloat? To tell me you and Elise are back on?'

Aidan shook his head. 'Nope. None of the above.'

'What then?'

'Can I at least come in? Or do you want me to say everything out here?'

Finlay stepped inside, shifting out of the way so Aidan could pass by, then he closed the door with an ominous snap. Aidan moved into the living area. A light breeze fluttered through the wide glass doors that opened onto a balcony looking over the river. Aidan drew a breath and stared out. Down river and on the far bank was the Cross Keys Inn, where just a few nights ago Finlay had celebrated his engagement and Aidan had danced with Lilah. How quickly things had changed for them both.

'I'm really sorry how things turned out for you. I know I was angry about you and Elise when I came home, but I never wished for this.'

'Didn't you?'

'I swear I didn't.'

'All she ever wanted was you. I'm surprised she didn't come crawling back.'

'She did.'

'What?'

Aidan turned to face his cousin. 'Yup. But I told her I'm done with her.'

'So... You and Lilah? Hayley said she'd gone off.'

'I'm working on things.'

'Good. Well, I hope you have better luck than me.' Finlay pulled a helpless face.

'You'll find someone,' Aidan said. 'When you do, just be more sensible about it than me. I've alienated the love of my life because I never told her how I felt.'

'Elise is still the love of your life?'

'No. Lilah is. I should have seen it. I was too obsessed with how angry I was with Elise – and you – and scared to let myself feel anything that would lead to more pain. I didn't see what was right in front of me.'

'What are you going to do about it?'

Aidan gave a little shrug. 'I don't know exactly.'

'I should never have dated Elise,' Finlay said. 'I certainly shouldn't have proposed. It was so stupid. Now I'm a sad guy who's passed thirty with two failed engagements to his name.'

'I'm sorry. But why did you do it in the first place? To piss me off?'

'That's why she did it. I see that now. I was her way of getting at you, but I stupidly believed she really liked me. You have no idea how much I wanted to believe it. I really thought this was a chance. It may sound cringe or whatever but I'd actually like to get married and have a family. Maybe it's not cool for guys to say so, but it's true. You know my relationships so far have been... pathetic. So when Elise approached me, you can imagine how easily I fell.'

'Hey, man.' Aidan stepped over to him and placed his hand on his shoulder. 'Don't beat yourself up... At least you're not a coward like me. If I'd had the nerve to spit out what I really felt, I wouldn't be in the mess I'm in now.'

'I said too much, you said too little. Relationships are such a mess. I'm taking a time out. No more dating for me until I've had time to regroup and really think about what I want.'

'You're a good guy, Finlay. I'm sure there are plenty of women out there just waiting to meet you.'

'Yeah, we'll see.' Finlay moved across the open-plan living area to the kitchen and opened the fridge. 'Let's drown these sorrows like old times.'

Aidan needed a drink, but he wasn't going to be wallowing. Tomorrow would be here before he knew it and, if he wanted Lilah back, he had to be ready.

CHAPTER THIRTY-ONE

Lilah chewed a cuticle as she watched the passing scenery. The bus hurtled down the dual carriageway between Dundee and Perth. In Perth she'd change to the bus for Glenbriar. She'd untangled the jewellery, polished it and wrapped each piece in tissue paper she'd found in her mum's house; it was probably at least five years old but no one would know. It felt better than handing over a mass of twisted chains.

The jewellery boxes were gone. Jaxon had ditched them at Zeb's but hopefully Aidan wouldn't mind that.

After she'd changed buses, her stomach got more and more knotted. What would it be like seeing Aidan again? Her heart yearned for it but dreaded it at the same time. His messages had been kind but changed nothing.

She'd never be Elise.

The familiar sights of Glenbriar came into view. This was where she belonged, not in a city. The quaint little streets and mix of houses, old and new, were exactly what she loved. The road to the riverside walk and the wobbly bridge. Everything she'd ever desired was here.

All the moments she'd shared with Aidan flooded back: when they'd worked in the garden, watched the bees, cooked, eaten, laughed and walked Maya together. She remembered the time she'd run away, and he'd taken her home on the bike. And the time he'd fallen in the pond. How she'd always had the sense of being seen and understood. But that had been what she wanted to see, not the love she'd so desperately craved.

As the bus passed the craft market, it looked so similar to the day she'd met Aidan at the fair. He'd shown her kindness despite everything being against her. She'd mistaken that kindness for love. She was coming back, but not for Aidan. It intensified the ache in her chest every time she thought about it, but she had to be strong. Marion had said she was welcome to accommodation at the Schoolhouse and that way she could keep her job. If she saw Aidan in the woods or the town, then she'd just have to learn to deal with it. She could say *hi* and walk on by. If he was with Elise... Well, she'd have to get used to that too.

As the bus approached the stop, Lilah's heartrate accelerated. The moment was getting closer. She stood up, adjusting her bag over her shoulder. The bus came to a halt, and she stepped off, reminding herself to breathe and act normally.

Warm air greeted her; weatherwise, it had been a great summer so far. Tourists bustled in and out of the shops, many of them heading to the market. Nerves jangled in Lilah's stomach and her shoulders tensed as she made her way closer. Glancing around, she caught sight of someone walking towards her.

'Ah, long time no see,' Brenda McManus said, folding her arms and stopping in front of Lilah. 'What you been up to? I've been hearing a load of rumours about you. None of them very nice. I really hope they're not true.' Her expression said otherwise. She was like a bulldog sniffing out a fat, juicy piece of gossip.

'Not sure what you've heard, so I wouldn't like to say.'

'Most of them are about you and Aidan McBride.'

Lilah tried to look past her but Brenda was very wide. 'Aidan and I were dating. What's wrong with that?'

'Dating? If that's what it was.' She leaned in. 'Just so long as he wasn't paying for the pleasure.'

'Seriously, Brenda? Why so mean? I honestly will never get your need to be so horrid to people.'

Brenda gaped at her but Lilah side-stepped her and walked on. No way was she going to take that kind of crap. So what if everyone thought she was easy or that her brother was a thief? She knew the truth.

As she approached the craft market, her eyes darted around. The Crafty Bee stall was instantly obvious with its bright yellow canopy and bee bunting. Her chest hurt as she thought about how much she'd helped with the barn. She'd won Patricia round and even Scarlett. But now, they'd be as good as strangers again.

Hidden safely behind another stall, she peered around. Patricia and Scarlett were at the stand but no sign of Aidan. Where was he? Would he show?

She took a deep breath and checked her phone. No new messages. He should be here. Where was he? Should she approach the stall and speak to Patricia or Scarlett? But what to say?

Doubts flitted around her head like the people perusing the stalls. Had he changed his mind? What if he turned up with Elise in tow? That would be her first test of strength.

As the minutes turned into an eternity, her shoulders sagged and disappointment settled over her. She walked around the stall and crossed to another one, pretending to browse the paintings while actually looking over at the Crafty Bee Stall.

The sound of laughter and the hum of conversations surrounding her was a stark contrast to the emptiness in her heart. She checked the time on her phone. He was late. She moved to another stall, keeping her eyes everywhere, trying to catch sight of anyone tall with dark hair, thick eyebrows and a stare that could turn her to molten gold.

Her gaze fell on a flash of silver and she caught sight of a pair of bright blue eyes. A husky dog trotted towards her through the crowd. Maya?

Her tail wagged and Lilah noticed something in her mouth. She approached Lilah almost smiling. Lilah ducked down and took a small bag from her mouth. She nuzzled against Lilah's leg as Lilah crouched at her side. 'Is this for me?'

Maya panted, as though she was nodding in agreement.

Lilah pulled a yellow envelope from the bag. Her name was written across the front. She ripped it open and prised out the card. Smiling, she read the slogan on the front. 'Will you BEE mine?' She unfolded the card and read the words inside.

Dear Lilah,

I know you don't want to speak about anything else, but if you'll let me, I'd like to say something. It's very important.

Aidan

x

Still crouching, Lilah scanned the crowd. Standing close to the bee stall was Aidan, hands in his pockets, looking brooding, serious, and wildly sexy. He gazed over at her, his dark eyes asking the question his lips couldn't. *Can I come over?*

Lilah clutched the yellow envelope in her hand and leaned close to Maya. She'd missed this beautiful dog. Getting to her feet, she nodded. Aidan raised one eyebrow slightly and slowly made his way towards her.

Maya waited by Lilah's side but watched Aidan intently. Lilah swallowed. As he drew near, their gazes connected. An electric current surged through her. The old feelings poured back, but she held them in.

The air crackled with unspoken words as they stood mere inches from each other. Lilah's grip tightened on the envelope.

'What is it you want to say?' she asked. 'Oh, but first I have your jewellery.' She pulled her bag off her shoulder and made to open it.

'I don't want the jewellery, Lilah.' His deep voice resonated through the air.

'You don't?' She frowned at him.

'No.' His gaze held hers. 'That's not what I want.'

'What then?'

'I want to ask you something,' he said, his tone serious.

The tension in Lilah's body held her in a grip lock. 'What?' she replied.

'Why do you think I asked you to be my girlfriend?' He took a step closer. Lilah averted her gaze, her mind racing.

'You felt sorry for me.'

'I can't deny it, but that wasn't the only reason.'

'You said it was to stop people talking about us, though that didn't really work. But I suppose what you really wanted was to annoy Elise.'

Aidan nodded. 'Maybe a little. But there was something else.' His expression softened, and he reached out, taking her hands in his. His touch sent warmth seeping into her soul. 'In the beginning, I felt connected to you, but I couldn't explain it,' he said, his voice low and sincere. 'I always found you attractive, but as time went on, it got stronger, until finally I realised what had happened...' He paused, his gaze unwavering.

'And what was that?' Lilah whispered.

'I fell in love with you.'

Lilah's breath hitched and her heart pounded in her chest. 'You what?' Her mouth must have looked like she was catching flies.

'I love you.' He ran his thumb down her cheek. 'I should have said it weeks ago. My own insecurities and doubts got in the way. I was terrified of being broken again. It was easier to kid myself I was seeing you for other reasons than admit how I really felt, even to myself.' He glanced at his feet. 'Which was wrong because I didn't stop to think how that would make you feel. That should have been my number one priority. You are my number one priority.'

'Really?'

'Yes. There's only you. I should have told you how much I loved you and cared about you every moment for months now. There's really only been you since the second I wrestled that log off you. It just took me a while to figure it out.'

'Oh my god, Aidan.' Lilah launched herself at him, flinging her arms around his neck. 'I've loved you forever. I never stopped and I never will.'

His low laugh rumbled and his strong arms held her. 'I know, Lilah. It's another reason I adore you. You've always loved me in a way no one else ever has. You didn't need to say it, I felt it and it's made me so happy. I don't want it to end.'

'It's not going to,' Lilah said. 'I can't imagine ever feeling like this about anyone else.' Maya nuzzled into Lilah's leg and she patted her head, still wrapped in Aidan's embrace. 'I think Maya's feeling left out.'

'Never. I've got both my favourite girls now.'

'Are you sure you don't want the jewellery? What will I do with it?'

'I'm glad you found it. Only because it has sentimental value to me, but I don't think it's worth much. It's been hidden away in a box for the longest time. If you return it to me, do you know what I'm going to do with it?'

'What?'

'Give it all to you. I don't know anyone else who'd suit it so well. You're beautiful anyway but you've got exactly the right look to pull it off. I think my dad would be pleased to know it was being used and not just shut away.'

Lilah sucked on her lip, holding back the rising emotion. 'No one's ever given me anything that precious before.'

'You're worth that and so much more. You're worth everything to me. Because I've never had anyone as precious as you before. What's mine is yours. I give myself to you.'

She smiled and ran her hand over his neatly cropped beard. 'You're even more precious than the jewellery.'

'Come home with me?'

She nodded.

'Good. I told the bees I'd do anything to get you back. They'll be so overjoyed we'll have happy honey for the rest of the year.'

She laughed and leaned her head on his chest. 'Happy honey. It's a good name for it. Happy honey in my happy place. Here with you.'

CHAPTER THIRTY-TWO

Aidan watched Lilah as she worked in the cottage kitchen. A sweet aroma of the gorgeous 'happy honey' from his bees filled the air. She dragged a spoon through the thick sticky goo in the pan, twirling it around and collecting a trail of hot golden gloop. The first batch of honey fudge was already cooling on the work surface while she worked on the next one.

'I really think this needs a tester.' He pinched an edge from the readymade tray and popped it into his mouth.

'Hey.' Lilah swatted his hand away. 'If you keep eating it, there won't be any left to sell. And you'll have your mum to answer to.'

Aidan nodded, still savouring the delicious taste. 'You're right,' he said with a chuckle. 'I'll make sure to control myself next time.'

'Are you sure you can do that?'

He moved in behind her and put his arms around her waist. 'It's always a struggle when you're around, but I'll do my best.'

She grinned, still stirring the fudge. He dipped in and placed a kiss on her cheek.

'I love you,' he whispered. *She's here with me.* Woodend Cottage wasn't his anymore, it was theirs. Together. She was channelling her baking skills into creating fudge and honey-based treats for Patricia to sell at the Crafty Bee Barn. Patricia had come up with a little arrangement and was paying Lilah for her time. Scarlett wasn't exactly her best friend, but they were on much better terms and the bitching had thankfully ceased.

'I love you too,' she said. 'But I need to stir this or it'll end up like cement.'

'Got it.' He backed off with a smirk. 'I'll go check on the bees. I thought I saw a little swarm last night. Better see it hasn't got too big.'

He strolled out into the fresh morning air and Maya jumped up from her resting place in the grass and followed him to the gate of the orchard. Tiny apples had started popping out and, on closer inspection, some of them were almost golf ball sized. All the sunshine had brought them on.

The bees were buzzing around hard at work, and Aidan smiled. The field beyond was safe. He, Lilah and Gabe were still in discussion with the councillors about a community buyout but without the worry of having a housing estate in his backyard.

The sound of the gate closing made Aidan turn, expecting to see Lilah. His eyes widened as Elise stepped through. He frowned. What was she doing here? She made her way towards him, her gaze downcast.

'Hi,' she said.

'What's going on?'

'I need to talk to you.'

Aidan shook his head. 'No. There's nothing more for you to say.' He walked past her.

'Please, Aidan.'

The side door to the cottage opened and Lilah peered out. Her focus landed on Elise almost immediately before she turned to Aidan, her expression clouding.

Aidan sidestepped Elise, went to the door, and put his arm around Lilah's shoulder. 'Elise wants to talk to me.'

'Oh,' Lilah said.

'But whatever it is, I want you to be here.'

Elise cast her eyes over them and drew in a deep breath. She would always be beautiful but nothing about her appealed to him anymore. He had everything he needed and wanted with Lilah.

'I just wanted to apologise. I put you' – she looked at Aidan, then at Lilah – 'both in an awkward position. I was angry with you, Aidan, but it wasn't right of me to take that anger out on innocent people. Hurting Finlay was...' She shook her head and glanced away. For someone so calm and collected, she looked on the verge of unravelling. 'Was awful. He's a good guy and he didn't deserve that. Neither did you.' She turned back to them. 'Either of you. I'm sorry for any hurt I caused you.'

Aidan stiffened. *Sorry?* Was that enough?

'It's fine,' Lilah said. 'We all make mistakes. I guess all we can do is learn from them.'

'Yup.' Elise nodded. 'I'm going to need some time to regroup. I might even look for jobs elsewhere, get out of town and make a clean break.'

Aidan cocked his head. 'I know how you feel.' It was exactly what he'd done after his dad died. 'Well, good luck.'

Elise nodded and gave them both a brief smile. 'Bye.' She turned and walked away.

'Do you think she's ok?' Lilah asked.

'She will be. She's strong and she knows deep down we'd never have got past all the negative stuff. I just hope she understands how strongly I feel about you. I don't want her thinking she can wheedle her way between us.' He tugged Lilah a little closer. 'I made a lot of mistakes in my relationship with her. It seemed that leaving her was the biggest one but actually that was the lucky one. Because I learned I didn't feel as much for her as I thought. If I had, I would never have left her. I know that now because I could never leave *you*. Ever. After my dad died, I should have found comfort with Elise, but I didn't. That situation wouldn't have arisen with you. You would have been there and I wouldn't have wanted to be away from you.'

She wrapped her arms around his waist. 'Let's always be here for each other.'

'We will be.' He kissed her brow. 'This is our home now. You, me, Maya and the bees. Whatever happens from here on in, we're in it together.'

Lilah smiled up at him. 'All my dreams have come true. You're my storybook boyfriend come to life, and this is my very own fairytale ending, except I don't have to imagine it anymore. It's real... And actually, it's not the end at all. It's the start of a whole new story.'

'So true. One where neither of us is alone and we'll always have each other.'

Lilah smiled. 'The perfect way to start over.'

Aidan hugged her and they smiled at each other. Maya nuzzled them both and the bees seemed to hum louder than ever. Everything was exactly as it should be.

The End

More Books by Margaret Amatt

The Glenbriar Series

1. Stolen Kisses at the Loch View Hotel

2. Just Friends at Thistle Lodge

3. Pitching up at Heather Glen

4. Two's Company at the Forest Light Show

5. Highland Fling on the Whisky Trail

6. Snowdown at the Old Schoolhouse

7. Starting Over at the Crafty Bee Barn

8. A Surprise Proposal in the Rose Garden

9. Cutting it Neat for the Wedding

10. A Classy Affair in the Country

11. Mix Up under the Mistletoe

12. A Fresh Start on the Bridle Path

13. Last First Kiss at the Village Church

14. Fight or Flirt on the Scenic Route

15. Love Match on the Road Home

Love on the Edge – Barra Series

ABOUT THE AUTHOR
Margaret Amatt

Margaret has told and written stories for as long as she can remember. During her formative years, she spent time on long walks inventing characters and stories to pass the time.

Writing books is Margaret's passion and when she's not doing that, she's often found eating chocolate, walking and taking photographs in the hills around Highland Perthshire. Those long walks still frequently bring inspiration!

It's Margaret's pleasure to bring you the **Scottish Island Escapes** series, **The Glenbriar Series** and the **Love on the Edge – Barra** series. Each series features interconnected stories for those who enjoy inhabiting Margaret's world but each and every book can be read as a standalone if you'd rather dip in and out.

You can find more information about Margaret on her website or by signing up for her newsletter

www.margaretamatt.com

Acknowledgments

Thanks goes to my adorable husband for supporting my dreams and putting up with my writing talk 24/7. Also to my son, whose interest in my writing always makes me smile. It's precious to know I've passed the bug to him – he's currently writing his own fantasy novel and instruction books on how to build Lego!

Throughout the writing process, I have gleaned help from many sources and met some fabulous people. I'd like to give a special mention to Stéphanie Ronckier, my beta reader extraordinaire. Stéphanie's continued support with my writing is invaluable and I love the fact that I need someone French to correct my grammar! Stéphanie, you rock. To my lovely friend, Lyn Williamson, thank you for your continued support and encouragement with all my projects. And to my fellow authors, Evie Alexander and Lyndsey Gallagher – you girls are the best! I love it that you always have my back and are there to help when I need you.

Also, a thanks to the editors at Leannan Press for their work on this novel.

Of course a huge thank you goes to the readers who continue to support me in so many ways. I appreciate each and every one of you and hope that I can keep bringing you more books to enjoy! Big love.

Margaret XX